AMULET BOOKS
NEW YORK

Dr. Critchlore's SCHOOL for MINIONS

-Twice Cursed-

BOOK FOUR

SHEILA GRAU

ILLUSTRATED BY
JOE SUTPHIN

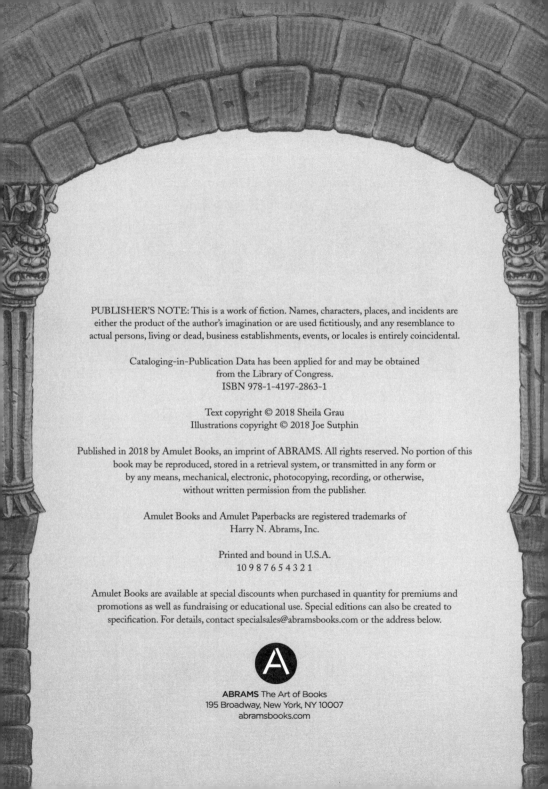

Cataloging-in-Publication Data has been applied for and may be obtained from the Library of Congress.
ISBN 978-1-4197-2863-1

Text copyright © 2018 Sheila Grau
Illustrations copyright © 2018 Joe Sutphin

Printed and bound in U.S.A.
10 9 8 7 6 5 4 3 2 1

Amulet Books are available at special discounts when purchased in quantity for premiums and promotions as well as fundraising or educational use. Special editions can also be created to specification. For details, contact specialsales@abramsbooks.com or the address below.

ABRAMS The Art of Books
195 Broadway, New York, NY 10007
abramsbooks.com

FOR LISA AND GORDY

CHAPTER 1

Don't hug zombies.

—GOOD ADVICE

I don't, as a general rule, hug zombies. Sure, the ones at school won't attack other students, but just being close to one leaves you smelling like death for the rest of the day. And bits of rotten skin fall off when you touch them. *Ew.* Just thinking about it makes my shoulders twitch.

Miss Merrybench, our former school secretary and current zombie, wanted a hug. From me.

Her sad, melty zombie face tilted sideways as she held out both arms, not in the usual zombie pose, with the hands hanging limp at the end of outstretched arms. No, her hands faced upward, waiting to catch a disgusted boy who'd rather hug his ogre-man friend Boris, a guy who only bathes once a week.

I backed up, looking for an escape. She'd cornered me in the dungeon, just as I was leaving Uncle Ludwig's secret library by the grotto entrance. Unfortunately for me, Uncle Ludwig was taking library security more seriously now that he was an official

1

Covert Librarian, and he'd installed a coded lock on the door. I'd be wrapped in a full zombie hug before I could enter the first number.

The string of dim lightbulbs circling the underground lake illuminated the grotto just enough for me to see that I was trapped. Locked door behind me, fish monster in the water to my right, rocky dungeon wall to my left, and directly in front of me a zombie with a skull-revealing smile who wasn't taking no for an answer.

"It's okay, Miss Merrybench," I said, holding up my hands in the "don't come any closer" position. "I forgive you for trying to kill me. And for telling me my parents were here to find me when they really weren't. We're good."

Miss Merrybench was in a twelve-step Afterlife Redemption Program, trying to make up for the mean things she'd done in her life. Step One was asking for forgiveness from the people she'd tried to blow up. She shuffled toward me, making small moaning noises that didn't increase her appeal in any way.

The signs around the grotto all warned against going near the water because of the flesh-eating fish monster, but I decided to risk it. I burst forward, ducking under Miss Merrybench's outstretched arms and stepping into the water next to her. My foot slipped on a wet rock and I fell to my hands and knees, scrambling away from the zombie and the water as fast as I could. An open passageway was in sight, but just as I thought I'd escaped, a tentacle fastened around my ankle and yanked me flat.

I screamed. Miss Merrybench screamed. I tried to kick my leg free, but the tentacle held tight, pulling me closer to the water. I desperately reached for a stalagmite and wrapped my arms around it.

"Clarence, no!" I yelled, because that was the fish monster's name. He didn't listen to me. "Miss Merrybench! The stun pole!" I pointed at the emergency box next to the warning sign. It held a long pole with electrodes at the end that would shock the fish monster into releasing me.

Miss Merrybench reached for the box, but she moved so . . . so . . . slowly. I held tight as she read the warning about the dangers of mixing electricity and water.

"Just do it!" I screamed right before I lost my grip and was pulled underwater.

I yanked the tentacle off my leg, but another one immediately took its place. This happened a few times, and I thought I heard monster giggles underwater. Clarence thought we were playing. Just as I was running out of air, something splashed into the water next to me.

A hand grabbed my arm and pulled me toward the surface. The strength of my rescuer was incredible. Not many creatures can win a tug-of-war with Clarence. I could only think of one: Frankie. I was pulled out of the water and lay on the gravel, gulping in air. Miss Merrybench stood above me and jabbed the stun pole at the tentacle still wrapped around my ankle, but she struck my shin instead.

I felt the quick, sharp sting of electricity, and I screamed again, closing my eyes and rocking back and forth. I heard an unearthly sound coming from the person who'd pulled me out, who'd also felt the jolt. I looked over and saw a small, freckle-faced girl wearing a Critchlore uniform with a first-year purple jacket.

"Sara?" I said.

Miss Merrybench looked down at the girl. In slow motion, her eyes went wide as she realized who this was: Sara, my vaskor friend. Sara was a monster, but she wore the glamour of a harmless girl. Miss Merrybench shuffled away, moaning. Even as a zombie, she was terrified of the vaskor.

Clarence, on the other hand, had a crush on Sara. His head popped out of the water and he burbled a greeting as he reached for her with a long tentacle, which she hugged, like it was a cute puppy or something.

"Sara, what are you doing here?" I asked. A large backpack lay on the ground next to her.

"Runt, I need your help," she said. "I think I made a terrible mistake."

But before she could say anything else, the secret door at the end of the grotto opened, and Professor Zaida stepped out.

She took one look at Sara and immediately frowned. Sara was supposed to be living at the Great Library with the rest of the vaskor, not sneaking around the dungeons here. Zaida tilted her head back toward the door.

"Both of you. Inside. Now."

CHAPTER 2

Clarence was a graduation gift to Dr. Critchlore
from his mother.

—INTERESTING FACT

Back in the library, Professor Zaida went from mad to furious as she emptied the contents of Sara's backpack onto a table. "One jar of black face paint. Two black beanies. Two pairs of gloves. Two Pravus Academy uniforms. One map of the Pravus Academy."

She looked at me. "What were you planning to do?"

I had no idea. "You tell her," I said to Sara.

"Rescue Syke," Sara said. Her voice sounded so hoarse and deep, which was odd, coming from that little girl body. "She's not safe."

Syke, my best friend, had gone undercover at the school of Dr. Critchlore's worst enemy, Dr. Pravus. She'd wanted to steal back the *Top Secret Book of Minions—Translated Edition* that Pravus had stolen from the Great Library, but that mission changed when she found out there were much more sinister things going on at that school. She'd been sending evidence of Pravus's plans for weeks now.

"And you thought you could sneak in there and get her out?" Professor Zaida said, looking at me. "Something Dr. Critchlore has been trying to do for weeks. The man is worried sick. One minute he's planning an all-out assault to rescue her, the next he's angrily vowing to ground her for a year when she comes back."

Syke was his ward, but I'd always known she was more to him than that.

"May we?" I asked, pointing to the dry clothes. At that moment I'd rather wear the uniform of our rival than have Uncle Ludwig catch me dripping near his precious books. She nodded, so I ducked under the table to change. Sara changed in the stacks.

"Runt, I realize it must be fun, knowing that you're a prince with an army of vaskor you can order to do as you please," Professor Zaida said. I nearly laughed out loud, because she had completely misread the situation. I couldn't order Sara to do anything anymore. "You cannot make these kinds of decisions on your own. There's too much at stake. I thought you understood that."

"I'm sorry," I said. "I'm just really worried about Syke."

"Mistress Moira is watching the Pravus Academy with her ravens," Professor Zaida said. "She'd tell us if Syke was in danger. You need to focus on your work here. Now, please order Sara back to the forest."

"I will," I said.

Sara and I left, and I wondered how I was ever going to explain to Professor Zaida that I'd freed Sara from her spell of obedience a few months ago.

"I'm not going back to the forest," Sara said as we walked upstairs. "Syke's been cuffed."

"Cuffed?"

"She has to wear a bracelet. It's impossible to remove. If Pravus doubts your loyalty, you have to wear one. That's why I couldn't take her out of there."

"Because of a bracelet?" I held the cafeteria door open and followed her inside. I assumed that she was hungry, mostly because she was always hungry.

"If she tries to escape, they can activate it remotely."

"Activate it to do what?"

"To kill her," she said. "With poison."

I gasped. That was so evil. "How are we going to get her out of there?"

"I thought you'd think of something," she said. "Like how you rescued me from the dungeon here."

The cafeteria was dark, so Sara and I snuck into the empty kitchen. I went to the pantry, where Cook kept a few clean uniforms for me. (Sometimes I showed up for meals dirtier than she liked.) I changed, stuffing the enemy clothes behind a crate in the corner.

I managed to dig up a bag of day-old doughnuts (literally, they'd been in the garbage), and Sara lit up with happiness.

"Awesome, I love doughnuts," she said. "Dr. Pravus fed us only meat, meat, and meat. The librarians feed us vegetables. I don't like meat. I don't like vegetables. I like doughnuts."

"Who doesn't? Look, Sara, you have to go back to the librarians. You heard Professor Zaida. I'm ordering you to go back."

"You can't," Sara said with a huge smile. "Runt, it's so great. Nobody can tell me where to go, or when to go to sleep, or who to maim. I can eat all the doughnuts I want." She stuffed another one into her mouth.

"Then what are you going to do?"

"I'm going to watch over Syke," she said, swallowing another doughnut without chewing. "I lived at the Pravus Academy for a long time before you freed us from him. I know where to hide so I can watch her. As soon as she earns Pravus's trust and gets that bracelet off, I will save her. I have to, she's my best friend."

"You've only known her a few months." It's possible I felt a little jealous. Syke was my best friend too.

"Yes, but she's done so much for me."

That was true. After Syke ran away from Dr. Critchlore's to go live with the other hamadryads, I thought she hated me, so when she asked me a few months ago to free Sara from her spell of obedience, I'd done it.

I'd been ready to free all the vaskor, but Professor Zaida showed up and stopped me. She'd been furious. She told me that I didn't know what I was doing. That Sara and the rest of her kind were the most powerful monsters alive, and there is nothing more dangerous than power without control. The spell of obedience was that control.

I'd wanted to argue with her, because I knew they weren't dangerous. During our first encounter, Sara had told me that she was Oti. I'd found a book in the Great Library that described the Oti as gentle pacifists. They wouldn't fight, not even to save themselves.

I knew that the vaskor were only dangerous *because* of the spell, because Pravus had ordered them to kill and they couldn't refuse. But Professor Zaida had been so angry, I couldn't explain that to her, or tell her that I'd already freed Sara.

"Sara," I said, "be careful. You can't run around Stull doing whatever you want. Actions have consequences. And what did you mean, you made a terrible mistake?"

"Someone saw me at the Pravus Academy," she said. "I couldn't let them think I was there to rescue Syke. They'd kill her. So I stole something to create a diversion."

"What?"

"I buried it out by the new forest," she said. "A bag of glowing green rocks."

"Sudithium?" I felt the blood rush out of my head. That *was* a mistake. It was a huge mistake.

Dr. Pravus and Dr. Critchlore were trying to create an Undefeatable Minion, and one of the essential ingredients was a mineral called sudithium, which, when ingested by a living organism, makes it much, much bigger. Dr. Pravus already had the mineral, and he didn't think we had any. Dr. Critchlore wanted to keep it that way. He said that if Dr. Pravus thought we were close to making our own Undefeatable Minion, he might do something drastic to stop us.

I sat there wondering what "something drastic" could mean.

CHAPTER 3

"We call them vaskor. It sounds much more
intimidating than Oti."
—KING DREDGEMONT, FIRST RULER OF THE VASKOR

I barely slept that night. I knew I had to tell Dr. Critchlore what Sara had done, but I didn't know how.

At breakfast, Professor Zaida sent a message, ordering me to report to the secret library. I asked Boris to tell Tootles that I'd be missing my mentor class. Boris worked in the stables first period, right next to Tootles's Forest Restoration Project (FRP).

When I showed up, she asked, "Is Sara gone?"

"I ordered her back to the Great Library," I said, which was technically true. "Did you talk to Mistress Moira about Syke? Sara told me that she's wearing some sort of bracelet—"

"A loyalty cuff," Professor Zaida said. "That's what Pravus calls them. As soon as he suspects someone isn't loyal, he puts one on them. One wrong move and they're punished with a jolt of electricity."

"Electricity? Are you sure?" That wasn't what Sara had told me.

"Yes," she said. "He told the EOs that he was testing a new training method. They like it."

"It's deranged."

"That's not the worst of it. Syke smuggled out a note using Mistress Moira's messenger crow. She says that Pravus trains his minions to be loyal to *him*, not to their EOs. He's been doing it for years. He uses the cuffs on minions he thinks might spill the beans to the EO Council."

"He's broken the Minion School Code?" I asked. "That's huge. Why doesn't the EO Council arrest him?"

"We need more evidence than Syke's testimony to prove it," she said. "Nobody would believe that she's an impartial witness. She grew up as Critchlore's ward."

"What about Tankotto's henchman?" I asked. "He was working for Pravus, not Tankotto, when he was trying to find the Great Library by poisoning librarians."

"Unfortunately, Dr. Critchlore can't tell the EOs about that. He'd be exposing the existence of the secret librarians."

"Oh, right."

"Imagine." She leaned back in her chair. "Pravus has been training minions for over twenty years, and he's placed minions in every realm except Upper Worb . . . and one other one . . ."

"The Forgotten Realm?"

"Yes, that one. All those minions, ready to turn on their EOs and fight for Pravus."

"Add in an army of UMs, and he'll be unstoppable," I said.

She sighed, then leaned forward. "And that's why we have to speed up your prince training. I thought we had more time. But I'm worried about Pravus, and I'm worried about the rebels."

"The rebels?" I asked. "In Andirat?" I didn't see how my home country had anything to do with Pravus. It wasn't even on the same continent.

"Yes," she said. "There are too many rebel groups fighting the generals. They need a leader, or at least a figurehead to unite them so they can confront the generals as one united group, rather than many small factions."

"A leader?" I asked. "You don't mean me?"

She nodded. "When you take your rightful place as ruler of Andirat, your armies could help us stop Pravus."

Eight years ago, the royal family of Andirat, my family, was murdered by five generals who wanted to rule the country themselves. Somehow, I was saved from execution and smuggled across the ocean to Dr. Critchlore's school, where I was left at the gate with no memory of my past. Since then, Andirat had fallen into civil war, because the generals couldn't agree on who should be in charge. They split up the country and now fight against each other, and against the rebels, which meant that everyone was suffering now.

I was the last prince of Andirat. Professor Zaida had been training me so that one day I could return as its rightful leader and end all the fighting.

"I'm not ready," I said.

"The generals are losing control, but since the many rebel groups aren't coordinated, the generals remain in power. You are someone who could unite the entire country, and force the generals to step down."

"I'm just a kid."

"Say it, Runt," Professor Zaida said. "Say what I taught you."

I sighed. "I can do this," I said. "I am Prince Auberon of Andirat, and I will lead my people out of their oppression."

"Now say it like you mean it," she said, and she made me say it five more times.

"Good," she said, standing up. "Now come, we have a meeting to go to."

We left the library through the grotto and headed for the dungeon hub, a giant room below the castle foyer that was filled with cubicles and offices.

Walking into the conference room was like entering the world of grown-ups. It was a serious room, so different from the classrooms I was used to. Here the table was free of graffiti and gum, and the walls weren't covered with student projects like sabotage plans or siege dioramas.

A painting depicting the battle that had given the Valley of Fears its name hung on the wall facing the door. The other walls were taken up by a whiteboard and a giant screen for teleconferencing. Professor Zaida and I took seats beneath the painting, which was good because I didn't want to look at it.

Dr. Frankenhammer, Coach Foley, Professors Murphy, Portry, Dunkirk, Twilk, and Vodum sat opposite us. Barry Merrybench, Dean Everest, Mrs. Gomes, and Mr. Griphold sat on our side.

"Why am I here?" I whispered to Professor Zaida.

"I requested it," she whispered. "You need to know what's going on in the world, so that you don't do stupid things."

Dr. Critchlore arrived. He held the door for Mistress Moira and then followed her in, taking his seat at the head of the table, beneath the whiteboard. He turned on the teleconferencing screen, and we all watched it flick on to reveal an enormous white-and-gold desk with fancy etchings, and an empty chair behind it.

"We're ready," Dr. Critchlore told the screen. "Please tell Her Charming Magnificence that we don't have time for her usual displays of grandeur."

The screen blasted out some peppy marching music as two sealmen took position on either side of the desk. The one on the right said, "All rise for Her Wise and Just Incredibleness, the Queen of Upper Worb." We all stood, and waited.

After a full two minutes, Irma Trackno strode through the door and took her seat. She wore her usual white tunic-jacket with its fur-lined hood.

"I don't have time to waste," she said, shaking out her white hair and removing her white gloves. "Let's get started."

"Hello, Mother," Dr. Critchlore said.

"Derek." She nodded. Then she sighed. "You never listen to me. Once, just once, I'd like you to take heed when I warn you that your life is in danger."

"You warned me every day of my life," he replied. "Until you left when I was seven."

"And I was right, wasn't I? We have enemies who wish to destroy us."

"Let's stick to the emergency at hand," Dr. Critchlore said. "We are meeting today because something happened at the Pravus Academy last night. This morning, our spies reported that there's so much activity there, it looks like Dr. Pravus is mobilizing for war."

Uh-oh. I tried to sink lower in my chair. I knew I should tell Dr. Critchlore that Sara had stolen sudithium from Dr. Pravus, which had apparently sent him into a panic. But I couldn't do it. Not now, in front of everyone.

"It's happening," Irma said, pointing a finger at her son. "Just like I warned you."

"Should Dr. Pravus go rogue," Dr. Critchlore went on, "and try to use the minions he's trained to conquer other realms, as we suspect he will, we need to warn the EO Council."

"No," Irma said. "You need to set up defenses at your school. You'll be his first target."

"That's ridiculous. Why would he waste time with me? He knows we're not close to making an Undefeatable Minion," Dr. Critchlore said.

"So what?" Irma said. "The man hates you. He told me he intends to destroy your school. He doesn't know I'm your mother. It took every ounce of self-control not to have my ice monster stomp on his smug, evil, handsome face after listening to all the names he called you. But at the time, I needed his giant gorillas."

"Why does he hate you so much?" I asked Dr. Critchlore.

Irma laughed out loud. "Oh, the stories I could tell! Those two have been rivals since school. Pravus was a pompous twit, and Derek humiliated him again and again. I was worried at first, because Pravus comes from a very powerful family."

"He does?"

"Yes. He's the son of Egmont Luticus, the banished overlord of Riggen."

Wait . . . was everyone the secret son of a powerful EO? I was beginning to feel less special about being a prince.

"His parents escaped Riggen before it fell to Fraze Coldheart. Of course I recognized the vile Luticus spawn as soon as I saw him in Derek's class picture.

"Listen to me now," she went on, leaning forward. "There is no more despicable creature in this world than the offspring of a tyrant. Entitled brats who have been given everything except the humility that goes with having earned things for themselves."

"But . . . isn't Dr. Critchlore the son of a tyrant?" I asked.

The room hushed as Irma stared at me. "Why aren't you dead?" she asked. She must have remembered my curse. At least, I hoped that was what she meant.

"Mother," Critchlore interrupted. "Let's stay focused on what's important."

"Right. Pravus and his desire to overthrow the EOs. But wait, I want to show you all something," Irma said. "The graduation video," she told her assistant, snapping her fingers. "Queue it up."

"Mother, please," Dr. Critchlore said. "Nobody cares about your home movies."

"Shhh, Derek. Watch this, everyone. It's important to know your enemy."

The video started. It was taken from the stands inside a large stadium. On the field were hundreds of students in their graduation robes, sitting in chairs arranged in an arc in front of a stage. Adults wearing fancier robes and sashes sat on the stage. A heavyset man stood at the podium.

"And now, for our most prestigious award. The top student of our graduating class in the Doctorate of Minion Studies is . . ."

Irma's voice cut in. "Look at the lower left—Pravus actually stands up before the name is called. Ha!"

"Derek Critchlore!" the man announced. A young Dr. Critchlore rose and approached the podium as the other students clapped and whooped enthusiastically.

"Look at my Derek," Irma's voice-over said. "Isn't he handsome?"

Her Derek was now leaning over the table with his head down, a hand to his forehead.

"Watch," Irma said. "The best part is coming."

Young Dr. Critchlore accepted his trophy, which looked like a bare tree with white and light-blue branches on a heavy marble base. He held it up shyly as his classmates cheered. Then, suddenly, another robed figure rushed the stage.

"That's Pravus," Irma said. "He kept screaming, 'That's my trophy! Mine!'"

"It's true," Dr. Critchlore said. "I knew he was extremely competitive, but have some dignity, man."

The camera zoomed in on the action and we could see young Dr. Critchlore trying to hustle down the steps. Pravus caught up with him and grabbed the trophy, but Critchlore didn't let go and yanked it away from him. An enraged Pravus then tackled Critchlore, but Critchlore held tight to the trophy. Pravus's face was crimson with rage as he struggled to grab the trophy while others pried him off Dr. Critchlore.

I'd always thought Dr. Critchlore had made this story up, or at least exaggerated it.

"You need to know who you're up against," Irma said.

"I've been rivals with him for twenty-five years, Mother," Dr. Critchlore said. "I think I know who I'm up against."

"No, you don't. True character comes out in times of stress. Dr. Pravus has kept that egomaniacal madman bundled up since that event. He's charmed all the EOs. They love him. *LOVE* him. But as you saw, this is a man who does not accept losing."

"Okay, he doesn't like to lose. Neither do I," Dr. Critchlore said, clapping his hands together for attention. "We need to stop him.

Now, I can think of only one reason why he would be in such a panic right now. He must believe we are close to making our own Undefeatable Minions. His plan will be ruined if we have them too."

"How close are you?" Irma asked.

"We've had the mutating virus and the sudithium for a few weeks—"

"So, make your own UMs and crush him already!"

"We can't," Dr. Critchlore said. "I won't allow it."

CHAPTER 4

*"Earning loyalty takes time and sacrifice.
My new cuffs guarantee loyalty in seconds!"*
—DR. PRAVUS, AT THE EO COUNCIL

W hy not?" Irma said, speaking for everyone in the room, because we were all shocked by this announcement. Wasn't creating a UM what we'd been trying to do for the last few months?

"We've known that creating an Undefeatable Minion requires three things: a mutating virus to make them indestructible, sudithium to make them huge, and a spell to make them obedient. But we need a human army to start with," Dr. Critchlore said. He was addressing the room, not his mother, which made me think that his decision was news to everyone.

"The problem is the mutating virus," he said. "It causes the subject's cell structure to change. Strength increases dramatically, skin hardens until it's like steel, senses are heightened, and these are just some of the changes mentioned in the *Top Secret Book of Minions*."

He paused for a second, then went on. "Dr. Frankenhammer has translated the footnotes, which contain a very serious warning.

Only ten percent of a population can survive the virus. The jolt to the cells is just too powerful."

"So, what's the problem?" Irma asked.

"To make an army of one hundred, I'd be sentencing nine hundred people to death," Dr. Critchlore said, looking directly at her. "I won't do it."

"Pravus will," she interjected.

"I won't do it," Dr. Critchlore repeated. "And so we have changed our objectives. We are focusing on neutralizing Pravus's UMs instead. Dr. Frankenhammer is working on antidotes to both the virus and the sudithium. If we can reverse those effects, it might make the Undefeatable Minions defeatable. But we need to know how much sudithium you've given Dr. Pravus."

"A truck full," Irma said.

"He must have used a lot for his giant gorillas," Professor Murphy said.

"A drop in the bucket," Irma said. "He's got enough to keep an army huge for years. You have to understand, he promised me that the gorillas he sent to Wexmir Smarvy would turn on Smarvy and fight for me."

"We get it, Mother," Dr. Critchlore said. "You gave the most dangerous man on the continent a rare mineral because he made you a promise."

Irma frowned. "Derek, you've never understood the politics of power. Of having to work with people you hate so you can achieve your objectives—"

Dr. Critchlore held up a hand. "We have a new objective: neutralize the Undefeatable Minions. I have gone to the EO Council to warn them that Dr. Pravus plans to start a war. I have shown them the evidence we've gotten from Syke, that he has been training his minions to be loyal to him, and not their EOs."

"What did they say?" Professor Murphy asked.

"They didn't believe me," Dr. Critchlore said. "They think I'm . . ." He shook his head, unable to say the word.

"What?" Professor Zaida asked.

"They think I'm . . ." he tried again. "That I'm . . ."

"Jealous," his mother finished for him. "They think he's jealous of Dr. Pravus."

Dr. Critchlore looked like he was going to throw up. "You need to convince them, Mother."

"I really can't help you," she said. "In fact, I go out of my way to oppose you any chance I get."

"Wonderful," Dr. Critchlore said with an eye roll.

"It's for your own good, Derek," she went on. "If anyone discovered that I'm your mother, it would ruin you. Nobody would recruit a minion from you again. They'd all think you train them for me, so I could use them to take over the world."

"Which is what Dr. Pravus is actually doing," Professor Murphy muttered. Dr. Critchlore nodded.

"I can't spare any more time," Irma said. "You all are dismissed." And the video cut off.

"Well, I had to try," Dr. Critchlore told the room. "Let's stick to the plan we have. Dr. Frankenhammer will work on the antidotes. Coach Foley, Mrs. Gomes, and Professors Portry, Murphy, and

Dunkirk will begin preparations to defend the school. Pravus may attack soon, to prevent us from making progress on the Undefeatable Minions."

"Mistress Moira could help with defenses," Professor Zaida said. "Her crows can monitor Dr. Pravus's minions."

"Mistress Moira and Miss Merrybench are traveling to Skelterdam to find the witch who cursed Runt," Dr. Critchlore said. "We all have our action items. Let's get busy."

He sat back down and motioned for Professor Zaida and me to come sit closer to him and Mistress Moira while the others cleared the room.

"Runt, we are in disagreement over what to do with you," Dr. Critchlore said. "Professor Zaida's plan has been to train you to return to Andirat. You could reestablish it as a united country with a strong army. An army that could help us fight Dr. Pravus."

I nodded.

"With this threat from Pravus, I'm worried about your safety here. It may be time for you to join the rebels in Andirat."

I swallowed a huge lump of fear in my throat. He wanted me to leave?

"However," he went on. "Professor Zaida isn't convinced that the rebels can keep you any safer. Mistress Moira also believes your life would be in danger if you left at this time."

"Because of my tether curse?" I asked.

"No. According to my research, your curses were cast in Andirat," Mistress Moira said. "The tether curse was cast to keep you in range of the death curse, and I believe that you triggered it when you moved north of Stull. First when you went to the Great Library, part of which lies in Burkeve, and then when you went to Polar Bay. Your tether will not be activated in Andirat, but I think you will be safer here with Dr. Critchlore, more so than if you joined a rebel group we know little about."

I wasn't ready to go to Andirat. Whenever I imagined going there, I always pictured Professor Zaida coming with me, and maybe Dr. Critchlore too. And my friends. Now Dr. Critchlore was talking about shipping me off to some rebels I didn't even know. I'd be all alone.

"What do you think I should do, Dr. Critchlore?"

"I trust the opinion of these two," he said, and I exhaled loudly with relief. "But I'm worried that if we wait too long, the opportunity to stop Dr. Pravus might be lost."

"Because I'm cursed to die, you mean? If we wait too long, I might not be around to unite the rebel army?"

"Miss Merrybench and I will find the witch who cursed you and bring her here," Mistress Moira said. "This type of curse can be removed two ways. First, if the witch dies. Second, if she removes it herself, which must be done in person. The witch will not risk returning to Andirat. She's cursed too many people there. Those people know their curses will be lifted if she dies."

"We don't have much time," Dr. Critchlore said. "Dr. Pravus could become too strong. Even if we neutralize his Undefeatable Minions, the man has tens of thousands of minions ready to fight for him."

"I'll contact the rebel leaders," Professor Zaida said. "We'll find someone we trust to take Runt back to Andirat after he's curse-free. Someone who will keep him safe."

Dr. Critchlore nodded, then got up to leave. Professor Zaida followed him out while I grabbed Mistress Moira's arm so I could ask her a question.

"I'm worried about Syke," I told her. "Sara says she's wearing a bracelet that will poison her if she tries to escape."

"Dr. Pravus keeps his minions loyal through fear," she said, shaking her head. "Don't worry, my ravens are watching her. I'm more concerned about you, Runt."

"It's just a lot of responsibility," I said. "I'm not ready to go to Andirat."

"And you mustn't," she said. "Runt, you must not leave this school under any circumstances. Do you understand?"

I nodded. Inside my head, I did a little happy dance of relief.

"Not until we remove your curses," she added.

"Do you know why I was cursed?" I asked.

She shook her head. "No, but I have my suspicions."

"Me too," I said. "I escaped when my family was killed. The generals must have hired the witch to curse me, right?"

"I don't think so," Mistress Moira said. "If the witch was working for the generals, she wouldn't have fled to Skelterdam. The generals would protect her. Instead, the generals have offered a huge reward for her capture—dead or alive. No, there has to be another reason."

"Could it be a mistake?" I asked, because it had to be.

"Not likely. You really don't remember anything?"

I shook my head. "I grew up thinking I was a werewolf, you know that. The only memories I have are of living with dogs. I don't know why."

"You could be blocking out painful memories," she said. "The

26

more I think about it, the more I believe that something happened eight years ago, and you were involved. Something more than escaping the coup that killed your family."

"Really? Why?"

"Because if she wanted you dead, the witch could have killed you instantly." She snapped her fingers. "But she chose a timed-death curse. Why? Because a four-year-old doesn't understand death, doesn't fear death."

"But now that I'm grown, I know what I have to lose," I said.

"That's right," she agreed. "This curse was done on purpose, to terrify you in the cruelest possible way. It feels like vengeance."

That didn't make me feel any better.

"I will find out why," she said, then she nodded to the door. "Now, off to class."

I tried to remember eight years ago, when I was four, but all I could remember was dogs: the smell of their fur and their doggy breath. The softness of their bodies as I fell asleep.

In the foyer, I saw Professor Murphy coming out of the cafeteria with a cup of coffee. Together we walked to his Junior Henchman class.

"Do you really think Pravus will attack here?" I asked.

"Yes. Not just because he hates Critchlore. I think his main objective would be to stop us from making our own UMs. However," he said, raising a finger, "attacking us is against the Minion School Code and will bring the punishment forces of the EO Council down upon him. So I don't think he'll attack until he has his Undefeatable Minions and can fend off the EOs. We know he was still searching for a witch as recently as last week, so he must still need a spell of obedience. Without that spell, unleashing the UMs would be like tossing grenades into a tornado—he'd have no control over where they strike. We may have some time."

"Do you think Dr. Frankenhammer can make an antidote before Pravus strikes?"

"Dr. Frankenhammer is a very skilled scientist, but we are in uncharted territory. We have to prepare for the worst."

We entered the classroom before the rest of the students. I took my seat at the end of the row of six desks.

Janet walked in first, making my heart feel ten times bigger in my chest. She seemed a little startled to see me.

"What's the matter?" I asked.

"Huh? Oh, I just remembered something I forgot to do."

"Homework?"

She laughed and rubbed my head. "No, silly." Then she whispered, "Something important."

Meztli and Jud came in next. They'd just found out that they were both practitioners of the ancient were-animal fighting style called Cadora, and had been hanging out together. Frieda followed, shaking the room as she sat down (she's an ogre).

Professor Murphy didn't wait for Rufus. He jumped right into his lecture on school defenses. Rufus showed up five minutes late, scowling. He'd gone from being a happy, popular bully to being an unhappy, friendless jerk. I almost felt bad for him, but his general jerkiness kept that from happening.

"We have to reinforce our weakest points—out by the aviary and Tootles's new forest," he said. "What do you kids think?"

"Surrender," Rufus said. "This school is filled with losers. We don't stand a chance against the Pravus Academy kids."

Professor Murphy ignored him and continued brainstorming. We took notes, but whenever anyone asked a question, Rufus scoffed like it was the dumbest thing he'd ever heard. Janet, instead of being angry, shot him a look of pity that would have embarrassed anyone else.

Rufus tore out of the class when it ended.

"I heard he wants to transfer to the Pravus Academy," Janet said as we left.

That was fine with me, although it did make me worry that Rufus had just learned all our weak spots.

CHAPTER 5

The Kidnapping Club was disbanded
after teachers complained that too many students
were missing classes.
—*HISTORY OF DR. CRITCHLORE'S SCHOOL*,
VOLUME EIGHT

At lunch, Cook was serving two of my favorites: thin slices of breaded chicken topped with cheese and tomato sauce on a bed of pasta, and cheesy steak sandwiches.

I looked from one tray to the other, unable to decide. "Why do you do this to me, Cook?" I asked as she waited with her serving spoon.

"The delivery of steaks came a day early; I didn't want them to go bad. And we'd already done the prep for the chicken. Just pick one."

I looked at the chicken, golden brown with crispy goodness. Then to the steak, all cheesy and oniony on toasted bread. *Arg*.

"The chicken," I said. "No, the steak!"

The kids behind me were getting restless.

"No, the chicken. The chicken," I said. She served me and I moved along, immediately thinking I'd made the wrong choice. I knew the steak would be gone by the time I went back for seconds.

I sat down with Frankie and Eloni. Boris showed up late, looking a little frazzled.

"I went to the new forest to tell Tootles that Runt wasn't coming to help him this morning," he said, "and someone put a bag over my head and dragged me away."

"No way," I said.

"I couldn't escape. I was pushed inside the aviary building, but when I pulled off the bag, there was nobody around."

"Did you report it to Dean Everest?" I asked.

"Yes, but he thought I was making it up to get out of my Dragon Training exam."

"No way," I said again.

"He's done it before," Eloni said, holding a steak sandwich that I wished I had. "This would be your fourth 'kidnapping,' right?"

Boris nodded. "But this one was real, I swear."

Conversation continued around me, but my thoughts returned to my own problems. I didn't want to go to Andirat, I was worried about Pravus, I hoped Syke was okay . . .

"Why so glum, chum?" Eloni asked me. He was so huge, but he had a smile that was more contagious than troll pox. "Wish you'd chosen the steak?"

"Yes," I admitted. "Plus, I went to a meeting in the dungeon this morning. Guys, Critchlore is worried that Pravus will attack our school."

They nodded, because rumors fly through this school faster than an angry bat.

Lunch was a bummer. All I could think about was that sandwich I didn't have, which was stupid, because I loved Cook's chicken. Instead of enjoying what I had, I couldn't stop thinking about the lunch I'd sacrificed.

Those thoughts vanished when I saw Darthin stumble toward us. He looked like he'd just been attacked by a family of feral swamp cats—there were scratches on his face and bandages covering his arms. A clump of hair was missing on the right side of his head.

"Darthin!" I said. "Who did this to you?" I handed him my glass of water and he took a long drink.

"I'm not supposed to talk about it," he said. We sat there silently for a second. "Okay, stop pestering me, I'll tell you. Dr. Frankenhammer has the virus that transforms humans into monsters, which is one of the things you need to make Undefeatable Minions. He's trying to make an antidote, so he's given the virus to whatever he can find in his lab—so far a rat, a lizard, and a cat. They've all transformed into wild, bloodthirsty monsters."

"They scratched you . . . won't you become infected?"

"No, the virus isn't contagious that way. But I've been fired. He needs someone more . . . sturdy. He needs Frankie."

"Really?" Frankie perked up. "Daddy needs me?"

"Yes, I'm supposed to tell you to report there after lunch. You're excused from your classes."

"Sweet!" Frankie looked so happy, but then he glanced at Darthin. "Oh, man, Darthin. I'm so sorry."

Darthin shrugged. "It's fine. I still get to work on the sudithium antidote in his secret, secret lab. But right now, he's focusing on the virus antidote. Be careful, Frankie. The rat attacks anything that comes into sight. The lizard is sneakier, and the cat grew horns that can slice through leather."

Yikes.

Darthin swayed a bit. "I've lost a lot of blood . . ." He fainted, falling sideways onto Frankie.

"I'll take him to the infirmary," Frankie said, lifting him with ease.

I eyed the steak on Darthin's plate, but before I could make a move, Eloni grabbed it, licked the top, and took a giant bite.

"Oh," Eloni mumbled through his full mouth. "Did you want it?"

He smiled, and I couldn't help it; I smiled back.

‡‡‡

Lunch was nearly over when I spotted Mistress Moira behind the counter with Cook.

"I've gotta go," I told the guys. I cleared my tray and ran to catch up with Mistress Moira as she left through the kitchen. Outside, two workers were loading luggage into a van. I stopped in my tracks when I spotted Miss Merrybench, her arms going wide for that hug.

I was torn. They were leaving to go to Skelterdam, where no human can survive, to try to find the witch who cursed me. I should be grateful. But then I noticed something crawl out of Miss Merrybench's ear and, *ew* . . . no.

"Mistress Moira," I said, dodging Miss Merrybench for the hundredth time. "How are you going to survive in Skelterdam?"

"I have some tricks," she said. "Don't worry about me."

Dr. Critchlore strode down the castle steps holding a small package. As I dodged zombie hugs, he handed it to Mistress Moira, and then they hugged good-bye. I may not be the most observant kid (I'd gotten a B in Strategic Reconnaissance last year), but I was pretty sure they liked each other.

"Be careful," Dr. Critchlore said, holding her face in his hands. "Pravus will have troops searching there too. He needs a witch to cast a spell of obedience."

"I can take care of myself," she replied. "You need to protect this school, and everyone in it."

"I will."

Now I was in an awkward situation. I wanted to hug Mistress Moira good-bye, but that would probably hurt Miss Merrybench's feelings. Thankfully, Professor Murphy came to my rescue.

"Time to go," he said, opening the van door for Miss Merry-bench. She gave up on the hug and climbed into the van. As soon as she turned away from me I went to Mistress Moira, who was gazing into Dr. Critchlore's eyes in a way that made me think I shouldn't interrupt whatever was happening there, but I did anyway. I shoved myself between them to give her a quick hug, and then I pulled away before Miss Merrybench could see.

"Good luck," I said.

"Thank you, Runt," she said. "And remember, don't leave this school until I get back."

I nodded, and she got in the van with one last look back at Dr. Critchlore. I jumped into her line of sight to wave, and then the van took off.

Behind us, six trees copied me by waving good-bye. Silly little toddler trees. This was their new favorite game, copying whatever I did.

I turned and put my hands on my waist. They all did the same, shaking with little tree laughter. I shook my finger at them and pretended to be angry, because they loved imitating that. And then I looked at Dr. Critchlore, who was still waving good-bye, but with a more concerned expression on his face.

"Don't worry," I said. "They'll find that witch."

"Yes, I believe they will. I just wish I'd . . ." His voice drifted off as he watched the van leave. I noticed he held an envelope in his hand.

"What?"

He shook his head. "Nothing." He stuffed the envelope in his back pocket. "Back to work." He walked up the stairs, leaving me standing with my trees.

They were growing up so fast. Each one was taller than me now, by a lot. Hmm . . . now that I thought about it, that was some pretty fast growth, even for a tree.

Uh-oh. There was a reason they might have grown so fast. Sara had hidden the bag of sudithium out by the FRP. Had they found it? Rather than ask them to come with me (which they wouldn't do), I turned and said, "Can't catch me!" and ran for the new forest.

And there I saw the evidence: The bag of sudithium had been dug up and spilled into the pond. The trees must have drank from it.

I picked up the empty bag. "Did you guys find this?"

"Treasure hunt game!" Googa said, hopping up and down. "Fun!"

Dr. Frankenhammer had to make those antidotes, quick, so I could cover up Sara's sudithium-stealing crime before people started asking questions.

I returned to the castle, heading for the dungeon and my afternoon lesson with Professor Zaida. A bandaged Darthin intercepted me in the foyer.

"Darthin, feeling better?" I asked.

"I'm fine, thanks," he said. "You're not heading for the dungeon, are you?"

"I am."

"Don't. Some of our giant insects have gotten loose. Ants, grubs, a praying mantis. She's got barbed arms that can slice through bone."

He patted me on the shoulder and headed for the stairs that led to the dungeon.

"Then why are you going down there?" I asked.

He held up a can of insect repellent. "I've got protection," he said. "I need to tell Mrs. Gomes to add these to the safety stations. Plus, I have an idea to help Dr. Frankenhammer with the bugs. It's a little crazy, but it just might work."

I was so proud of Darthin. He was focusing on controlling monsters, instead of hiding from them, like he used to do.

"Can you let me know when Dr. Frankenhammer shrinks them?" I asked. "I may need some of that antidote."

He was about to answer when he looked behind me and an expression of dreamy surprise took over his face. I turned and saw Janet. She was smiling, which always made me feel light and floaty all over.

"Runt, I have something to show you," she said, flipping her dark hair over her shoulder. "It will only take a second. Come on." She pulled me out the front door.

"Where are we going?" I asked. Janet was holding my hand, and I couldn't keep a big smile from stretching across my face.

"To the sports field."

The sports field? Janet didn't play tackle three-ball, or dodge boulder, or any sport that I knew of. "Why?"

She touched my nose. "It's a fun surprise."

"Okay, but I have to get back for class." Professor Zaida would be angry if I was late.

We walked down the road, hand in hand, and I realized that I didn't care about Professor Zaida. The sky was blue, birds were chirping, and two manticores were growling at each other as we passed by. The day was perfect.

"Let's take the shortcut," Janet said, leading me through the buildings next to the main road. Earlier in the term this was where some imps had trapped me by crying for help. Ha! I would never fall for such a lame trap now. I'd really grown over this school year.

As soon as I stepped onto the field, I was tackled by Janet's skeleton friends.

"See?" Janet said to them. "It's really not that difficult. You just have to make sure you have the right guy, and then lure him away."

"Janet? What's going on?"

She didn't answer. She sprayed something misty right in my face and I passed out. The last thing I heard was Janet saying, "Take him to the car outside."

CHAPTER 6

*There are ~~twenty-two~~ twenty-one realms in the
Porvian Continent, and one neutral territory, Stull,
where the EOs gather for meetings.*
—*MAP OF THE PORVIAN CONTINENT*, UPDATED MONTHLY AS
EOS STEAL TERRITORY FROM EACH OTHER

I woke up bouncing around in the back of a sedan driven by a skeleton. It took me a few blinks and a moan to return to consciousness. Two more skeletons sat in the front, and there was another one on my left. Janet sat on my other side, watching the scenery outside.

"You're awake," she said. "Sorry about that."

"What's going on?"

"I'm taking you to meet someone. I knew you wouldn't leave school without asking permission, so I had to kidnap you. I told my associates to do it"—she raised her voice to say the next part: "but they are completely incompetent! Setting up ambushes in the wrong place, grabbing Boris by mistake. Ridiculous."

Bones rattled angrily from the front seat, then we bounced over a pothole and I was thrown into the skeleton beside me, who shoved me back into Janet.

I checked my wrists. "You're not taking me north, are you? I have a tether curse."

"Don't worry, we're only going to Stull City. You went there before, remember? The field trip to the capital? You were fine."

"Why are you taking me?"

"My father doesn't trust Professor Zaida. She's too cautious. We need you to make some appearances. To rally the people behind you so that the generals can be overthrown. There's no time to waste. Our people are suffering!"

"*Our* people?"

"We're both from Andirat. My father worked for King Natherly, your grandfather, before the coup. He's now the leader of the rebels. He's been working against the generals ever since they overthrew the royal family."

I closed my eyes, because my head was still foggy.

Janet handed me something to drink. "This will clear your head."

I took it, but didn't drink. "I don't know if I trust you, Janet."

"Runt, we're on the same side. I've spent the last year protecting you."

I drank. "You're a spy," I said.

"Yes, I'm not a siren. I was sent by my father to find you. He's been looking for you ever since he heard you might still be alive. You were kidnapped during a parade right before the coup. Everyone thought the kidnapper killed you, but we found out he couldn't do it. He took you across the sea and left you at his former school. We knew you were at a minion school in Stull, we just didn't know which one.

"I thought you were a dead ringer for little Aubie from the moment I saw you. And then I noticed your medallion. I pointed

40

you out to my father in the capital—remember, the man I was talking to in the library?"

"Yeah," I said. At the time she wouldn't tell me who he was.

"My father thinks it's time for you to take your rightful place as prince of Andirat. We need to take the country back from the generals who've destroyed it. The people are counting on you."

"They are?"

"You're their shining hope for a better future."

I was their shining hope? Oh, jeez. Those poor people.

I shook my head and looked out the window, trying to make sense of things. Janet was a spy? She wanted me to take my rightful place as prince? Fear crept into every nerve in my body and I had to force myself to take a few deep breaths.

I repeated the lines Professor Zaida made me recite ten times a day: "I can do this. I am Prince Auberon of Andirat, and I will lead my people out of their oppression."

"That's right," Janet said with a smile.

I didn't know what conviction felt like, but I knew I didn't have it.

We drove down a winding road into Castle Valley, which was just outside of Stull City. Stull was the only neutral country on the Porvian Continent. It wasn't run by an Evil Overlord, but it was where they met peacefully to negotiate treaties and stuff. Every EO kept an embassy here, for when they came for EO Council meetings.

We drove past tall walls and huge stone gates guarded by enormous monsters. On field trips we often detoured down this road.

"That could be you," our teacher would say, pointing to one of the guards. We would all oooh and ahhh, because those guys were living the minion dream—cushy job in a nice neighborhood with full benefits.

Our skeleton driver turned abruptly onto a road that ended at a tall stone gate with three arched entranceways. As our car approached the middle archway, two giant ogres thumped out to intercept us.

"Janet!" I cried. "We can't go in there."

She smiled at me. "Of course we can, silly."

The ogres standing guard dipped their heads at us, and we drove beneath the massive central arch. Past the gate, I could see a castle in the distance—a dark, gothic structure that looked like it had poked its way out of the ground; the pointy spires and towers rose to an incredible height. The immense castle sat on slightly higher ground, overlooking a grassy meadow in front, and flanked by forests on either side. We drove up a long road that ran along the side of the field.

"What is this place?" I asked.

"Historically, this was the summer palace of the rulers of Erudyten. There's a lake and stables behind the castle."

"Erudyten, the land of my ancestors," I whispered, still in awe. My people used to live there, before the EOs took over and ran them off to Andirat.

"Now it's the Andiratian embassy."

Embassy? It was the most enormous castle I'd ever seen. And the grounds went on forever. I looked at Janet, to see if she was serious.

"This is all yours, Your Highness," Janet said. "Welcome home."

I had to have heard that wrong. "Wha-what did you say?"

"This castle is yours," she said. "It belongs to you."

My heart was jumping and pounding and thumping in my chest as I looked from Janet to the castle and back again. "You're joking," I said, because she had to be joking. I could fit everything I owned into a duffel bag I kept in my closet. There was no way the castle could be mine.

"You're joking," I said again.

"This embassy belongs to the royal family. And *you* are the last direct descendant."

"If this is Andirat's embassy, why haven't the generals taken it over?"

"The generals are afraid to leave Andirat. Each one thinks that if they leave, another general will take over his region. So the exiles took over the embassy and made it the home base for the rebels."

"The exiles?"

"Many wealthy Andiratians fled after the generals took over. They live in Stull now. They fund the rebellion. And they can't wait to meet you, Your Highness."

This was too much. I mean, I knew about this in theory, but seeing the castle and hearing Janet address me as "Your Highness" felt so unreal, like I was floating through a dream, or a nightmare; I couldn't decide which. Maybe I hadn't really woken up from whatever it was she'd sprayed in my face.

Stop being a baby, I told myself. *You are a prince. You're going to be a king someday. If Professor Zaida has confidence in you, you should too!*

It was a pretty good pep talk, but I didn't believe a word of it.

CHAPTER 7

Erudyten is gone, but not forgotten. It will be ours again.
—THE LEGEND OF ERUDYTEN, TAUGHT TO
CHILDREN IN ANDIRAT

We drove closer to the castle, past some low hedges and a flowerbed filled with white and red flowers. The red flowers formed two giant letters, an *E* for Erudyten and an *A* for Andirat.

"Everyone thought the entire royal family was killed," Janet said. "When your grave was discovered empty, people got so excited, and started asking, 'What if he's still alive?'"

We continued driving past a topiary garden. A line of sea serpent–shaped hedges circled a zoo of other giant hedge animals—giraffes and elephants and bears and a rabbit almost as big as the one I'd seen in Upper Worb.

The car stopped near the entrance. I stepped out and took it all in. The castle had looked huge from the gate, but standing next to it, I really felt how enormous it was. It towered over me like a mountain, story after story of dark-gray stone topped with pointy roofs and towers stretching to the sky.

Two lines of uniformed people stood on the steps leading to

the entrance. As I walked past they bowed their heads and said, "Welcome home, Your Highness."

At the door a man and a woman in dark suits stood apart from everyone else. They bowed before introducing themselves. "Paula Ambrose," the woman said. "I'm in charge of affairs at the Andiratian embassy, Your Highness." She had light hair that fell to her shoulders and very red lips that did not smile.

"Dante Fox, your personal valet," the man said with a quick bow. He looked more like a bodyguard than a valet. His suit strained to contain his muscles, and he had the face of a henchman, with a round, bald head, thick eyebrows, and bushy mustache. "Please, follow me."

Mr. Fox led the way into the palatial entrance hall, where a string quartet was playing. "'The King's Tribute,'" Janet whispered in my ear. "For you."

We veered into an enormous room with tall, red velvet–draped windows on one side, life-sized portrait paintings along the other. More grown-ups in suits stood in groups, most of them huddling around one tall man—the man I'd seen Janet talk to in the capital library. Her father.

He was also dressed in a dark suit, and he still had that hunched-shoulder look of a crane. He stood thoughtfully, holding the lapels of his jacket while listening to the woman next to him. It reminded me of how fathers look when they're holding a child on their shoulders, with strong hands clinging tightly to chubby shins.

I could tell in an instant that he was the most important person in the room. The people around him snuck glances his way, straining to listen in on his conversation.

I felt self-conscious. In this fancy room filled with elegant grown-ups, I was wearing my Critchlore uniform: black cargo pants, tan jacket with black trim, Critchlore T-shirt. Janet had somehow changed into a navy blue dress while I'd been sleeping in the car.

She edged by Mr. Fox and headed toward her father. Mr. Fox held out a hand, preventing me from following her. "If I may announce you, Your Highness?"

He took my confused look for a "yes" and stepped forward.

"Ladies and gentlemen, may I present His Royal Highness, Auberon Gabriel Titus Kenton Valdemar Natherly, Prince of Andirat."

The music got louder as I stood there in view of everyone. Or maybe it just seemed that way because the room had gone quiet. Everyone turned to me, staring for a moment. But then they clapped. The clapping grew to cheers.

They were cheering . . . me? I felt so awkward. Like when people sing "Happy Birthday" and you have to stand there smiling while everyone is looking at you, and all you can do is hope the song ends quickly.

Janet's father strode forward and bowed.

"Welcome, Your Highness," he said. "I am Brian Tinsforth Seizemore. You may call me Commandant."

"Nice to meet you." I held out my hand. "I'm Runt Higgins."

Everyone laughed, but the Commandant frowned. He glared at Janet, who hustled over and whispered in my ear, "You are Prince Auberon . . . Runt Higgins is no more."

I froze as my situation hit me with the force of a troll tackle. Runt Higgins was no more?

"You probably don't remember me," Mr. Seizemore said as he led me toward the other adults, "but I knew you as a child. I was an advisor to your father and grandfather. And now, I'm here to serve you."

"Okay, uh, Commandant."

Well, this was new, having grown-ups tell me they were at my service. I was more used to them telling me what to do, and then screaming at me as I did it.

"We're working on staging your glorious return to Andirat," he went on. "And we don't have much time."

He introduced me to many people—rebel leaders, exiles, strategists for this and that. They all had titles and they all began to blur together in a giant collage of smiling adult faces. Once that was done, Mr. Fox suggested that I visit my quarters, so that I could dress in something "appropriate" for dinner. I followed him upstairs to the third floor, where he stopped in front of an elaborate pair of double doors and opened both sides, throwing them wide.

"Your quarters, Sire."

My jaw dropped as I walked into the fanciest room I'd ever seen. Gold-trimmed everything, rich red velvets, polished wood. To my right was a bed big enough for a troll; to my left, there was a sitting area in front of a fireplace. In front of me, across a carpet that was itself a work of art, a pair of doors made mostly of glass opened to the balcony.

I walked over to look outside. The backyard was warmly lit by the setting sun, and I saw a man and woman in uniform riding horseback on a path that curved around a rose garden. Beyond the garden lay a lawn big enough for a game of Giants vs. Villagers, bordered by forest on two sides, and, in the distance, a sparkling lake. There were more perfectly trimmed hedge animals everywhere. It was as if I'd been transported to a fantasyland at the Evil Overlord Adventure Park, but without the crowds.

Mr. Fox suggested I take a bath. He led me down a short hallway, and we passed a walk-in closet filled with clothes, all for me.

I couldn't remember the last time I'd taken a bath. It was amazing. I poured in an entire bottle of bubble bath and sculpted my very own bubble world, full of hills and valleys. My fingers were prune-like when Mr. Fox knocked on the door and told me it was time to join the others.

Something "appropriate" for dinner turned out to be a dark suit with a white bow tie and shoes that were uncomfortably stiff. Mr. Fox helped me dress and then escorted me back downstairs to a long dining hall filled with people, where he announced me again. After everyone stood up, he led me to the head of the long table. The Commandant sat on one side, with Janet on the other. Everyone sat after I did.

Walking into this grand room, I felt exactly like I had when I'd walked into my first Junior Henchman class and seen twenty-seven kids show up for the five available spots. I'd known, looking at my classmates, that each one would be a better henchman than me.

I knew, looking at this room of adults, that any one of them would be a better prince. I wanted to hide under the table and wait for someone to tell me this had all been a terrible mistake.

CHAPTER 8

The two-pronged fork is not for eating.
It's the King's Stabbing Fork.
—ANDIRATIAN ETIQUETTE

I turned to Janet, and she must have sensed my dread, because she smiled at me. *You can do this*, she seemed to say. I took a deep breath and smiled back.

I was served a thick gray soup with black shavings floating on top, like bits of bark in a puddle. It even smelled like dirt. I was starving, but this wasn't what I'd had in mind.

"Do you have any chicken nuggets?" I asked the server. He shook his head.

"This is the chef's famous cream of wild mushroom soup," the Commandant said. "The truffle shavings on top were flown in especially for you. They are a very expensive delicacy."

Truffles? They looked like imp poop. I swirled them around while listening to the Commandant talk to the person next to him. During the meal, the Commandant kept whispering instructions to me, telling me when to start eating, how to address people, and why everyone jumped when I picked up the wrong fork. His manner was gentle, and I liked him. He didn't yell at me when I spilled sauce on my shirt.

People told me stories about Andirat. I smiled through it all, barely tasting the food because I was so overwhelmed by everything. That morning I'd woken up and gone to class, training to be a junior henchman. Now I was at the head of a table with everyone thinking I was their shiny hope for a better future. It made me feel both big and incredibly small at the same time.

Just as my eyes were starting to droop, Dante Fox appeared at my side. "I can return you to your quarters now," he said, like he was reading my mind.

"That'd be fantastic," I said.

Back in my room, Mr. Fox lifted the coat from my back before I had a chance to kick off my shoes.

"I've laid out some nightclothes." He pointed to the bed and then walked over to the windows to close the curtains. "I will come dress you for breakfast at seven."

"Thank you," I said. "Good night, Mr. Fox."

He bowed and backed out of the room. I changed into my pajamas and then went to the bathroom. As I brushed my teeth, I couldn't help but notice that I looked the same. I don't know what I'd been expecting, but no magic had worked its wonders on me to make me feel more prince-like. I'd felt like an imposter all through dinner. I knew I didn't belong here.

"I am Prince Auberon of Andirat," I told my reflection. "I am going to lead my people out of their oppression."

Sure you are, my expression seemed to say. *And then you're going to single-handedly win the Hoopsmash World Cup.*

I got into bed. The comforter was a mile thick and the mattress felt like a cloud.

Back at Critchlore's, I shared a room with Frankie and Darthin, in an old building that was freezing in winter and roasting on hot days. I slept on a lumpy mattress with a thin pillow next to one guy whose snoring sounded like thunder, and another guy who was too afraid to get up to use the bathroom, so he kept a jar under his bed.

I had to admit, this was nicer. But while I knew I should be thrilled at my new situation—this room, this castle, I had servants!—a heavy feeling in my gut kept that thrill from lifting my mood. I was scared. Terrified. What if I wasn't good enough to be prince? What if they didn't like me? What if I made a mistake?

Janet's words echoed in my brain. *Runt Higgins is no more.* I had abruptly switched lives, and I hadn't even said good-bye to the old one.

I needed to talk to Dr. Critchlore, to Professor Zaida, to Cook. They had to be worried about me. Tomorrow I'd ask Janet how I could get in touch with them. She'd help me. She knew how important they were to me. And let's face it . . . I was the prince. That meant people had to do what I asked, right?

I snuggled into the comfy dreaminess of my bed and drifted to sleep, remembering how Janet had smiled at me through dinner.

I was awoken in the middle of the night by scratching noises near the fireplace.

My first thought was that my foster brother, Pierre, had put another two-headed swamp cat in my dorm room. Pierre was Cook's real son, a fact he never let me forget. He'd played lots of pranks on me when I was little, including one that made me believe I'd morphed into a werewolf one night.

The room was dark, and it took me a moment to remember where I was.

The noises started by the fireplace, then traveled along the wall, like sharp claws tapping across a wooden floor. I reached for the lamp and turned it on.

"Who's there?" I called. My voice seemed as frightened as I was, leaving my mouth in a trembling whisper.

A small, startled face looked up at me before scurrying off in panic. The little creature—a brownie or a kobold—ducked behind a wingback chair near the fireplace and disappeared. I jumped up and raced after it, but there was no trace of him, or where he'd gone.

I checked the wall, the fireplace, and the floor, but I couldn't figure out how he'd escaped.

I ran to my room's double doors, but they wouldn't open. I'd been locked inside.

CHAPTER 9

*Terror grips with a stronger hand when
you wake in the night.*
—TRUE FACT

I was wide awake now, my heart racing. I made a barricade of furniture along the wall by the fireplace, so the creature wouldn't be able to get back into the room. If it was a kobold, who knew what sort of tricks it would play on me? I got back in bed, wishing Frankie and Darthin were with me now, even if they brought their snoring and pee jar with them.

I lay on my back, covers pulled up for protection. I told myself that nothing was in the room with me, but I couldn't go back to sleep. I turned on every light and stayed up for what seemed like hours, listening to every creak and rattle as the wind rushed by outside.

I woke to a shove on my shoulder.

"Hmm," I mumbled.

"Time to get up, Your Highness," a deep voice rumbled through the fog of my dream.

"No, thank you," I said.

Another, sharper shove. "Get up."

I bolted upright. "Mr. Fox," I said, looking up into his wide, expressionless face.

"It's time to get dressed." He held an outfit on a hanger.

I stood and grabbed the clothes. "I got it," I said, uncomfortable at the idea of someone else dressing me.

He nodded and turned to the windows, opening up all the curtains he'd shut the night before. I noticed that the furniture I'd rearranged had been moved back to its original placement.

"Why was I locked inside?" I asked.

"For your protection," he said. "You're not aware of the castle's defenses. If you were to wander, you might meet something . . . unpleasant."

"Like what?" I was used to unpleasant. At Critchlore's I'd been attacked by Clarence (twice), a giant muscle-blob, a werewolf, and a swarm of carnivorous cockroaches. And that was just this school year.

"Step over here," he said. "And I'll show you."

Mr. Fox talked with such formal precision, which was surprising, because he looked like a dangerous henchman. He had a scar through one eyebrow that I had a feeling didn't come from ironing clothes or making appointments or whatever it was that valets did.

I joined him by the balcony door. He removed a key from his jacket pocket and pointed to the stone gargoyles perched on the edges of the roof. Then he opened the door and we stepped outside.

"The gargoyles have always protected the castle," he said. "They are made of the same stone." He nodded at one with huge, pointy ears and stubby horns. The gargoyle's rocky head turned to peer at us, and his eyes suddenly burst into flames. I jumped backward.

"They cannot always tell friend from foe," Mr. Fox said, guiding me back inside. "Don't go out there again."

I didn't think I'd be able to, since he had the key, but I nodded.

"I will take you to breakfast with the Commandant," Mr. Fox said. "After you've dressed."

I grabbed my clothes and headed for the bathroom. Funny, the bathroom door was the only door that didn't lock.

Mr. Fox led me downstairs to the ground floor, where I met Janet and her father in his private office. The high-ceilinged room was bigger than a classroom, with bookshelves, leather chairs, dark wood, and thick carpets. A beautifully detailed map of Andirat hung over the fireplace.

The Commandant sat at his desk by the window, talking on the phone. When he saw me, he nodded and raised a finger, indicating he'd be a minute. Janet floated over to greet me, wearing a swirling pale-green dress, and dismissed Mr. Fox.

"I hope you slept well," she whispered.

"Not really," I said. My brain still felt foggy from the lack of sleep.

"It's a big change, I know." She touched my arm and led me to an adjoining room, where breakfast was laid out on a round table: fancy pastries and eggs and little sausages and fruit cups. Tall windows showed a wide terrace outside, perched above the rose garden, and beyond it, the lake.

"We have important work to do this morning," Janet said, pulling out a chair for me. "Father wants to make sure you have the right memories. You need to forget all that dog business and remember what it was like growing up in the palace."

"I've been studying Andirat for months now," I said. "With Professor Zaida."

"Yes, but we need to make sure you have *authentic* memories. Professor Zaida doesn't know what it was like to live in the palace. Which paintings lined the hallways, what activities the family did for fun. Personal, intimate stuff."

"Oh, okay," I said.

"You don't need more than a few specific memories," her father said, taking his seat next to me. "After all, you were only four when you were kidnapped."

"Can I call Cook?" I asked. "She's probably worried about me."

"I've talked to her," Janet said. "She's fine. I've told everyone at Critchlore's how vital it is for you to focus on this and nothing else. They understand. They know how important you are, and they're very proud of you."

She smiled at me and passed the plate of eggs to her father. He swished out his napkin and served himself, then handed the plate to me.

"Here's the problem," he said, getting right to business. "There's another rebel leader here in Stull. He leads a group as large as ours and he doesn't believe you're the missing prince."

"Syke never believed it, either," I said.

"She's just jealous," Janet said. "She's that type, you know."

I didn't, but the Commandant held up a hand for attention.

"Like me, this man worked for the royal family before the coup.

He swears that he saw the entire family murdered, and that there's no way you could have survived. Obviously, he's wrong, but without the support of his people, our job will be difficult. Maybe impossible."

"A prince can't lead if nobody will follow," Janet said, in explanation.

"Can't you do a DNA test?" I said.

"He doesn't trust them," the Commandant said. "He believes that such tests are often used to confuse the gullible. There are too many ways to manipulate the data, all while the results are supposed to be incontrovertible. He's a suspicious man who sees conspiracies everywhere."

"He trusts his own instincts over scientific tests," Janet added. Apparently she felt that her job was to translate what her father said, in case I didn't understand.

"Since this is the case," her father went on, "we need to be ready for any type of question he may ask. He knew the castle, the family, the grounds. But at the same time, it's important that you not appear too rehearsed."

"Got it," I said before Janet could jump in to reiterate. "Know things, but look natural about it."

The Commandant smiled, and I smiled back. I'd been so frightened that I'd have to do this alone, but I wasn't alone. I had Janet and her father. I forgot about my night terrors and my worries about responsibility, because they were going to help me learn to be a prince, and together we would save our people.

We finished eating, and then the lessons began, right at the breakfast table. I was shown pictures, home movies, and journal entries. I searched for memories in my brain that matched the pictures, and sometimes I found them. Having a picnic by the lake behind the castle in Andirat—I remembered that! The stables and the forest, I remembered those too.

After sitting for two hours my legs got twitchy. The Commandant noticed. I had a feeling he noticed everything.

"Why don't you take a walk outdoors," he said. "We'll convene back here in thirty minutes.

"And Janet," he added with a stern look. "Remember your assignment. No mistakes this time."

CHAPTER 10

The Swamp Tromp, the Monster Relay,
and the Crash and Smash.
—ANNUAL ALL-SCHOOL COMPETITIONS

What did he mean by that?" I asked her, but she was already by the door to the terrace, heading outside.

The day was bright and sunny, and very warm. I took off the button-down shirt I was wearing over an undershirt, and draped it over a chair. Janet, wearing a short-sleeved dress that looked as light as air, frowned, but then shrugged.

"What did your dad mean about mistakes?" I asked.

"I was babysitting the child of a visiting exile and he got away from me back here," she said. "It wasn't my fault. Mrs. Ambrose distracted me." We walked down the terrace steps and onto a gravel path. "*He could have been killed*," she mimicked someone's high-pitched voice. "*The monsters would've eaten him if Mr. Fox hadn't been there.* Blah, blah, blah."

She laughed. "Why don't we forget all that prince stuff and just enjoy this beautiful day?"

"Okay," I said. I scanned the backyard for monsters, but found my gaze returning to Janet. It felt like I was in a dream. Just me and Janet, hanging out together with nobody else around.

"It's fantastic, isn't it?" she said, her arm sweeping to include everything.

"It is," I agreed.

The field, the gardens, the lake, they were all so beautiful. Maybe later I'd ask Mr. Fox if he wanted to throw a ball around. I also daydreamed out loud about installing a zipline leading from my third-floor balcony to the lake house. Maybe a few rope swings to sail over the water, and a go-cart track next to the rose garden, or a mini-golf course. I could create my very own Evil Overlord Adventure Park.

Janet laughed. "And you can hire your own minions. Imagine! You could make Rufus's life as miserable as he's made yours."

"I'd rather forget about Rufus," I said. "Professor Zaida told me that leaders obsessed with personal vendettas are unfit to rule."

"Sure, it's much better to be obsessed with amusement parks," she said with an eye roll, which, if I'm honest, stung a bit.

We headed for the lake. Giant ogres patrolled the edges of the woods, some of them accompanied by the largest manticores I'd ever seen, with powerful lion bodies and human faces on keen alert. Their scorpion tails swished threateningly in the air. There were also flying monkeys perched in the trees, and some human guards on horseback.

"They've upped security, of course," Janet said.

"Why 'of course'?"

"The generals know about you. Everyone in Andirat is talking about how you might have survived. The generals will do anything to keep you from returning to Andirat."

I nodded.

"There's Mrs. Ambrose," Janet said, nodding to a group in front of us. "Your first act as king should be to fire her. My father tried, but she's been here forever and nobody knows the castle like she does. Plus, the exiles like her, and they control the money."

Mrs. Ambrose stood with a trio of manticores, feeding them from a bucket of fish with a gloved hand. She did a double-take when she saw Janet. "And here's our new prince now," she said to the manticores.

"Hello," I said, smiling at the group.

Three faces stared back at me, scowling. One licked his lips after drool escaped out of the side of his mouth. Manticores have a lot of teeth. It's a little creepy, like someone put a shark's mouth on a person.

"Mrs. Ambrose, can I talk to you?" Janet asked. "Privately?"

Mrs. Ambrose didn't look happy, but she nodded and they walked away, leaving me standing awkwardly with the manticores. They watched their bucket of food swing away, and then turned to look at me, like it was my fault they'd lost their meal. The one with the dark mane and beard made me nervous. He was as tall as me, even on all fours.

"Hot day, isn't it?" I tried. They just kept staring at me. I glanced over at Janet, hoping she'd rescue me, but she was busy arguing with Mrs. Ambrose.

"Uh . . . so do any of you know Tiffany Smithers-Pendelton?" I asked. "She's a manticore from my school."

Dark Mane scowled. He took two steps toward me on those

powerful legs. I backed up, nervous now, but then he smiled and said, "You know Little Tiffy?"

"Yeah," I said, exhaling with relief. I wouldn't call her "little," but okay. "She was the only first-year to make it through the Swamp Tromp."

"Hey, Roger," a female said. "Isn't that William's niece? The one who didn't get into the Pravus Academy?"

"That's right, Elsie," Roger said. "She had a nasty cold and accidentally sneezed a few teeth at her interviewer. He lost an eye, but if you ask me, that should have earned her a spot." He turned back to me. "How is she?"

"Good," I said. "Well, I hope she's good. I'm a little worried about the school, what with the rumors—"

Janet returned and pulled me away.

"Bye," I said to the manticores with a wave. They waved back.

"Do *not* talk to the help," Janet whispered in my ear. "It's not what a prince would do. You are above them. A ruler, not a minion. I thought Professor Zaida was teaching you this stuff."

"I guess we hadn't gotten to that part," I said.

"Stay away from the manticores," she said. "They're dangerous and you do *not* want to run into one if you're alone. They maimed one of my father's aides when he stepped out for some fresh air. They won't listen to my father, only to Mrs. Ambrose, who recruited most of them." She looked back and shivered. "I hate them. They always look like they want to bite off my arms."

"Why were you angry with Mrs. Ambrose?" I asked.

"Mrs. Ambrose doesn't know her place," she said. "She's lived here too long, running the embassy like her own little kingdom.

It's gone to her head. When my father arrived a year ago, Mrs. Ambrose was reluctant to give up control to him. But my father is the Commandant of the rebels. *He's* the one in charge."

We walked beneath giant redwood trees and giant ogres, who bowed as we passed. I asked if we could take a boat out on the lake, but Janet pointed to the seven-headed hydra splashing in the shallows. "She wouldn't like it. And we should be getting back."

"Right. We don't want to make your father angry." I said it in jest, but Janet nodded her head.

"You really don't," she said. "I should warn you about my

father . . . he's got a temper. He's such a great man, and he expects everyone to live up to his high expectations. If he sounds mean, it's because saving Andirat is so important to him. To us."

As we headed back to the castle I looked for my room. My quarters were on the third floor, and I found my balcony and the gargoyle guard, the one with huge ears and stubby horns. Above the fourth floor, the many pointy tops of the building seemed to hold individual rooms, separated by pitched rooftops.

I noticed movement in one of those upper rooms. Someone was watching us, but when I focused on the window, the curtains fell shut. I stopped to tie my shoe and stretch, and then quickly

looked back at the room. A girl stood by the window. She wasn't fast enough this time and I saw her.

"Who lives on that top floor?" I asked Janet.

"Oh—those are attic rooms, mostly used for storage."

At lunch I sat at the head of the long table and listened to stories from the exiles about what Andirat was like before the coup.

The afternoon was boring. I tried to memorize my favorite foods, the names of our pets, the different pranks my siblings played on each other. My lack of sleep the night before caught up with me, and I dozed off during a slide show of relatives. I woke up to whispered arguing between Janet and her father, but they hushed when they noticed my eyes flutter open.

Before dinner, Janet took me for another walk behind the castle.

"This embassy is a replica of what Andirat used to be like," Janet said. "The trees and flowers were flown in from across the sea. The architecture is the same. We are very proud of our artists and architects. But back at home, the generals have destroyed everything. So much history . . . gone."

"But we can remake it," I said. "Rebuild the country. And then come back here whenever we want, to visit friends and stuff."

"That's right," she said, smiling at me in that way that made me feel all fluttery in my chest. "You're doing great. I'm sure you're going to convince Mr. Cordholm, the other rebel leader, that you're authentic. And then we can all go home."

Home. For a second I thought she meant back to Critchlore's, but of course she meant Andirat. How could I call a place home if

I didn't know anyone there? And what would happen to the home where I'd grown up?

"What about Critchlore's?" I asked. We passed by the dark-maned manticore, Roger, who looked like a statue, his focus was so intense. "Dr. Pravus might attack them. They need help with their defenses."

"What you need to realize, Your Highness," Janet said, using her patient, teacher voice, the one she used when we sat with her father, "is that the problems at Critchlore's are insignificant compared to what's going on in Andirat."

We walked back toward the castle. Janet seemed annoyed, and I regretted asking about the school.

"Listen," she said, after being lost in thought for a few moments. "Millions of people are starving. Millions. Without trade, the country has no money. Without money, they can't buy food. And any food they grow is stolen or sabotaged by rival gangs working for the generals. I thought you cared about people. I thought you wanted to find your family."

"I do. But my family is gone."

"Darn it, Runt!" she said, really angry now. "*We're* your family now. All the people of Andirat. Your family needs you."

My family needed me. She was right.

"When Andirat is reunited we'll bring our armies here and reclaim Erudyten," Janet said. "We will take on Dr. Pravus. Just like Professor Zaida said."

"How do you know what she said?"

"My father knows *everything*," Janet said.

"Then you know that I'm cursed to die on my sixteenth birthday, right?"

"Of course we do," she said. "When Andirat is reunited, we'll find the witch, and we'll kill her."

"Kill her?"

"Yes, that's how curses go away. You kill the witch who cast them." She made an audible exhale of disappointment at my ignorance.

"Can't we just ask her to remove it?" I asked.

Janet didn't answer. She looked at the sky instead, shaking her head a little. I looked too. But where Janet sought relief from my stupidity, I only saw monkeymen swooping from one side of the lawn to the other in the soft light of dusk.

And then I noticed the swishing curtain in the attic room of the castle again. There was a girl up there, I was sure of it. She was small, like me.

"Are there any kids our age here?"

She shook her head. "No. Just the embassy staff."

Either Janet didn't know everything about this place, or she was lying to me.

CHAPTER 11

"Beware of people who try to make decisions for you."
—WARNING FROM PROFESSOR ZAIDA

At dinner the lady sitting next to Janet told me stories about the museums that the generals had looted. This after someone else reported that the generals were training children to fight in their armies. I had to stop listening. My brain was getting crammed so full of depressing news that it felt like all my happiness was being squished out of me.

And then, during dessert, the Commandant said something to the person next to him that caught my attention: "He's a brilliant minion trainer. Have you seen his giant gorillas? With his help we could subdue the generals without a fight."

The fork I was holding slipped from my hand and clattered against my dish. "Are you talking about Dr. Pravus?"

The Commandant turned to me, his smile disappearing in a flash. He didn't answer.

"Dr. Pravus is evil," I said. "What do you mean, 'With his help'?"

The room went quiet. The Commandant clenched his teeth. I'd

made him mad, which Janet had specifically warned me not to do.

"He wants to destroy my home," I said again, but quieter.

"I think what Prince Auberon is saying," Janet, my translator, said, "is that he would find it difficult to work with a former rival." She looked at me. "Your Highness, don't worry. If we accept his help, we'll demand that he leave Critchlore's little school alone."

Was she serious? Accepting help from Pravus? I was too stunned to say anything. Everyone else started talking in hushed voices, and the Commandant ignored me for the rest of the meal.

My mind raced with thoughts, none of them making me feel better. Why did we need Pravus's help? And if we accepted his help, how could we stop him from taking over this continent without looking like a backstabbing ally? Professor Zaida told me that every action has consequences. Other leaders will judge us for what we do, not what we say.

I remembered what Irma Trackno had told Dr. Critchlore: sometimes you have to work with people you hate to achieve your objectives. That it was naïve to think otherwise.

But defeating Dr. Pravus *was* one of our objectives. He *had* to be stopped. That was just as important as overthrowing the generals.

After dinner, Mr. Fox escorted me to my room. He was rigid and quiet, like a caged animal waiting for the door to crack open so he could charge out. Once in my room, he turned to me, anger blazing in his eyes like a gargoyle. He gripped his hands in tight fists, and it looked like he was struggling to keep himself from throwing me across the room.

"You do NOT interrupt the Commandant. You do NOT contradict the Commandant. The Commandant has been working to save our country for EIGHT years."

"But . . . I'm the prince."

"YOU are nothing but an IGNORANT child."

I backed away from him, my heart racing. He was going to punch me, I was sure. "I'm sorry," I said, holding my hands up in apology. "I . . . I . . . I won't do it again."

"You won't," he said. "Think before you speak. Now, get some sleep."

As if I could sleep now, with all that adrenaline charging through my body.

He left, locking the door with an emphatic click. I took some deep breaths to calm myself. Dante Fox, the man I thought was there to do my bidding, had just scared the truffles out of me.

Why was everyone so mad? All I'd done was state an opinion about Dr. Pravus. I knew I wasn't an expert or anything. I was just a kid. Of course these people knew more than I did. But shouldn't I be allowed to have an opinion? I was the prince.

Tomorrow I would explain to the Commandant why Pravus had to be stopped. Maybe he just didn't know the truth about him. In the meantime, I sat in a wingback chair by the fireplace and munched on one of the big oatmeal chocolate chip cookies that had been left on the desk. Someone didn't want me to go hungry, since I was locked inside. I placed a few on the floor, a peace offering to my nightly intruder. Angry kobolds (or brownies) are dangerous creatures.

I fell asleep in my bed with the lamp on and woke up to a pale ghost face floating right above me. I know that for most people this might be terrifying, but I'd lived with ghosts all my life. This one lacked that touch of decomposition that made a ghost really scary. He was actually kind of good-looking, even though he was frowning at me. He wore the formal attire of a castle servant, but the clothes floated around him, like he was swimming underwater.

"Hi," I said. "What's your name?"

The ghost looked startled, and I realized that he'd wanted to scare me. I felt bad, so I screamed, pulled the covers up to my chin, and pointed at him with a shaky finger. "G-g-g-g-g-host!"

He didn't buy it and left, sulking. Then the scratching noises came back, which was weird, because ghosts can't affect the physical world.

I realized that I *did* have two roommates, the kobold/brownie and the ghost. They just weren't as friendly as Darthin and Frankie. They didn't answer any of my questions, even though I knew they were there, listening.

"Okay, roomies," I said to what looked like an empty room. "I'm going to tell you a story, because I can't sleep, and there's nothing to read in here. It's called 'The Troll and the Brownie.'"

"The Troll and the Brownie" is an old fable about a brave brownie who saves her family from an attacking troll by using cleverness and tricks. It's a funny story, unless you're a troll. Midway through I paused to sip some water and heard chewing sounds from behind the chair. Soft laughter interrupted me a couple times too. I kept telling the story. It was the distraction I needed.

"Tomorrow night I'll tell the story of the Sad Ghost of Well-more Manor, who couldn't scare anyone because he was just too handsome. Good night."

The room was quiet. Eventually, I slept.

When Mr. Fox came the next morning, I was already up and dressed. I did not want to spend one more second alone with him. He silently escorted me downstairs, then left me outside the Commandant's office when someone asked for his help with two ghosts who kept disturbing the Commandant at night.

The door to the office was open, and I heard Janet and her father arguing.

"... too much at stake. I think we made a big mistake."

"No, this is better," Janet's voice said. "He's not that sharp, but he'll do whatever I say. Always has."

Wait ... were they talking about me?

"That won't matter if nobody believes he's the prince because he's such a buffoon. He asked for chicken nuggets! He can't remember his father's favorite food."

They *were* talking about me. And not nicely, either.

"This will work," Janet said. "It will."

"... I'm this close to returning to Plan A," the Commandant said.

"I can make him work harder," Janet said. "He's got a sensitive temperament. He's easy to manipulate."

I wanted to burst in and say, "What the heck?" I can take being yelled at, it happens all the time, so I'm used to it. But hearing Janet say I wasn't "that sharp" felt like a punch to the gut. Did she really think so little of me?

Then again, I hadn't exactly been at my best here. I could blame my lack of sleep, or the shock of the situation, but either way, I knew I could do better.

Prove them wrong, a voice inside told me. *Be the prince they need you to be. Prove them wrong and make them proud.*

CHAPTER 12

*"The ghosts here don't like the Commandant because
he only listens to patriotic marching music,
which gets really annoying."*

—MRS. AMBROSE, WHO ALSO DOESN'T SEEM TO LIKE
THE COMMANDANT

I spent that morning being the most perfect prince I could be, but the Commandant grew more and more agitated anyway. No matter how hard I worked, he was never satisfied, until finally it seemed like he was going to explode with anger.

"GET OUT OF HERE!" he yelled, after I couldn't remember my father's favorite quote. "You've got to be perfect by the time Cordholm arrives. Perfect means *no* mistakes. Come back for lunch with the rest of the team."

Janet and I walked outside in silence. I felt sick with nervousness, and fear.

"I can't do this," I said.

"Don't worry," Janet said. She stopped and held me by the shoulders, looking into my eyes. "Oh my, you're shaking like a leaf." She laughed. "Relax. You're doing great. You really are."

I felt like a fool. I didn't want Janet to think I was a little kid who quaked with fear when someone yelled at him, even though I kind of was. But there were other things besides her father's anger that were upsetting me.

"Janet, we can't work with Dr. Pravus," I said. "He tried to kill me. Twice."

"Don't worry about that, either," she said with a wave of her hand. "I talked to my father. Like any great leader, he carefully considers every course of action. He didn't have all the facts about Pravus, but once I told him, he agreed with me. That man is too dangerous."

"Thank you," I said.

"Now that you don't have to worry about Pravus, you can concentrate on convincing Mr. Cordholm that you're the prince. Once you do that, you'll see how nice my father can be."

"Maybe he'll get me a new valet," I said.

She laughed.

"I'm serious, Janet, Mr. Fox is really mean. Why can't Mrs. Ambrose be my valet?" Despite what Janet had told me, I thought she was nice. I imagined her bringing me books and a glass of milk to go with my cookies. She'd tuck me into bed with a kiss on my forehead, instead of threats.

"Good grief, no," she said. "Listen, Mr. Fox is the best person for the job. It's just . . . He's always been really protective of my father. I'll talk to him." She patted my arm. I used to really like it when she touched my arm, but now it felt condescending. She was treating me like a stupid little brother instead of someone she might like.

"Truthfully," she went on, "Mr. Fox was right to yell at you. You shouldn't talk about things you know nothing about."

I stopped walking, startled. Where had nice Janet gone?

She turned to face me with a tilted head. "Oh, come on. Did

Zaida tell you that you'd just walk into Andirat and take over by yourself? That's ridiculous and you know it. We each have our jobs, and right now yours is to convince Cordholm that you're the prince."

That didn't make me feel better. It seemed that everything was riding on whether I could convince this Cordholm guy.

We walked down to the lake again, passing a number of guards along the way. We skipped stones on the water until it was time to go back. I kept an eye on that attic window. Twice I saw the girl before she could hide.

I wondered if the Commandant had someone locked up in there. I started making up stories about her. Maybe she was my very own sister—a princess who had also survived the coup, but was now disabled or disfigured, so they'd decided to hide her, because they were ignorant bigots.

Or maybe it was some other royal family member, a cousin or a niece. Or the child of a cousin . . . what was that called again? Second cousin? Maybe that's what they meant by second cousin, once removed. They're the ones hidden from the rest of the family.

And then I realized how stupid I was being. I was imagining that she was somehow related to me, because deep down I knew I wanted my family to be alive.

Maybe she was a captured spy, or an assassin. Or Janet's evil twin. (Or was Janet the evil one, and the nice one was locked up?)

"Why are you laughing?" Janet asked.

"No reason."

She sighed and shook her head.

Yep, it's definitely the nice one up there.

‡‡‡

That night I wanted to catch the noisy creature that always snuck in around midnight. I waited for it, hiding in the chair by the fireplace. As soon as I heard those scratching noises I flipped on the lamp. It was a brownie—a furry creature with human features but only as tall as a cat on its hind legs. She—it was clearly a girl—was dressed in slacks and a wool vest over a soft shirt. Between her large, pointy ears a floppy newsboy cap rested over her short, curly hair. Thick, dark eyebrows were perched over surprised eyes.

"Hello," I said.

"Wasn't 'spectin' you to be wakeful," she said, backing away.

"I couldn't sleep," I said. I was too worried about my school, my friends. Was Syke safe with Dr. Pravus? Had Mistress Moira and Miss Merrybench found the witch who'd cursed me? Had Dr. Frankenhammer made an antidote for the Undefeatable Minions?

"Most times, I'm quiet as a feather fallin'," she said, nervously twisting her hands together. "I'm a regular sound-vacuum. But I didn't think—"

"It's okay," I said. I almost laughed, because she was the opposite of a sound-vacuum. "Want a cookie?"

She eyed the plate on the table next to the chair and licked her lips. She looked from the plate to me, and back and forth a few more times.

"I'm not going to eat them all," I said. "Here." I held one out and she took some tentative steps toward me. "Have you worked here long?"

She snatched the cookie and nodded.

"What's your name?"

"George," she said, between taking small nibbles of the cookie. "George?"

"Named after my grandmother, George Henry Snicklesby."

"Oh. You can call me Runt," I said. "Have you seen another kid around here? A girl, about my age?"

"The Commandant's daughter?"

"No, not Janet. Another girl."

"No kids here 'cept you and the Commandant's daughter."

She munched on her cookie, while I thought about Janet. I wished George hadn't mentioned her. I'd been trying to forget our latest conversation. It hadn't been nice.

She'd grown upset with my constant worry about everyone at Critchlore's. *Forget about them! You have to move on. This is so much more important. Why can't you see that? For goodness sake, you're like a child.*

I am a child, I'd said.

Well, it's time to grow up. Growing up means making sacrifices. You can't have everything. Most kids learn that when they're eight. She'd looked at me with an expression of disgust. It wasn't pretty, not even on her.

You can't be a doctor and *a firefighter,* she'd said. *And you can't be a minion* and *a prince. You're a prince. Act like one.*

It's always harsh when grown-ups yell at you, but when your friends yell at you? That really stings. I felt angry and embarrassed at the same time. And then more embarrassed when I realized that she was right. I was acting like a child.

"Got another story?" George asked, so I told her the fable of the Five Little Imps.

‡‡‡

As the days went by, my lessons grew more stressful. Janet and her father got mad if I forgot any small detail. They got mad when I shared something Professor Zaida had taught me. They got mad when I asked about Critchlore's. I was mad at myself for not being perfect. I had to be perfect.

But I made mistakes. And when I did, the Commandant would curse at me. I began to think he was kind of a jerk, but then I felt bad for thinking that. The responsibility of saving our people weighed heavily on him, and he was allowed to be nervous and demanding.

At night the ghost kept me awake by floating around and pointing at me and at the wall, shaking his head "no." George was so noisy when she cleaned my room. She'd knock something over and I'd bolt upright. Then she'd say, "Oh, you're awake. How about a story?"

My restless nights always caught up to me after lunch, and I fell asleep every afternoon during my lessons. I was sure that my need for an afternoon nap only reinforced Janet and her father's opinion that I was a baby, but I couldn't fight it. I was just too tired.

"I can power through without a nap," I told Janet one afternoon. "If I could use that time to talk to someone at Critchlore's."

"You can't talk to anyone there until you're perfect here," Janet said. "You have to work harder."

"I know," I said. "I will."

We had been at the castle for five days when Janet brought me a package after one of my naps in the Commandant's office.

"It's from Cook," she said.

I smiled. Finally, some contact with my old life. I tore open the package, barely able to contain my excitement, but the box was filled with cookies and nothing else.

"She knows you're working hard and wants to make sure you're eating enough. That's so Cook, right?"

"It is," I agreed. "But there's no note or anything." I looked all through the box. Nothing.

"She must have forgotten," Janet said with a shrug.

No, she wouldn't have. I looked closer and I knew that Cook hadn't sent this package. First, because some of the cookies had coconut flakes on top and Cook knows I hate coconut. And second, because most were the exact same oatmeal chocolate chip cookies that someone left in my room every night. Janet had tried to make them look homemade by chipping some of the edges and putting them in a plain box.

Janet was lying to me, and I wanted to know why. Never mind, I knew why. She was sick of me asking about Critchlore's and not focusing on my work here. Still, it bothered me. Come to think of it, there were a lot of things bothering me here. I'd been ignoring them because I knew what we were doing was important, and maybe because I was grateful that responsible people were taking charge of the decision making.

But why was I still locked in my room at night? Why wasn't I allowed to share an opinion? Why wouldn't anyone listen to my zipline idea? Why was I constantly warned about the dangers of the guards who were there to protect me? Which was it? Were they dangerous or were they protecting me? It didn't make sense.

I couldn't figure out the Commandant. Professor Zaida had been teaching me to lead. I know it's ridiculous to think that a kid could rule a country, but she'd told me that I'd grow into my role as a leader as long as I had capable advisors.

The Commandant wasn't teaching me to lead. He was teaching me to be a prop. "Say this," and "Stand like this," and "Don't smile like an idiot." Despite my asking, they wouldn't include me in any of the planning sessions. How could I learn to lead if I wasn't included?

"This is it," the Commandant said the night before the meeting. "You *have* to convince him, or our plans are shot." He started rubbing his temples, then he pointed at me. "If you fail, you'll be history, like your parents."

Okay, was it me, or was that kind of a mean thing to say? He stood by the window, hunched over in his typical manner. I began to think that if he did have a child perched on his shoulders, he would probably pluck her off and toss her aside so he could get back to work.

Janet put a hand on my arm and looked me straight in the eye. "You can do it." Then she patted my head like I was Pizza, Dr. Critchlore's dog.

CHAPTER 13

Richer households prefer brownies to kobolds because
they're less belligerent, they smell better, and they don't lie.
—ACCORDING TO BROWNIES

Mr. Cordholm came the next day and spent the morning with the Commandant. I was told he would interview me after lunch. I knew that Seizemore wanted to unite the rebels, and just like the generals, the rebels couldn't agree on who should lead their cause. Mr. Cordholm and Seizemore were leaders of the two largest groups. If I could convince Cordholm that I was the prince, his group would join ours. And once they did, the other rebel groups would join us too.

I was dressed in slacks and a button-down shirt. My shoes were stiff and uncomfortable. On the way downstairs, Mr. Fox told me through gritted teeth that I "better convince this man, or else." I didn't ask what he meant by "or else." His clenched fist seemed obvious enough. If I blew it, I would be history, like my parents.

"Just be honest," Janet told me when she met us in the foyer. "If he suspects you're lying about any little thing, or holding something back, he'll never be convinced that you're the prince."

With the exception of being in the presence of Dr. Pravus, I'd never been so nervous. Not when Professor Murphy hit us with a pop quiz, not when I'd been trapped in the hedge maze with an angry dragon and a swamp monster. Not even when I'd pelted Killer the mountain lion with a rock to see if fear would make me morph into a werewolf.

We entered the Commandant's office, where her father stood with a dark-skinned man dressed in a sage-green military-style coat. He was nearly bald, and his face was smooth. Wearing glasses and a thoughtful expression, he looked like an intellectual, someone more comfortable with a book in his hand than a weapon.

"And here is our young prince," the Commandant said. "Prince Auberon, this is Mr. Jason Cordholm."

Mr. Cordholm's gaze traveled from my feet to my face before he acknowledged me with a slight tilt of his head in greeting. His expression gave nothing away. "He certainly looks the part, Seizemore," he said.

"Commandant," the Commandant corrected.

"We'll see." Mr. Cordholm reached for something on a nearby table. "I brought you a delicacy from home." He handed me a small box tied with a pale-purple ribbon. "It's Snagfluke. Your father's favorite candy."

I opened the box and found little brown lumps frosted with powdered sugar, each in an individual paper cup. I looked to the Commandant, because if there was one thing I'd learned as a junior henchman trainee, it was this: Don't Trust Food from Strangers.

Mr. Cordholm laughed. "They're fine," he said. "Select one for me to eat if you don't trust me."

I picked one out and handed it to him. He popped the candy

into his mouth and seemed to swallow it without chewing. "Commandant?" He nodded to the box and I held it out for Janet and her father. They each took a candy.

I selected one and popped it into my mouth like Mr. Cordholm had. Immediately my gag reflex kicked in. I turned away from him as I winced and spat the Snagfluke out into my hand. Ugh, it tasted like hot, spicy barf. I turned back around, trying to conceal the disgusting lump behind me.

Mr. Cordholm frowned. "You know, a prince would have eaten the candy without a grimace."

"I'm sorry, but that . . . ugh, that tasted terrible," I said. "Gah! My mouth is still burning." I looked at Janet and her father, both frowning at me as their eyes watered.

"Come, let's take a walk," Mr. Cordholm said.

I followed him, dropping the spit-out candy into a potted plant on my way out. "Sorry," I whispered to the plant. I wanted to dump the whole box, but I'm pretty sure that would have been rude.

The flavor clung to my tongue, so I grabbed a hose by the back door and took a quick drink. Mr. Cordholm gaped at me.

"Oops," I said. "I guess that wasn't very princely, either."

He frowned, and I thought I'd failed already, not one minute into the interview. But then he smiled and took a drink himself. "I don't blame you." He leaned toward me and whispered, "That stuff is awful. It was fun seeing Seizemore eat it, though. That alone was worth the trip. Let's go. Tell me about you. Where have you been hiding?"

We walked down a path. "I haven't been hiding. At least, I didn't think I was." And I told him my whole life story. I told him about Dr. Critchlore's school, and my foster family, and the classes I'd taken. I told him about how I'd met an Archivist for the Great Library who figured out that I was the missing prince. I asked him if he knew any librarians.

"That's a very secret organization," he said. "You shouldn't mention that you know of it."

I slapped my head. Gah! Failed again.

I thought about the lists I'd kept this year. First, my list of reasons I thought I was cursed, which kept getting longer and longer. Then my to-do list, same. And finally, my good list, which Cook had told me to keep because writing down things you're grateful for is supposed to make you a happier person. After these last few days I thought of another list I could keep—a list of times I'd failed, and failed, and failed.

Cursed, To Do, Good, and Fail—those were my lists.

"Why do you think you're the prince?" he asked.

"Because the smartest person I know told me I was," I said. "Because all the evidence fits: The timing of the coup and when I showed up at Critchlore's, the clothes I was wearing, my medallion." I showed it to him.

"The vaskor obey me," I said. "Because I'm family."

"The vaskor," he said with a gasp. "You have the vaskor?"

I nodded.

We passed Roger the manticore, and he looked at me expectantly. Lately, I'd been tossing him pastries I'd grabbed from the breakfast table. I shrugged an apology and offered him a candy. He seemed to like it, so I left the box with him. Mr. Cordholm laughed.

"What's your impression of Mr. Seizemore?" he asked.

"He's serious," I said. "He's very worried about our people, and I think that comes out as gruffness." I paused, and then added, "But . . . there are things that make me uneasy."

"Like what?"

"Like . . ." I was worried that I was breaking a confidence, but Janet told me to be honest. "The Commandant admires Dr. Pravus, a man I know is really evil."

"Yes," Cordholm said. "They went to school together."

I felt sick. The Commandant not only admired Pravus, he knew him. "I know that I'm supposed to put the needs of our people first, but Pravus is just as dangerous to the people of this continent as the generals have been to Andirat. He rules by fear and intimidation. I can't imagine that we'd accept his help, because I know he'd expect something in return."

Mr. Cordholm frowned. I wasn't sure if he was disappointed in me, or in the Commandant. "Ruling is difficult. Sometimes you have to accept help wherever you can get it, for the greater good."

"I've heard that," I said. "But would *you* accept help from Dr. Pravus?"

"I feel like you've been very candid with me, so I'll be honest with you. No, I would not accept help from Dr. Pravus."

"Maybe we can convince the Commandant not to work with him," I suggested.

He smiled and nodded and we walked in silence until we reached the lake.

"Back home, the water in Lake Grandora is as clear as glass," he said. "Willows dip their branches into the water. It's beautiful." He sighed, lost in his memories. "They've done an amazing job re-creating it. Even that boathouse over there looks the same, with that porch facing the water."

I looked at the boathouse porch and was hit with a memory of my own. I closed my eyes to see if I could capture it before it slipped away. "But it smells wrong," I said.

"Pardon?"

I opened my eyes and looked at Cordholm. "The last time I was by the lake, it smelled like goose poop. It was everywhere, all around the lake. There were so many geese."

"Yes, that's right." He smiled. "Before the coup, the geese were a gift from another realm. We only had them that one year."

"We used to hide under that porch and throw rocks at them. There was one goose that terrified us all. He would've charged a full-grown troll, I bet."

"We called him Bruiser," the man said, laughing. "Yes! He was very aggressive."

"I was so scared of that goose," I said.

Cordholm tilted his head. "I don't think Seizemore ever went down to the lake. He hates moisture. He wouldn't have remembered the geese."

"I just remembered them now, when you mentioned that porch."

He nodded, and we turned to walk back to the castle. I figured it was my turn to ask questions.

"Why are you so sure I was killed?"

"Well, actually, I lied," he said. "I did not see you killed."

"You didn't? Then why—"

"I don't trust Mr. Seizemore," he said.

"The Commandant?"

"Exactly. I don't trust people who give themselves titles they haven't earned. He was an aide to the royal family, nothing more. He may have saved you from the coup, but that doesn't make him a leader of our rebellion. You're very young. I'm worried that he's using you to further his position in the rebellion. If we're successful, he'll be very powerful. He would say the same about me, I'm sure. But I've learned to be wary of people who crave power too obsessively."

He paused before adding, "And that man is as obsessed as they come."

CHAPTER 14

Don't give geese as a gift unless you want
the recipient to hate you.
—GOOD ADVICE

Janet and I waited in the foyer while her father and Mr. Cordholm talked. Janet paced, not looking at me.

"I think it went well," I said.

She harrumphed at me, which I found a bit rude, if I'm honest. If I'm extra honest, Janet had lost most of her appeal during our time at the castle. I reviewed all her actions through a new lens now, a suspicious lens.

I used to feel such a rush of happiness when she smiled at me. Back at school, I went through my days just hoping to catch a glimpse of her. And if she actually talked to me? I'd spend the rest of the day reliving our conversation. But now, every smile seemed fake. I knew she thought she was manipulating me.

Syke had never liked her. She'd called her faker than Darthin's gargoyle horns. I really missed Syke.

Mr. Cordholm came out to say good-bye. Janet rushed past him and straight into her father's office, so I walked our guest to his car.

"I'm glad you're alive," he said. "I've told Seizemore that I'll support you. He's asked me to travel to Andirat to deliver our demand that the generals surrender."

"He told me that the generals hate him, and would never surrender to him," I said.

"I admire him for that. Most castle workers quickly switched sides when the generals took over. Not Seizemore. He was loyal to the royals." We reached his car. "I'll be leaving soon, but . . . " His voice took a quieter tone as he leaned in closer to me. "If you feel like he's being too controlling, you can get a message to me. There's an old beggar woman by the library in Stull City who knows how to contact me."

"I've met her," I said. "She recognized my medallion." My mouth may have dropped open as I remembered that she was a CLOUD—a covert librarian. If she was a CLOUD . . . and she knew how to contact Cordholm . . . then maybe he was one too.

He laughed at my expression. "Good luck, Your Highness," he said.

"Thank you, Mr. Cordholm," I said, and I shook his hand.

I returned to the Commandant's office to find Janet and her father huddled over some spreadsheets on his desk.

"How'd I do?" I asked.

Janet looked up briefly and said, "Very well," before her attention went back to the papers. "He's convinced you're the prince."

If I was expecting any kind of praise, I should have known better. Her father continued talking.

"While Cordholm is in Andirat, I'll take control of the rebel groups, and then we'll all return as one army. If the generals haven't surrendered by then, seeing the prince at the head of the united rebels will surely do the trick."

He looked up, seemingly startled that I was still standing there.

"Prince Auberon," the Commandant said. "You're free to return to your quarters. You must be tired. You missed your nap today."

You've got to be kidding me. How lame did they think I was? "I'd like to know what you're planning," I said, stepping forward.

"This is just logistics," he said. "It's far too trivial for your attention."

Janet took me by the arm and led me out. "What he means is that we're figuring out dates and times and boring stuff like that."

"I know what logistics are, Janet," I said, only barely managing to keep an angry scowl from my expression. "I'd like to help."

"I know this situation is overwhelming," she said. "But a prince doesn't involve himself in piddly little stuff like this. It's unseemly. Please, you need your rest."

"Fine," I said, pulling my arm free. "But now that I've convinced Cordholm, can I talk to Dr. Critchlore?"

Janet looked at her father, who was busy writing notes on his master plan. She re-grabbed my arm and dragged me to the door.

"Dr. Critchlore is busy at the EO Council," she said.

"Then can I talk to Cook, Professor Zaida, Murphy, anybody at Critchlore's?"

"You need to focus on what we're doing now."

"You're not telling me what we're doing now."

"Look," she said in a harsh whisper, "there's still a lot of work to do. I thought I was being nice, letting you have the evening off while we work, but if you don't appreciate the break, we can start on

93

the next phase of training. I don't think you realize how unprepared you are for what's coming."

"I just want to talk to someone at Critchlore's," I said.

"Runt Higgins is in the past," she said, pushing a button on the wall I hadn't noticed before. "Forget about him."

Forget about my friends? My foster mother? Dr. Critchlore? That was impossible.

I stood there, feeling so conflicted. When I'd arrived, I'd been worried that I wasn't ready to be a prince. I wasn't ready for the responsibility of making decisions that affected so many people.

Well, it turned out that I didn't have that responsibility. The Commandant was running everything. He made all the decisions. All I had to do was learn which fork to use at dinner and how to address different heads of state.

I should have been happy that someone else was running things, but I wasn't. I wasn't happy at all.

Dante Fox appeared out of nowhere to escort me to my quarters. The sight of him scared the fatigue right out of my body. I could feel my heartbeat galloping wildly in my chest.

And then I thought: *What am I? A prince or a prop?* Janet and her father didn't tell me anything, they locked me in my room, and they treated me like I was denser than one of Cook's fruitcakes. I was angry at them, and at myself for letting them treat me this way.

As we reached my door, I stood in front of it, blocking Mr. Fox's access to the handle. It was time to stand up for myself. What did I have to lose?

"I'd like something to read," I said. "I'd like you to go to the library. I saw some fairy tales from Andirat. Bring me a few of those while I change into my nightclothes. If you do that, it will restore some of my trust in your ability to serve as my valet."

"I don't need your trust," he said with a scoffing laugh.

I hesitated, unsure if I really wanted to test him or not. But then I remembered my anger.

"Are you sure?" I asked. My heart may have been hammering out a warning to stop talking, but I concentrated on keeping a stern expression on my face. "I think the Commandant needs me a lot more than he needs you. We could go forward as friends, or you could continue to treat me like an untrained pet that you need to scare into obedience. That treatment upsets me. I may not be able to perform my functions as prince if I'm upset. I have a very sensitive disposition."

Might as well use Janet's description of me to my benefit.

He stared at me for what seemed like a full minute. I was worried my approach wouldn't work, but finally he reached around me and unlocked the door. He pushed it slightly open for me to go inside, then closed and locked it from the other side. I hoped he was getting me the books, but either way, he wasn't in the room with me, and that made me happy.

The lights were off, but the drapes were open. I flopped into a cushy chair next to the bed and closed my eyes, releasing my anxiety with some calming breaths and mentally celebrating my small victory.

But then I heard scratching noises by the fireplace and a few whispers. Dark shapes zipped around by the fireplace, cleaning up George's cookie crumbs. I sat in the shadows, unnoticed.

"Thanks for the help, guys," George said. "He's awake-like at night, so I have no time to clean."

Ha! The little liar. She didn't clean up at night because she was too busy eating cookies and listening to stories.

"You help us when the Commandant tears through his room like an angry tornado. It's only fair we return the favor."

"Not much to do here," another voice said. "This kid's not a slob like the last one."

Last one? Did he mean Janet?

"You're supposed to be watching him. Isn't that what the Commandant wants? Make sure he doesn't go exploring or nothing?"

"Yeah. I'm s'posed to let him think he's befriending me," George said. "That's what the daughter said—'Let him think he's tamed you, then he'll believe anything you say.' He tells me stories at night. And get this—the big guy told him not to open the windows and he's never tried it. Not once."

"You didn't magic him?" one of the voices asked. "To make him stay away from the windows?"

"Can't magic him," George replied. "He's got the royal family protections. But it doesn't matter, he's just an obedient little lamb, this one."

I was beginning to feel like I couldn't trust anyone around here.

"Makes your job easier," one said.

Dante Fox returned, and at the sound of him entering the room, the brownies scattered. He placed a pile of books on the nightstand, and then pulled the covers back for me.

"Shall I draw you a bath?" he asked with a stony face.

"That would be fantastic," I said. "Thank you, Mr. Fox."

"At your service, Your Majesty."

I smiled. That was just me being me, making friends with people who thought I was an idiot.

CHAPTER 15

Dante Fox's real name is Marilyn Dooglepits.
—THE COMMANDANT SUGGESTED THE CHANGE

Mr. Fox told me that I would be studying with my tutors while Seizemore met with the rebels and made preparations for our departure. There were routes to plan, decoy dragons to hire, rebel forces to coordinate, and so much more.

I wanted to be part of the planning, to learn about tactics and strategies and stuff. Professor Zaida had been teaching me to be the kind of prince who listens to advisors and learns how to choose the best course, but whenever I tried to listen in, the Commandant dismissed me. I felt like all the prince lessons I'd gotten from Professor Zaida were for nothing.

If they weren't going to let me use my prince training, then maybe it was time to use my minion training. I had to do something.

After my morning "family history" lesson, Janet stood up for our walk. As I followed her out to the terrace, I detoured to the serving table next to the wall. The dishes from breakfast were still there, and I grabbed a piece of toast and a banana for Roger. I also palmed a pair of scissors I'd noticed next to a package of pastries, and slipped them into my pocket. I didn't like being locked inside my room at night. Maybe I could use them to wiggle the lock open.

"A Minion Prepared Is a Minion Not Snared"—as the sign says above the Strategy Room at school.

In the afternoon I met with the Commandant and his assistants. We stood around a table that held a mock-up of a city square.

"Your Highness, we need to rehearse your arrival," the Commandant said. "It's important to make a powerful first impression. When the people see you, they need to see someone in charge. Someone who's angry at what's become of his country. Those are the emotions you need to rehearse."

Rehearse? Wouldn't they be my genuine emotions?

"You will lead a march on the capitol, climb the steps, and turn to address the crowd. I've written a speech that I want you to memorize and practice until you repeat it in your sleep."

I nodded.

"That's all you need to do," he said. "We'll take care of the rest."

"The rest?"

"The rebel forces will secure the capital. If they haven't done so already, we will demand the generals surrender to you. Then the real work begins. Establishing a ruling body, capturing the anti-royal agitators . . ."

"And finding the witch who cursed me, right?"

"What?"

"I'm cursed to die on my sixteenth birthday, remember?"

"Of course. Of course. That's one of our top priorities."

It didn't seem like it.

Mrs. Ambrose came in and whispered in the Commandant's ear. She nodded to the hallway, where a man holding a ridiculously ugly briefcase stood. I was so focused on that briefcase—seriously, orange and brown stripes with pink polka dots?—that it took me a moment before I looked at his face . . .

. . . and recognized him as Dr. Pravus's henchman.

He was wearing a disguise, but I knew it was him. He was using the same distracting technique he'd used when trying to poison the secret librarians. Before it had been a flashy suit, and then a bushy mustache. Now it was that briefcase. But I'd never forget those oddly shaped ears, those cold eyes. It was him.

"Excuse me a moment," the Commandant said.

While the Commandant met with Pravus's man, Janet showed me a copy of a video that they had Mr. Cordholm take to show the generals. It began with a long montage of rallies held throughout what I assumed was Andirat. The people held up banners with my picture. They chanted for my return. In one part, soldiers formed a wall to prevent the protestors from reaching the Monoliths of Andirat, but the crowd overwhelmed the troops, and the soldiers gave up and joined the mob, removing their shields and jackets.

"The generals are losing support every day," the voiceover said. "But you don't have to lose everything. Join the reunification movement. Don't you think it would be better to be a part of a powerful nation rather than the ruler of the small province you now control? The Andiratian army was once feared the world over. Now we are vulnerable to invaders because you can't—you won't—defend each other.

"Together, we are more than the sum of five armies. We will be the strongest nation in the world."

I paused the video. "Do you think the generals will just surrender? Without fighting or anything?"

"They'll surrender," Janet said, "with the right incentives. Most tyrants cling to power because they know as soon as they lose it, they'll be jailed, or killed. But we'll offer them a safe way out. We are all Andiratians. It's time for us to stop killing each other."

I nodded. "Professor Zaida says that diplomacy is better than war."

"Sure . . . right. Whatever." Janet nodded. "There's more." She pressed play.

The voiceover continued, this time over a map of Stull and the surrounding realms: "After reunifying our armies, we will cross the ocean to conquer our homeland on the rich Porvian Continent. Think about it. Erudyten will be ours again. You just have to support the prince."

I slumped in my chair. This wasn't diplomacy. I'd thought that Janet and her father wanted me to help take Andirat back from the generals and end my people's suffering, but they just wanted more war. The four countries that made up what was once Erudyten—Brix, Carkley, Delpha, and Riggen—had enormous armies. A war between them and Andirat would result in thousands, maybe even hundreds of thousands, of deaths. The deaths of minions who'd trained at Critchlore's. Minions I knew.

Why didn't anyone care about the minions?

"We will defeat the EOs," Janet said. "And rule those realms ourselves. Isn't that what you want? To reclaim what's ours?"

"Not like that," I said.

This was not how my grandfather had wanted to regain our homeland. He'd been working on a diplomatic solution with the EOs who had taken it over. The generals had wanted to fight instead, and that was why they'd staged the coup. Now it looked like they would get what they'd wanted all along—war. But I would never get my family back.

After their meeting, I saw Pravus's man back in the hallway with the Commandant. His briefcase was heavier, it seemed, because he kept switching it from one hand to the other.

At dinner, the Commandant announced that we would be leaving for Andirat sooner than expected, and that everyone should start packing.

I should have been terrified about this development, but I was too full of rage. Janet had promised that we wouldn't work with Pravus, an obvious lie. It was time to confront them. I took a deep breath and turned to the Commandant, asking him about the man with the ugly briefcase.

"That was a dreadful briefcase," the Commandant laughed. "Funny thing, he called it his 'lucky case,' because nobody has ever tried to steal it. Who would?"

He turned to talk to someone else.

"You didn't answer my question," I said.

"Hmm?"

"Who was he?"

"Oh . . . nobody important."

"You seemed very anxious to meet with him. Why?"

"We need to work with a few local people to ensure your safety when we depart. That man works for an EO in Stull City. He has connections."

"Connections with Dr. Pravus?" I asked with a hard stare. For the first time since I'd been here, the Commandant looked nervous. Good.

"As a matter of fact, I do believe he went to the Pravus Academy."

"He not only went to the Pravus Academy," I said. "He works for Dr. Pravus now. He's an assassin. Why do you need the help of an assassin?"

The Commandant's discomfort turned to anger. I could sense it building inside him. His lips pursed before he answered.

He leaned over to me and whispered, "Your Highness, this isn't the place to discuss sensitive strategic operations. You'd know that if you paid attention in your etiquette class."

I whispered back, "There seem to be no other times when I can ask you questions. And I need to know why you met with a man who works for Dr. Pravus. Do you know what Pravus is planning to do?"

"Of course I do. Pravus is about to attack Stull City. We need safe passage, so I bribed that man to get it."

"You can't trust anyone associated with Dr. Pravus."

"I only gave him a down-payment bribe. One standard EO gold bar. When we reach safety, a third party will release the three other bars I've promised him. Dr. Pravus needs the money. To feed his army, and—" He cut himself off before saying any more.

"If you know his plans, then you must know that he's going to attack Dr. Critchlore's school first."

"I know no such thing."

"I'm telling you, so now you do. We have to help them. With your security forces, you practically have an army here. We could go to Critchlore's—"

"We have our own priorities, Your Majesty," the Commandant interrupted. "Any delay, and millions will suffer. Stop whining about your little school."

"I won't allow us to support Dr. Pravus," I said, standing up. "I'm getting that gold back."

The Commandant grabbed my arm, hard. "You will not ruin everything again. I won't let you."

"Again? What are you talking about?"

He let me go, but held my gaze. "Dr. Pravus is our ally. He has been for some time. With his help, we will take back Andirat. And then we will take back Erudyten from the EOs who stole it. We will be the strongest nation in the world."

Was he insane? Pravus wanted to rule this continent, we *knew* that. His father had ruled Riggen, which was the *capital* of Erudyten. There wasn't enough gold in the world to convince Pravus to hand it over to us.

Dante Fox appeared at my elbow. "It's time for you to retire," he said. I wasn't sure if he meant that I needed to go to bed, or to stop being a prince.

I walked upstairs fuming. The Commandant was working with the man who wanted to destroy the only home I'd ever known. A man who couldn't be trusted. Why wouldn't he listen to me?

CHAPTER 16

"The secret to good decision-making is to always . . .
oh, drat, we went the wrong way!"
—GENERAL FORGE, INTERVIEWED DURING
THE FAILED ARCTIC EXPEDITION

I paced in my room, once again locked inside. I did not trust these
people. I did not like these people. They'd lied to me, and I was
pretty sure they were using me. There had to be another way to
help Andirat. A way that didn't involve working with Dr. Pravus.

My Critchlore family needed me. Now more than ever. They
had no idea that Dr. Pravus was getting aid from the rebels here.
We were helping to feed his army with our gold!

What was I supposed to do?

During one of my sessions with Professor Zaida, she'd warned
that one of the most difficult aspects of leadership was the feeling
that you had to make decisions alone. *You will have to make tough
choices. Sometimes unpopular choices. Trust your instincts and training.*

My instincts were telling me to run back to Critchlore's. I needed
to be around people I trusted. But if I did that, the generals in
Andirat would cling to power. They would never surrender to the
splintered rebel groups, but they might surrender if I, the rightful
prince, united those groups.

I had to choose one: was I Runt Higgins or Prince Auberon? Should I help my school or my country? I couldn't save both. I didn't know if I could save either of them, really, but I had to choose. My heart wanted me to go home to Critchlore's. My head told me that more people needed me in Andirat.

Should I trust my instincts, or my training?

Why couldn't I have both the chicken and the steak?

I'd never felt so conflicted. I continued to pace the room, changing my mind with every step.

In the end, I think it was the box of cookies that made up my mind. Janet had lied about them being from Cook, but what made that lie even worse was that she hadn't even tried to make it convincing. They thought they could lie to me easily because I was too dumb to notice.

They thought they had me figured out. I was a sensitive guy who needed a nap every afternoon and wanted everyone to like me. I was no threat. Well, it was time to surprise them. I was going to find out what was really going on around here. First, I'd escape my room. I'd find Mrs. Ambrose and talk to her in private. She didn't trust the Commandant, and I wanted to know why. I also wanted to know why that girl was locked in the attic.

After I got some answers, I was going to escape and return to Dr. Critchlore's, so I could be with people I trusted.

I pulled out the scissors I had taken earlier and tried to unlock my room's door, but that didn't work. I moved to the glass door that led out to the balcony. After wiggling the tip of the scissors into the keyhole, the door unlocked with a twist.

I stepped outside. I was about to walk to the balcony's edge when movement caught my eye. The gargoyle. I'd forgotten about him. His stony head swiveled my way, but he didn't move. Would he stop me from escaping?

I walked over to the opposite side of the balcony, away from the gargoyle. Leaning over, I saw what I knew I'd see from surveying the castle on my many walks with Janet: an escape route. I could climb over my balcony, slide down the slanted roof, and drop down to another balcony one story below.

The gargoyle's eyes burst into flames, and he flapped his wings in warning. I boosted myself up to the edge of the balcony.

The gargoyle pushed off his perch and flew straight at me. I held up my scissors, but immediately felt foolish. Rock beats scissors, everybody knows that.

I dodged him, diving back inside just before he reached me.

Okay, time for Plan B. I waited for George.

She showed up earlier than usual, eager for cookies and stories.

"Good evening, Your Highness," she said, grabbing a cookie and jumping up into one of the chairs by the fireplace.

"Hi, George," I said. I stood by the window, watching the gargoyle, who'd returned to his post and once again looked like a statue.

"What're you gazin' upon there?"

"The backyard. Those lanterns light everything so nicely. It's so beautiful, even at night."

"Sure, I guess." George shrugged. "Don't get out much myself."

"What's that building over there?" I asked.

George hopped down and came over. She jumped on the chair next to me so she could see over the balcony's edge.

I called up all the anger and frustration I'd been feeling, because I knew I had to be convincing. I grabbed George by the waist with one arm and threw open the door to the balcony with the other. Before she could squirm out of my grasp, I grabbed her by the legs and hung her out over the edge of the balcony, upside down. She was lighter than my fully loaded school backpack, so I wasn't worried about dropping her.

She screamed. "Hey! Pull me in!"

"Let's play a game, George," I said. "This is one of my favorites. It's called I Know You're a Stinking Little Spy, So Fess Up and Tell Me How to Get Out of Here or I'll Drop You on Your Head."

The gargoyle tilted his head our way.

"You can't," George said. "Rothor will catch me."

The flaming eyes watched us, so I pulled out my scissors. When the gargoyle looked like he was coming our way I said, "Don't," and pressed the blade against George's neck.

It looked like the gargoyle was going to call my bluff. He flew toward us, but right before he landed on the balcony edge beside me, the ghost swooped out and froze between us. The ghost and gargoyle faced each other, and I'm not sure what was communicated between them, but soon they both flew off, leaving me alone with George.

George yelped. "I'll magic you."

"You can't," I said. "I know things. You have no idea what I know and what I don't. So as soon as I hear another lie, I'll . . . I'll make sure you never lie again. Got it?"

"Please, they'll kill me," George said. "I have to do what they say."

"I don't know if I believe that." I put the scissors away and grabbed her with both hands. I really didn't want to drop her. "So let's do a little test. You lie—you fly. Got it?"

She gulped and nodded.

Back at Critchlore's, we'd just started studying interrogation techniques in my Junior Henchman class. I knew how to start, with rapid, easy questions that get quick responses. Then you throw in the question you really want an answer to, and if your victim pauses before answering . . . well, that might tell you what you need to know.

"Question one," I said. "How long have you lived here?"

"All my life. I worked for the Natherlys when I was little."

"Who do you report to?"

"Mr. Fox. I used to report to Mrs. Ambrose, 'til Seizemore showed up."

"Mrs. Ambrose doesn't like the Commandant, does she?"

"No. And Seizemore doesn't trust anyone who's loyal to Mrs. Ambrose. He brought in his own brownies, but they don't know the secrets of the castle. I do. I've had to pretend to be one of them, for my own safety. He sent the rest of the old ones away. Honest."

"Who is the girl in the attic?"

George didn't answer right away.

"Listen, George," I said. "I might know the answer, or I might not. Do you think it's worth the risk?"

"I can't tell you," she said. "Mr. Fox'll kill me."

"It's funny that you're worried about Mr. Fox, when I'm holding your ankles and I'm REALLY MAD right now. Good-bye, you scheming little spy."

"No! I'll tell you. Please!"

"I'm waiting. Who are they hiding in the attic?"

"Prince Auberon."

CHAPTER 17

I nearly dropped her.

"Hey!" she shouted.

"But . . . I'm Prince Auberon."

"No, you're not," George said. "Honest. Brownies don't lie."

I pulled her up. "But it's a girl, I saw her long hair."

"The prince keeps his hair long, but it's him."

I carried her back inside and shut the door. Then I collapsed to the floor, with my back to the bed.

"You have *got* to be kidding me." I was beyond stunned. How many times did I have to find out I wasn't who I thought I was? I'm not a werewolf, I'm not a vaskor, I'm not a prince. A violent storm of emotion raged through my body, and I felt sick. I crumpled over to my side.

"I'm done for," George said, sitting next to my head.

I had so many questions, but part of me thought, *Why bother? Just lie here in a ball. Don't get up, the universe will only punch you down again, just like it always does.*

112

"Mr. Fox is going to kill me," George said, crying now.

"George, I won't let anything happen to you." I sat up. "Why have they locked him up?"

"He fought with Seizemore," George said. "Wouldn't do what the Commandant told him to do. Seizemore kept telling him he could get a new prince. And then he did."

"Me," I said. "Can you take me to him?"

"Might as well, now that I'm doomed. My brownie family . . . before they left, they told me to help him, but I just couldn't risk it, see?"

"Let's go. I need answers. And then we'll get out of here."

She nodded. I followed her over to the fireplace, where she picked up a poker. She moved it around the wall, making scratching noises as she did. She paused deliberately at different spots until a three-foot-tall panel next to the fireplace popped open.

"It's magnetic?" I asked.

"Yeah. There's a sequence to release each latch."

She walked into the crawl space. For once, I was happy that my nickname was Runt, because the passageway was brownie-sized and I barely fit on my hands and knees. We snuck through dark tunnels, behind walls, and up a secret staircase. All the while, my mind was racing.

I wasn't the prince.

What kind of prank was this? If I wasn't the prince, why was there all that evidence that I was? The medallion, the memories, the clothes, the vaskor. I still wasn't sure I believed George, and I expected a trick at every turn.

We reached what looked like a dead end, and George turned to me. "I should warn you," she said. "The prince . . . he's not real nice. Seizemore ruined him, raising him like he did. That's why none of us have tried to help him."

"None of you?"

"Mrs. Ambrose, she hates him most of all. She told us to wait and see, maybe the new prince would be better."

She turned to the wall and opened a panel. We stepped into a musty attic room lit by a very dim lightbulb and one bright desk lamp where the boy—I could see now he was a boy—sat reading.

"Your Highness," George said, "it's me, George. I've brought you a guest."

I stepped into the light as he stood up, and we faced each other. It was like looking in a mirror, except for the hair. Just looking at the way he stood, I could tell he was a prince. He had a sort of quiet dignity and self-confidence about him.

And then he screamed like a deranged chicken and charged me.

He tackled me around the middle and I fell backward, beneath his flailing fists. Unfortunately for him, I was trained in hand-to-hand combat, hand-to-paw combat, and hand-to-stinging-tail-barb contact. I quickly twisted free and pinned him, sitting on his arms as he squirmed.

"You think you can just steal someone else's life?" he asked, livid.

"I don't want to steal your life," I said. "They lied to me. They told me I was the prince and I believed them." Sitting on top of him, I saw the medallion he wore around his neck. I pulled out mine.

"Why do I have this?" I asked. "Why do the vaskor obey me? Why was I wearing the prince's clothing when they found me eight years ago?"

"Let me up," he said.

I let him up. He grabbed my medallion and pulled it so hard the chain broke. "You shouldn't have this!"

And then he attacked me again.

I pinned him easily. "We're not getting off to a trusting start, Your Highness. I'm not your enemy and I do *not* want to take your place. I just want some answers, and then I'll go. I'm only here because I was kidnapped by the Commandant's daughter."

He scowled, but eventually stopped squirming. "Okay, I'm sorry. I've learned I can't trust anyone." He sighed. I let him up. I thought that by this time we both knew who would win a wrestling match, but he tried to tackle me again. It was pathetic, and I changed my mind about him having any sort of princely dignity.

"What's your problem?" I said, pinning him again. His face pursed in anger, like he couldn't handle not being able to defeat me. "Do you want to escape, or not?"

"I have to escape."

"I'll let you up," I said. "But come at me again, and I won't tell you how to find Cordholm, the rebel leader who hates the Commandant."

"You know where he is?"

"Yes."

"Fine. I give you my word as Ruler of the Lands of Eldercot and Grand Master of the Royal Order of Mortezi."

"That doesn't mean anything to me, but you're a pathetic fighter, so I'll let you up."

He stood, panting. "I've been locked up," he said. "I'm out of shape, or I'd have bested you." He picked up my medallion and shoved it in his pocket. "So . . . you're my double." He looked me up and down again. "Not much of a resemblance, if you ask me." He nodded at George. "Hi, George. You're looking pitiful, as always."

"Your Highness," George said with a bow.

"You're really Prince Auberon?" I asked.

He nodded, standing up straight. Once again the princely manner was back.

"You're supposed to bow when I acknowledge your existence," he said. "Because, here's a news flash for you—you are *not* a prince."

I bowed.

"Wow, they got the perfect little pawn, didn't they," he scoffed.

I sat down on the small bed next to the wall. "Who am I?"

"You were my doppelganger." He sat back down at his desk.

"Your what?"

"Don't you remember? You lived at the castle. You were the funny little boy who thought he was a dog, probably because your father was the royal houndsman. Your parents let you sleep with the dogs. You used to howl with them at night."

"My father was . . . the what?"

"The royal houndsman. The keeper of the dogs. Until someone noticed that you were a dead ringer for me. There were rumors about an assassination attempt coming, and my grandfather thought it would be wise to use doppelgangers for outdoor events. So that's what you were—my double."

"That explains the lack of princely memories. Wait . . . my parents lived at the castle?" My parents. I had parents. "They could still be alive. What were their names?"

"I don't know," he said. "I was four."

"The Commandant must know."

"Don't trust anything he says. He's a liar and a traitor. He helped the generals kill my family."

"*What?*"

"Eight years ago my grandfather was about to fire him for failing to report some suspicious dealings by the generals. Seizemore was actually helping the generals plan their coup. He made sure the vaskor were sent on a bogus mission so they couldn't protect my family. Then he told the generals where we were hiding, so they could kill us."

"That's so evil," I said.

"Seizemore was promised a position of power after the coup in return for his help, but the generals cut him out completely. I think he was suspicious of them, and that's why he saved my life. I was his little insurance policy. He's kept me hidden in the Forgotten Realm, feeding me lies and plotting his return to power."

The prince stood up and went to the window. "This past year, whenever I wouldn't do what he asked, Seizemore would tell me that he could replace me in an instant. He said I had a double, and nobody needs two princes."

He turned to me. "Don't believe anything they say. They want to use you, because you're . . . simple."

"Hey!" I said. "It didn't take *me* eight years to figure out they're using me. And here's a news flash for you—I'm the one who actually managed to escape my room. So I think some respect is in order—"

"They're going to kill me," the prince said. He was angry and scared, I could tell. "I've watched you. You're a convincing prince. They don't need me. But you're not safe, either. Once they've taken control of Andirat, you'll have to do what they want, or they'll expose you as a fraud. Posing as a royal is an offense punishable by death, and they've got evidence of you doing it here."

He leaned against the windowsill and crossed his arms. "It's funny," he added without a smile, "but right now *you* are more a prisoner than I am. So I will withhold my respect until you've actually earned it."

"I don't have time for this," I said, standing up. "I'm getting out of here."

"And I have to reach Cordholm. Where is he?"

"Heading to Andirat," I said. "But there's a beggar woman in Stull City who knows how to contact him."

"I cannot let Seizemore take control of my country. Andirat ruled by that megalomaniac would be as bad as it is now, run by the generals."

"What are we waiting for?" George said. She opened a panel near the front door. "Let's go."

The prince stood up and pushed past me to follow George. "You are not coming with us," he said to me.

I followed him out into the hallway. "Why not?"

"You're going to get caught," he said, very softly now. He and George tiptoed down the hallway, with me following. They both crouched low as they passed a bust on a pedestal, but I didn't and got hit with a net that swooped out of its mouth.

George turned around to free me.

"You're slowing us down already," the prince said. "It would be much better if you just got yourself caught, and didn't put *me* in peril."

"I won't put you in peril," I said, struggling out of the net.

"You have no idea about the defenses of this castle. I've lived here for the last year. I know the creatures who work here. You will be alone and ignorant." He sneered at me. "I'm sure it's a situation you're familiar with."

He took off down the hallway, but the handsome ghost from my room came through the wall to block his way. The prince yelped and ducked behind a curtain. I sprinted to catch up.

"You've been trying to tell me I'm not the prince, haven't you?"

I asked the ghost. He nodded. "Well, here he is. Can you help us escape?"

The ghost pointed behind me, telling us to go that way. The prince ran off, and I followed.

"Do the noble thing," the prince yelled as he ran. "Be a distraction, so I can escape. Millions need me."

"I have people who need me too," I said, racing after him.

He reached the door to the servants' staircase, but couldn't open it. I came to a stop next to him.

"It's funny," I said, repeating it exactly as he'd said it.

"What?"

"You're just like Seizemore, aren't you? Another selfish jerk trying to manipulate others to get his way. I offered to work together, but you just want to use me. You don't care at all what happens to me."

He nodded. "That's right. I don't."

"I'm from Andirat," I said. That much I knew was true. "I'm your subject, Your Highness. A leader takes care of his people. That's his *only* job. To care about his people. What a sad excuse for a prince you are."

Wow, that felt so good.

A bright flash burst through the windows. I was still basking in my verbal victory and standing in plain view of anyone outside, while the prince and George dove out of sight.

CHAPTER 18

"They came in the night, destroying everything in their way."
—ACCOUNT OF THE ATTACK ON STULL CITY

It took me a second to realize that the bright flash wasn't a searchlight. The flashes were short and intermittent.

From the window, I saw a flurry of movement down below. A line of armored buses stood ready to evacuate the embassy. Men and monsters were racing toward the front gate, while Seizemore stood on the steps, directing the embassy staff.

"Something's happening outside the gate," the prince said.

"It's Pravus," I said, my heart sinking. "He's beginning his assault on Stull City. That means he's already attacked my school."

Oh, no. I was too late.

I cracked the window open and heard Seizemore yell, "Everyone to the buses! We're evacuating NOW!"

"It's the perfect time to escape," the prince said. "They're distracted and think we're safely locked in our rooms. I'm going to the capital to find Cordholm's contact."

"She's not going to be there now," I said. "The place is under attack."

"Then I'll find out where she went."

"Oh sure, just talk fancy and wait for people to do your bidding, while monsters are destroying everything in sight," I said sarcastically. "I'm going to Critchlore's. You can come with me. I know an Archivist of the Great Library there. She can find Cordholm."

"I don't know what you're talking about," the prince said. He turned around and headed back the way he'd been going before the ghost had turned us around. "I'm escaping out the front. George, you will come with me. I may need your help."

"George, come with me," I said. "That way isn't safe, the ghost told us. I can protect you."

George took a step toward the prince.

"Well, good luck," I said. "To both of you." I added that last part because I wanted the prince to know I was escaping on the high road.

I stood by the door to the servants' staircase, trying to figure out how to open it. My blood boiled with anger and desperation, but mostly anger. What an eye-opener this week had been. I'd grown up dreaming of becoming a minion. I was told that minions were loved and cared for by their EOs. One big happy family out to rule the world.

But the truth was, nobody cared about the minions. They were just used. A powerful weapon or a ready sacrifice. And really, what was a tyrant without his minions? He was nothing. Well, I was done being a tool for anyone but myself and the people I cared about.

The ghost pointed to a secret latch, and I opened the door.

But then I hesitated. I needed a disguise. I felt exposed in my white shirt, and I couldn't move comfortably in stiff shoes. I decided to detour back to my room. I sprinted downstairs, knowing I'd only have a few minutes before Mr. Fox came looking for me.

My ghost friend pointed to a potted plant, where I found the key to my door. I unlocked it, then relocked it from the inside, hoping that would slow down Mr. Fox. I rushed to my closet and found some dark, comfortable clothes and shoes. I even found a bag I could sling across my back. I loaded it up with supplies I might need: a throw blanket, a few candles, the matches I saw by the fireplace, the fireplace poker, and the box of cookies Janet had told me were from Cook. Then I headed for my balcony. Maybe I could sneak by the gargoyle if I was quiet.

I opened the balcony door very, very slowly. Just as I crept outside, I heard banging on my door. I dashed across the balcony, climbed over the balustrade, and hid on the other side, crouching low on the roof. My room door flew open.

"Your Majesty! It's time to evacuate!"

I expected to feel the talons of the gargoyle grip me, but when I turned I saw that he was gone. All the gargoyles were gone.

I heard Mr. Fox tearing through my room. "WHERE ARE YOU HIDING, BOY!" he screamed. "We have to get out of here!"

In seconds he would realize the balcony door was unlocked. I had to move. I started sliding down the slanted roof. Oh, boy, it was high. One slip and I would fall three stories and splat onto the stone terrace. The pitch was steeper than it had looked from below. I turned my body so that I was facing the building and could scuttle down the slope like a crab, carefully testing each tile before putting my weight on it.

The balcony door crashed open above me. I moved faster, fearing that Mr. Fox would lean out and see me. My feet hit the gutter, and I sidestepped across the roof until I reached the wall of the round tower. I saw Mr. Fox on the balcony as I grabbed the ledge my feet were resting on and hung down.

The drop to the next lower balcony was not far and I landed easily, pressing my body against the wall and out of view. I snuck around the tower's narrow walkway, ducking beneath the windows until I made it to the far side. I heaved myself over the low railing once again. The drop to the ground was too high to jump, but I knew there was a stone column with grooves I could stick my toes and fingers into. I climbed down to the ground floor and hid in the shadows.

I'd mapped out this escape route during my walks with Janet. I knew I'd be able to escape if I could get past the gargoyles. Fox must have known, too, which was why he tried to scare me into never opening my window.

Now I just had to wait for the horse patrol to pass by, as it did every ten minutes, and keep from being spotted by the six flying monkeys, the eight ogres, and the fourteen manticores stationed in the backyard. Most importantly, I had to avoid activating any of the motion-detector lights by the rose garden.

And to think I'd gotten that B in Strategic Reconnaissance last year. I was acing things here, I knew I was. I'd memorized every beast, every patrol, and every obstacle on every escape route.

I wondered what Janet would think of me now. Stupid, smiling Runt had actually been plotting his escape during each and every leisurely stroll.

I took a deep breath and headed for the side of the castle. I'd have to get to the main road out front if I was to have any chance of finding my way back to Critchlore's. Hopefully there were others fleeing the fighting in Stull City and I could blend in with them. I just had to get past that long stretch of land in front of the castle.

Unfortunately, the front of the castle was currently filled with monsters. And by monsters, I meant Janet and her father. Plus their minions, who were actual monsters.

The backyard, by contrast, was quiet. Lanterns were on, but there was no sign of the normal patrols.

I stuck close to the castle wall. The stone was so dark and heavy it seemed to suck in light. I was well camouflaged, but I moved carefully. I crept around the castle's corner, where a monkeyman stood in the middle of the path, glaring at me. He came at me quickly, but I dove under his outstretched arms, rolled on the ground, and popped up, sprinting for the nearest door.

I opened the door, darted in, and quickly closed it behind me. There was no way to lock the door, and I was worried the monkeyman would wrestle it open, but he didn't even try. I peeked out a small window on the top half of the door and saw his wings flapping outside. Why wasn't he trying to come in?

Why was the door covered in scratch marks?

No time to wonder, I had to move. I took the fireplace poker out of my pack and was ready to battle that monkeyman if he came inside.

It was dark, but I could see a faint glow at the opposite end of the room, which I assumed was another door. I had never been inside this room, but I'd seen the horse paddock behind it and assumed it was a stable. My nose confirmed this; the scent of hay and horses was strong. As my eyes adjusted to the dark, I noticed one wall with saddles and harnesses and . . . uh-oh.

Barb cuffs.

The manticores wore protective cuffs over their scorpion tails when they weren't on duty, to make sure they didn't accidentally poison anyone with a wayward jab. There was a wall of them here.

Janet had told me to avoid the manticores, and I'd run right into their home. The monkeyman wasn't trying to get in, he was making sure I didn't get out.

CHAPTER 19

*A manticore's sting feels like being stabbed with fire while
your body is exploding from the inside.*
—IT'S QUITE PAINFUL

Stalls ran down both sides of the building. As I tiptoed through the aisle I could see that the stalls were filled with hay and, more distressingly, sleeping manticores. I wondered how they could sleep through the blasts, and then I realized I couldn't hear anything from outside. The stable's walls were incredibly thick, and the windows were boarded closed. Safety lighting glowed along the wall, so it wasn't completely dark.

Stupid, stupid Runt. I slapped my head. That B in Strategic Reconnaissance made sense now. Our teacher's motto was "One mistake, that's all it takes," and now I knew why. I should have learned what was inside this building.

The monkeyman opened the door and saw me standing in the center aisle. I backed away from him, one careful, silent step at a time. He smirked, and then screeched loud enough to wake everyone in Stull City.

I took off sprinting away from him, but a paw reached out from a stall and swiped at my legs. I went sprawling to the ground. A few manticores charged at the screeching monkeyman, and he darted back outside.

"Oh, good," the manticore who'd tripped me said, sauntering out of his stall. "My midnight snack has arrived."

"Hello," I said, backing away from his approaching paws. "I command you, as Prince Auberon, to back off." I stood up confidently, pointing my fireplace poker at him.

He chuckled. "You're not the prince. Mrs. Ambrose thinks you intruders have killed the real prince." He took another step forward, licking his lips.

"Wait!" I said. "You're right, I'm not the prince. I just freed the real prince. He's not dead. We split up to escape. You can help us."

"More like you can help me. Seizemore locks us up in here and doesn't feed us enough."

"Let me talk to Roger," I tried.

"You don't know Roger, little mouse."

"Roger!" I yelled as all the manticores seemed to circle in closer and closer. The safety lights cast their faces in a sinister glow. They were so huge.

"Stay back!" the first one ordered. "He's mine."

"You can share, Nigel," another said with a sniff. I hoped he wasn't about to sneeze any teeth at me. "We're all hungry."

I backed away, right into another manticore. Just as he turned his head sideways to take a bite out of my midsection, a loud roar echoed throughout the stable. The rest of the pride backed away.

"The boy asked for me, Nigel," Roger said, his dark mane lost in the blackness of the room. "Step aside."

Nigel growled, but backed off.

"Roger, I need your help," I said. "Dr. Critchlore's school has been attacked. I have to escape and go back to help them."

He circled me slowly, eyeing me from his great height. "That's brave talk coming from one so small."

"I know the school," I said. "I know I can help."

"Where is your friend, the girl?"

"She's not my friend. Janet and her father have been lying to me and I have to escape. Please."

"You do not like the Commandant's daughter?"

"No."

"Good answer," he said. "I will help you." To the others, he said, "This is the boy who gave me that box of candy."

"Got any more?" one of them asked.

"No, sorry," I said. "But if you help me, I'll try my best to get you some."

"Elsie, Ingrid." Roger nodded at the group. "I'll need your help."

Two manticores stepped forward while the others went back to their stalls. We headed for the door I'd come through. The monkey-man was still outside, but one look at Roger and he flew off.

"You may climb on my back," Roger said. "It will be faster."

"Perhaps he should ride on my back," the manticore Elsie said. I recognized her from my first day. "He won't get a face full of mane, and you can lead the charge unencumbered."

Roger nodded.

"Thank you, Elsie," I said. I grabbed a barb cuff off the wall. "Do you mind wearing one of these?"

"No." She lifted her tail for the cuff.

"If we help you," Roger said while I attached the cuff, "you must

129

promise to come back here and rid this place of the Commandant, his daughter, and his people. You must make sure they never return."

"I will," I said. "The real prince will. He hates them too. After saving my school, that will be our number one priority."

"You know that to break your word to a manticore means that you and your descendants will be forever cursed by our kind," Roger said.

I didn't, but what was one more curse?

"I think speed is our best option," he said. "The element of surprise. We shall sprint for the front gate, maim the guards there, and let you escape."

"Okay," I said, climbing onto Elsie's back and grabbing her collar. "Except for the maiming. I'd like to keep the maiming to a minimum if you don't mind."

He snorted, but took off. We raced down the side of the castle, stopping to check the situation out front. The gargoyles that had been missing from the castle were out here. Mrs. Ambrose was directing them to protect the front of the castle as everyone evacuated. I saw Janet and her father at the top of the steps, laughing about something, but then Mr. Fox burst out of the front door screaming, "THEY'VE ESCAPED! BOTH OF THEM!"

Roger nodded at his friends, and we burst out of the shadows so quickly I nearly fell off Elsie's back. She was incredibly powerful and fast, keeping pace with Roger. Ingrid positioned herself behind us. We flew through a group of ogres standing near the armored buses, then bounded over a wall of hedges between the road and the field. I heard shouts and screaming coming from Seizemore and Mr. Fox.

The topiary animals were moving. I blinked a few times, because I thought I was seeing things, but no, they were trying to stop us. The giant bear stood like a tackle three-ball catcher, arms wide.

Roger charged through the bear while Elsie dodged around it. The sea serpent swished over the grass, coming to intercept us. Elsie jumped over one of its humps and ducked under the reach of the giant bunny. Roger blasted through an elephant, leaving it a pile of leaves and branches and clearing a path for us. Watching Roger crash through obstacles, I was really glad I was on Elsie's back.

We reached the open field and trampled through the giant *E* made of red flowers. Two buses had taken off, one on each side of the field, racing to reach the entrance gate before us. We raced next to topiary giraffes, who swung their heads down to knock us over.

Okay, those topiary creatures were pretty cool. I'd have to remember to tell Tootles about them.

I saw a couple of small shapes running across the open lawn toward the front gate. The prince and George. A pair of trolls were laughing as they herded them into the open, where two ogres stood waiting to grab them.

"Roger!" I screamed. "We have to save those two!"

"An added challenge! How delightful!" He changed course and ran for them. The trolls thought he was on their side at first, and they backed off when Roger roared at them.

"Prince! George! Jump on!" I said. George jumped on Ingrid, ducking under her stinging barb and grabbing her collar. I held my hand out to the prince, so he could jump on Elsie. He shook his head. "I must be in front!" he yelled.

"Fine, get captured then," I said.

A troll knocked Roger out of the way and reached out to grab the prince, who yelped and jumped on behind me. Elsie took off, easily bounding out of the troll's reach. A monkeyman swooped down to try and grab us, but the manticores were too nimble, and their stingers too dangerous.

The prince hugged my waist as we dodged ogres, leapt over the barrier hedge, and raced for the gate. The buses screeched to a halt in front of us, blocking the three arched entrances. The ogre guards at the gate turned, preparing for a fight.

Elsie slipped between the buses and zigzagged through the guards like they were slalom flags before seeing that the gates had been closed with iron bars. She cut to the left, running back to the forest that bordered the field.

Roger passed her. "I know another way," he shouted. We raced through the trees. None of the huge minions could keep up, because the trees grew so close together. Roger came to an abrupt halt in front of the perimeter wall, which was covered with vines. He brushed the vines to the side until he found the stone he was looking for. The front of the stone pulled off, revealing a button behind it. When he pressed it, a narrow passage opened in the wall. The prince and I slid off Elsie's back, and we all squeezed through. Roger found a similar button behind another stone, this one with a scratch mark across its face. He pressed it and the wall closed behind us.

We were free! And far enough from the entrance that the guards couldn't see us. Far-off explosions shook the ground, and the glow of fire lit the sky in every direction. The valley was under attack.

"That was great fun!" Roger said. "I wasn't sure I'd make it past those buses."

"Thank you, Roger, Elsie, Ingrid," I said. I was so grateful to be free, I hugged each of them.

"Yes, thank you, noble servants," the prince said, pushing me aside. "Let us continue onward."

Roger snorted in his face. He scanned the road for pursuers, and once he saw that nobody was coming for us, he turned to reopen the passage. "We stay with our pride," he said.

While the prince followed to argue with him, I pulled George aside.

"George, come with me," I said, nodding to the road leading out of the valley. It was crowded with people fleeing the attack. George stood twisting her hands together, worry crinkling her brow. "I think we've seen who's more capable."

"I didn't choose the prince 'cause I thought he was more capable," George said. "He's my sovereign, and he needed my help."

"Come on, then," I said. "We should get out of here."

"I'm bound to the castle," George said, backing up. "But you must take the prince with you. I know he seems arrogant—"

"Seems?"

"He is arrogant, but he can't take care of 'imself," George said. "Please."

"I can't make him come with me," I said.

"I'll convince him."

I waited while George talked to the prince, who kept shaking his head. But then he seemed to think about something and nodded. When he and George returned, George nudged him to speak.

"I owe you an apology," the prince said, very reluctantly. "I shouldn't have cast you away back at the castle."

"Apology accepted," I said.

"Further," he said, "I have decided to accept your offer of assistance."

"My what?"

"You said you could help me contact Mr. Cordholm," the prince said. "This will be our primary objective. Let's go."

I looked at George, who shrugged before waving good-bye.

CHAPTER 20

"Ahhhhh!"

—HEARD THROUGHOUT STULL CITY

With Pravus's army attacking the capital, the road through Castle Valley was jammed with refugees trying to escape the fighting. Cars and buses and hundreds of people and monsters crowded the road. Explosions echoed all around us, and smoke filled the night sky. We caught bits of conversations as we walked next to the road.

"Did you see them?" someone said. "The monsters . . . they're enormous!"

"They destroyed everything. Everything."

"I saw one swallow a troll. Just picked him up and stuffed him in its mouth. A troll!"

The prince and I hitched a ride with a family of humans who let us jump in the back of their truck. We made it out of Castle Valley and past a town that looked like the moon had fallen on it because every building had been smashed flat. We drove through the Valley of Fears and down Sure Death Highway, until we had to jump off when the truck passed Pitfall Road, which led to Critchlore's school.

It was late and we were exhausted, so I suggested we take shelter for the rest of the night away from the road. The prince acted like it was his idea and ordered me to find a place where we could sleep. I spotted a barn not far from the road, and we snuck inside.

It was empty, and it looked like it had been that way for a while. There was a hole in the roof, but even the moonlight didn't want to venture inside. The place was abandoned, alone, and smelled bad, just like me. I propped open the doors to let in a cross breeze and then lit a candle for myself, and one for the prince.

I found a dry, clean-ish spot in the corner and made a little bed of hay I'd collected from around the barn. I lay down, pulling the blanket from my backpack and covering myself.

The prince had done nothing while I'd been working. He stood next to me holding his candle, his sneering, condescending face glowing in its own little amber spotlight.

"I shall be needing a blanket," he said.

"Then you should have brought one," I said, hugging mine closer.

He sat down next to me, plucking hay from his pants like a fussy little Mr. Fussypants. I really did not like this guy.

"Must be quite a blow," he said. "Finding out you're not the prince."

"Yep," I said. "I'm devastated."

He didn't like my tone, apparently. "So what kind of a dimwit believes he's a prince, just because someone tells him?"

I ignored him and stared up at the ceiling. I could see a small constellation of stars twinkling through the hole in the roof.

"Have you always been so gullible?"

Probably.

"The funny little kid who pretended he was a dog," he said. "I bet you really thought you were a dog, didn't you?"

Inside I was fuming, but I wasn't going to let him see. I reached for my medallion, but of course it was gone.

"Do you know my real name?" I asked.

"No, I was four," he said. "And you were a peasant."

I turned away from him, hugging my blanket.

"I know you must be worried about the fact that you struck me," he said to my back.

"That doesn't even make my top twenty."

"The punishment for striking a royal is death. But I will pardon you if you give me that blanket."

"How gracious."

"Is that sarcasm?"

"Yes."

"Now listen," he said. "I am your better. You shall treat me with respect."

"*You* attacked *me*," I said, turning back around. "Not the other way around. I just saved your life, and you respond by threatening my life? You're not my better, you're a joke. But because some people might need you, I've decided to help you. But don't push your luck."

He didn't have a quick reply for that.

"I can't call you Prince Auberon," I went on. "What do people call you?"

"Prince Auberon."

"No, your friends, what do they call you?"

"Your Highness."

"Seriously? Do you even have any friends?"

"Of course I do," he said, but I could tell I'd stung him with that question.

"Well, I can't call you either of those," I said. "How about Aubie?"

"*Ew*, no."

"You have a bunch of names, maybe we can shorten one. Gabe? Titus? Ken? Val?"

He shook his head at each suggestion.

"What then?"

"I had a nanny who used to call me Ronny," he said. "Auberon, Auberonny, Ronny. Maybe just Ron."

"No, I already know someone named Ron," I said.

"So what? I know lots of Larrys," he said. "I could be The Ron."

"Just Ron," I said. "Fine."

I knew I needed sleep, but my thoughts were fighting each other and the battle kept me awake. I wasn't who I thought I was, yet again. When one part of my brain tried to remember my "royal houndsman" family, another part told it to stop. *Don't do it. Don't build another maybe-family in your mind, because it will only be stolen from you again.*

My werewolf family had been a lie. My prince family had been a lie. Who knew if my royal houndsman family was real or not. I didn't want to imagine that I might have parents who loved me, or an older brother who didn't prank me, or a little sister who liked to play dress-up. I couldn't do it again . . . I couldn't lose another family.

Daydreaming was out, but I didn't want to think about reality, either. Dr. Pravus may have destroyed my school, and everyone in it.

I'd never felt so alone. My future and my past were both gone. What was I going to do now?

I rolled to my side and outlined a circle in the dirt. Then I picked up a piece of hay and put it inside the circle. I imagined it was Cook, and she was safe. The next piece of hay was Syke, and I put her in the safe circle. Then Darthin, Frankie, Meztli, Boris, and Eloni. Pierre. Dr. Critchlore, Mistress Moira, my professors.

Maybe Dr. Pravus hadn't attacked my school. Maybe the Critchlore minions had fought him off. Maybe everyone was safe. I focused on these thoughts as I added everyone I knew to my pile of safe hay.

As I was trying to remember the names of all the sixth-year students, I fell asleep. I slept for a few hours and woke up with the sun and the realization that I didn't have a blanket. The prince had stolen it and now slept beside me. Even in sleep he had a condescending look on his face. I grabbed my blanket and stuffed it back into my bag.

"Time to get moving," I said, munching on one of my cookies. I handed him a coconut one before he could order me to share.

He stood up and brushed himself off. He noticed my little pile of hay, and then shuffled his feet through it, sending rocks and hay flying. "Let's go," he said.

I had a feeling I might be heading for a similar scene of destruction at my school. I took a deep breath and told myself to focus on my job. I had to help whoever was left, if anyone was left, and I had to find a way to get the prince to Cordholm.

We headed to Critchlore's, sticking close to the cover of trees whenever we could. The school wasn't far, but I'd wanted to approach it in daylight, while rested, so I'd be prepared for any dangers.

"Look . . . uh," Ron began, "er, what was your name again?"

"People call me Runt," I said.

He laughed. "How appropriate."

"Says the guy who lost three wrestling matches to me," I said.

"I've been locked up," he said, still trying to make excuses. "But it doesn't matter. I shouldn't have attacked you, Runt."

"That's okay."

"I've been betrayed by everyone I've ever known," he went on. "I guess I'm not the trusting type."

"Have you always lived with Seizemore?"

"Since my family was murdered, yes," he said. "He hasn't always kept me isolated. I did have friends before, at school in the Forgotten Realm. But a year ago he brought me here and hired private tutors." He kicked a rock. "He's going to ruin me now."

"How?"

"Once, in jest, I told him that he'd have to earn his place in my palace," Ron said. "My little joke enraged him. He was livid. He threatened to discredit me with my people. Said he has hours and hours of video of me being awful. He told me that once people see the lie, it's very difficult to convince them to believe the truth. Especially if they've made up their minds."

"He told me first impressions are important," I said. "He had a whole scene set up for my arrival back home. To make me look prince-like."

The prince nodded. "They were using you to pressure me into cooperating with them. They let me watch you stroll around the grounds. Janet told me, 'We don't need you now. If something happened to you, nobody would care.'"

"She said that?" Wow, that was harsh.

"Yes. At first I thought they were going to kill me, but then I realized that Seizemore never does anything rash. Better to keep me around for insurance."

I nodded.

"In case something happens to the simple kid they found to take my place," he added, and just when I was starting to feel sorry for the guy, I hated him again.

We were approaching the road that led to Critchlore's front gate, so I steered us into the woods for cover, heading toward the area that had been deforested by Kumi, the giant gorilla.

Once we reached the edge of Kumi's clearing, I noticed the guards. Two towering giants stood on either side of the school's main entrance, where the sign that had read "Dr. Critchlore's School for Minions" had been torn off and cast aside.

"Oh, no," I said.

"What happened?"

I'd had a sliver of hope that Dr. Pravus wouldn't waste time attacking my school, but that hope had just been crushed flat.

"Those are Pravus minions at the gate," I said.

Not only that, but I saw smoke rising in the distance.

CHAPTER 21

Defending Your School from an Egomaniacal
Madman Obsessed with Revenge
—NEW CLASS AT DR. CRITCHLORE'S,
ADDED A LITTLE TOO LATE

This was a brilliant plan, wasn't it?" Ron said. "Tell me again how your friends are going to help me?"

"My friends could be dead, and you're only worried about yourself? That's real nice, Just Ron," I said.

"My people need me," he said, and when I pointed to my chest, he added, "You don't count. What do we do now?"

"We find out what happened to everyone. We have to get inside."

"Past those two? Not likely."

"I know a way."

His arrogance had knocked the feeling of despair out of me, replacing it with resolve. I led Just Ron around the outside of the perimeter fence. The school was as big as a village, so it took us a while to reach the site of the FRP. I silently prayed that my toddler trees had gone unnoticed by the invading Pravus troops.

We had to duck out of sight a bunch of times, because Dr. Pravus's ahools were patrolling the skies. I didn't want to run into

one of those giant bat creatures here, especially without Frankie to fight it off.

We made it to the right spot. I cupped my hands to my mouth and made a sound, starting very softly and rising, like the roar of the wind: "WoooOOOOSH! GoooooGGAAAAA! Fffffffthhhh-hhiiiiiip!"

"Fthip?" Ron asked.

I shrugged. "It's his name. Or hers. Thems? It's a tree."

The perimeter wall was over twenty feet high, but we could see the trees towering over it. They'd grown even bigger.

"Great me!" Ron said. "They're moving. Those trees are moving!"

Long branches reached over the fence. I grabbed one in a bear hug and nodded at Ron to do the same. The prince stepped closer, tentatively, but as the branch lifted me away he jumped on. Once we were over the wall, they placed us gently on the ground.

My toddler trees were so huge! Nearly as tall as the castle's towers. Their faces were still toddler-ish images in their now-wide trunks. An ahool swooped overhead and the trees froze. The giant bat-like creature seemed to do a double take, then shrugged and flew on.

We stood in the middle of the trees. Ron kept turning around, like he was expecting an attack.

"Thanks, guys," I said. "Where's Tootles?"

"Tootles gone," Googa said.

"Everyone leave," Plang said. "Then bad creatures come."

"Bad creatures?"

They nodded. Plang pointed to the ahool. "Bad creatures."

"What about Dr. Critchlore?"

"Crishlore gone," Fthip said. "Tootles gone. Riga gone. Tree house gone." He pointed toward the lake. The smoke I'd seen from the front gate rose from where the tree house used to be.

"Where'd they go?" I asked.

"They go bye-bye." Googa seemed to slump after that, so I gave him a hug.

"Why didn't you go with them?" I asked.

"Too big," Googa said. "Tootles say, 'We have to sneak away,' and big trees can't sneak."

"'Can't sneak,'" Fthip repeated. "No more hidey seek."

"Tootles say, 'Play freeze tag,'" Googa said. "'Don't move.' He'll come back soon."

"Okay, you guys stay here. I'm going to find out where they went."

I nodded at Ron to follow me through the FRP, which offered

lots of cover. As we tiptoed carefully past some hedges, I turned and noticed five trees mimicking our every move.

"Freeze tag, remember?" I said.

"You didn't tag," they said in a singsong voice, laughing. I ran back and touched each one, saying, "You're caught," and then Ron and I continued toward the stables.

"Those giant trees . . . you command them?" Ron asked.

"What? No, they're my friends."

"And the giant manticore. He obeyed you as well. It must be because you look like me."

"Wrong," I said. "Roger wouldn't obey you. He only obeys Mrs. Ambrose. And he only helped me after I told him I hated Seizemore and Janet and everyone who came to the embassy with them. Oh, and I promised we'd return to the embassy and rid it of Seizemore's people. If we don't, we'll be cursed forever, just so you know."

He looked like he didn't believe it, but I had no time to explain. If Pravus had ahools patrolling the skies here, who knew what other minions lurked on the ground.

I led us between the aviary and the stables, but froze when I heard Ron yelp behind me. I turned and saw him being lifted into the air by a giant beast who'd been hiding in the shadows.

How had I not noticed Kumi? Maybe that B in Strategic Reconnaissance had been generous. Either that, or Kumi had aced his Sitting Still So Nobody Notices You class. His black fur blended in with the shadows of the trees. Plus, he'd shrunk a lot more. Now he was only double the size of a regular gorilla.

The last time I'd seen Kumi he'd been heading back to the Pravus

Academy with Syke. If he'd been sent here with the Pravus team, then maybe Syke was here too.

He lifted Ron to his face, smiling, but then the smile turned to confusion.

Ron looked like he was about to wet his pants, but he was trying to be brave. "Release me!" he squeaked. "I command it!"

"Kumi!" I waved my arms around to get his attention.

Kumi saw me and smiled again.

"Put him down, okay?" I said, and he did.

He signed "Runt" and "Happy." I wasn't fluent in Gorilla Sign Language, but if he spelled out words one letter at a time, I could understand.

"I'm happy to see you too," I said. "Are you here with the Pravus team?"

He nodded.

"Have you seen any Critchlore people around?"

He shook his head and then made some motions with his hands that I didn't understand.

He noticed my confusion, and signed the letters: "G-O-N-E."

"They're gone?"

He nodded.

"What are you doing here? What's your job?"

He mimed some things, and I made a guess.

"You're going to destroy the school," I said. He nodded. "Where are the rest of the Pravus minions?"

He pointed to the castle. Then he signed, "S-Y-K-E."

"Syke's here?"

He nodded. "H-E-L-P pause S-Y-K-E."

"I will," I said.

He tapped his chest, then signed, "M-Y pause B-E-S-T pause F-R-I-E-N-D."

I nodded. Of course she was.

"Kumi, do you want to be big again?" A huge Kumi could be very helpful in a school full of Pravus minions.

He nodded, so we took him back to the FRP and I introduced him to the toddler trees. I mimed drinking from the pond and Kumi drank.

"Come on, Just Ron," I said, pulling him away. "We've got to get into that castle."

"Didn't that giant beast just tell you that all the Pravus troops were there?"

"Yes, but I know how to sneak in."

I led Ron behind the castle, down a seldom-used pathway. Peeking between trees, I could see that the castle was heavily guarded with ogres and werewolves and other monsters, all wearing Dr. Pravus's green military-style uniforms with the giant *P* on the front.

We reached the other side of the castle and continued toward the lake. Two human-looking guys came out from behind the Wall of Heroes, so I quickly pulled Ron into the organic garden. We ducked behind a high mound of strawberries as they passed.

"You need to report to Victus in Critchlore's office," one said. "I'll check that shack on the other side of the waterfall."

"I thought Syke was doing that."

"She's helping Victus find something for Pravus."

Victus. Man, I hated that guy. I'd played against him in hoop-smash, and he was such a dirty player. He was obnoxious in Polar Bay, too, where he'd led a Pravus team that tried to stop us from finding sudithium.

"This way to the castle," I whispered. I led Ron through the organic garden. "Don't touch the berries." It looked like he wanted to do it just to spite me, so I tossed a rock at one and we watched the vines whip out and wrap around it.

Ron said, "It seems we are venturing farther *away* from the castle."

"It does, doesn't it?" I said. "How clever of you to notice."

"Is that more sarcasm? Directed at me?"

"You sound surprised. You really don't have any friends, do you?"

"I've had enough of your insolence. When this is over you'll see what happens to people who displease the royal family."

"When this is over, maybe you'll realize that you're not a better person just because you were born into a family of wealth and privilege, Just Ron."

"It's Ron. Only Ron."

"Okay Only Ron."

"You are so annoying."

"No, you are."

We made it to the boathouse by the lake and ducked inside. It was dark and musty, but enough light snuck through the dirty windows that I was able to see the dim outline of shapes. I found a flashlight and a freezer full of fish. I stuffed a couple fish into my backpack and motioned for the prince to grab one too.

"You're kidding, right?" he said.

"Suit yourself," I said. "But if I were to run into a hungry monster, I'd like to have something to offer him to eat, besides my limbs."

He grabbed a fish by the tail, very gingerly.

The secret dungeon entrance was underneath a box in the corner. I pushed it aside and started down the ladder built into the side of the tunnel that went straight down. My footsteps clanged on the metal rungs.

As we reached the bottom, the prince asked, "What's down here?"

"Normally it's full of bat-men, mole-people, spiders, and giant bugs," I replied. "But the Pravus team might have stationed something really scary down here."

We snuck through the cave-like hallways. It was eerily quiet, which, if I'm honest, was the normal vibe down here. But this time it felt even eerier. We passed one of Mrs. Gomes's security stations, and I pulled out a can of insect repellent, just in case. I tested it out in Ron's direction, because he bugged me.

"Hey!" he said.

I looked at him for a second, and then at the can. "Doesn't seem to work."

He rolled his eyes. "Oh, how you wound me," he said with a big dose of his own sarcasm. Sometimes sarcasm makes you laugh, sometimes it makes you want to punch a person in the face. His was the second type.

We continued through the tunnels. Twice we heard growling noises coming our way and had to duck down alternate passageways. Ron was growing more and more terrified, I could tell.

"I'm getting out of here," he said. "Now."

He threw his fish at me and turned to leave.

CHAPTER 22

*"You can't beat me, so join me. Accept this bracelet
as a welcome-to-the-team gift."*
—DR. PRAVUS, TO THE MINIONS OF HIS ENEMIES

N o, you'll get lost," I said, grabbing his arm. "Come on, we're
close to Critchlore's office. Those Pravus guys said that Victus
and Syke are there. If we can spy on them, maybe we can figure out what happened to Critchlore and everyone else. We have to
find Professor Zaida. She's the only person I know who can contact
Cordholm."

He sulked, but I was able to lead him to Critchlore's secret bun-
ker. Once inside, we climbed a spiral staircase until we reached a
hidden door to Critchlore's office that was concealed on the other
side by a bookshelf.

"We might be able to overhear the Pravus team from here," I
said.

Ron found a panel that opened a small window behind the
bookshelf. Now we could clearly hear what was said inside, and
even get a narrow peek.

"We have one of these at the embassy," he said. "George showed
it to me, before I was imprisoned. I would hide and spy on Seizemore. That's how I discovered how despicable he is."

"Hey, Ron," I said, serious now. "I'm really sorry about your family."
He nodded.

The office was empty, so we waited. And waited. Ron had never played rock-paper-scissors, so I taught him that game. Then I taught him a shoot-'em finger game, twenty questions, and the alphabet sentence game. He was terrible at all of them, and a poor loser, so I switched to two lies and a truth, the game where you tell three things about yourself and the other person has to guess which one is true.

Ron started. "One: When I turned five, Seizemore gave me my very own whipping boy, who would be punished when I misbehaved because nobody is allowed to touch a royal. Two: When I turned six, Seizemore gave me my own whip, and taught me to use it on the servants myself. Three: When I turned seven, my best friend didn't come to my party, and I later learned it was because Seizemore had had his parents executed for stealing food."

"Those are all terrible," I said. "I hope they're all lies."

"Actually, they're all true," he said with a sad smile. "I was trying to trick you."

"Okay, I'll go," I said. "One: I've never had a birthday party, because I don't know when my birthday is. Two: My foster mother, Cook, has had so many foster children she can't remember their names, so she gives them nicknames she can remember. Three: I don't remember what my parents look like."

"The second one is true?" he asked.

"Actually, they're all true," I said.

We sat quietly for a moment, then Ron said, "I remember your father. He whistled a lot, and the dogs loved him. He always seemed so happy."

I smiled, adding that one mental picture to my empty family photo album. "Thanks," I said.

We played the game straight after that. I learned that he hated snails (me too, though I meant plucking them out of the garden and he meant eating them). We liked the same movies, but he had horrible taste in music.

We ate the last of my cookies and were about to give up and search elsewhere when someone entered Dr. Critchlore's office.

"Let's have a little fun, shall we?" a voice said.

It was Victus. Tall, pointy-nosed, arrogant Victus. "Which building should we destroy first?" he asked.

"The one by the cemetery," a girl-voice answered. Syke! "It's dangerous. They used to raise a lot of zombies over there."

I grabbed Ron's wrist and mouthed the word "friend." He nodded.

She was right inside Critchlore's office. I could open this secret door and grab her. She could escape! But then I caught a glimpse of her wrist. She was wearing an orange "loyalty" cuff. Pravus still didn't trust her.

"What about the dungeon?" another voice said. A big guy, by the look of his back. "My patrols say there are some giant bugs down there. They might be protecting something important, or some minions we missed."

"It's possible," Syke said. "The dungeon is a maze of tunnels, but I can't help there. I hate the dungeon. It smells like root rot and there's no sunlight, which I kinda need."

"Okay, we'll start with the buildings by the lake and work in from there," Victus said. "I'll send the ogres to start. Dr. Pravus said to film everything so he can broadcast it. He wants Critchlore to see his school destroyed, bit by bit. The werewolves can root out the dungeon. What about booby traps? Hiding minions? Has everything been checked out?"

"Mostly," Syke said. "The patrols have swept through the dorms, stables, and fields and found them clear. I told you Critchlore wouldn't booby trap his school. He loves it too much."

Victus slammed his fist on the table. "THOSE COWARDS!" he shouted. "I wanted a fight. I wanted to destroy them, make a name for myself. But no, they evacuated. Critchlore minions are the worst."

"Why do you think I left?" Syke said.

Victus pulled all the drawers out of the desk, dumped their contents on the ground, and kicked stuff everywhere in a tantrum that would have made a two-year-old proud.

Once that was out of his system, he sat in Dr. Critchlore's chair and put his feet up on the desk. "I have another assignment, and I need your help, Syke. This is your chance to prove yourself and get rid of that cuff. Tell me, where are Critchlore's awards?"

"Awards?"

"Yes, Dr. Pravus has a wall in his office that's covered with awards. Plaques, framed certificates, a shelf of trophies. When Pravus came here to steal the book, he couldn't find a trophy case in this office, and there's nothing in his private quarters. Where are they?"

"I don't think I've seen anything . . . but I wasn't allowed in here, no students were. Maybe there's a hidden room? What does that button do?"

Clever Syke! She was trying to get herself trap-doored.

Victus pushed the button and Syke screamed as the floor dropped away beneath her.

I replaced the secret panel and pointed down the steps.

I was halfway down the stairs when I heard a sharp exhale from the prince. A scoffing sound.

"What?" I asked.

"Your people ran," he said. "Like cowards."

"They probably thought Pravus was coming with his Undefeatable Minions," I said. "It was the smart thing to do."

"What am I doing here?" Ron asked himself. "I've tagged along with an imbecile who wants to take me to his fainthearted friends, who are hiding who knows where."

"I'm not an imbecile," I said, turning to face him. "Tell me again how you escaped the embassy? And my friends aren't cowards. Well, except for one, maybe."

"They didn't stay and fight," he pointed out.

"You don't know what you're talking about."

"I know what I see."

I wanted to punch his sneering, condescending face, but I was too worried about Syke. I raised a finger to his face. "We'll finish this later," I said. I walked down the stairs and darted next door, where Syke stood, brushing hay off her clothes.

"Runt!" she said, rushing over to hug me. "Thank the Goddess you're okay. What are you doing here?"

"Trying to find out where everyone went," I said. "Come on, we need to get you to Dr. Frankenhammer's lab and remove that cuff."

"Wait," she said, grabbing my arm before I could leave. "Who's this?" She nodded at Ron.

I sighed. I really didn't want to have this conversation right now. I'd been spending so much time with Ron, whose constant insults were wearing me down, and now I had to confess to Syke something that would make me feel even worse.

"Syke," I said. "Meet Prince Auberon."

She looked at him, then at me. *Oh, great, here we go.*

"Nice to meet you," she said to Ron, her smile widening so much it looked like her face was about to split in two. He nodded a reply, looking haughty and self-important, while I braced myself for what was coming. She turned to me and said, "I knew it! I knew you weren't the prince."

That got a big smile from Ron, who almost laughed out loud.

"Come on, we have to move," I said, leading the way out of the trapdoor pit. "They'll be looking for you."

"I so knew it," she said, not willing to let this victory go without an award ceremony and a parade, it seemed. "Ha! Where'd you find him?"

"Long story," I said as we rounded a corner. "But I was kidnapped by Janet, who is—"

"A spy! I knew it!" She did a little hop of glee as we ran. "Wow, I have fantastic instincts. I really should trust myself more."

"Yeah, you're a regular Psychic Sally."

"Oh, quiet, you," she said, punching my arm. "Be a good loser. I'm probably right about Vodum being part swamp monster too."

"You should quit while you're ahead," I said.

We raced down tunnels and dark passageways. As we got closer to the secret lab, I thought I heard a clicking sound, followed by a soft fluttering. And then I turned a corner and ran right into a giant praying mantis. One of its forelegs shot out and pinned my jacket to the wall.

CHAPTER 23

*"Dr. Frankenhammer also had two giant mole crickets.
Nobody knows where they went, but there are a few
more tunnels now."*

—DARTHIN, EXPLAINING THE INSECT EXPERIMENT

Ron screamed as I slipped my backpack off my free shoulder and pulled out the insect repellent, spraying the mantis in the face. It jumped back, bumping into a humongous fluttering moth and some enormous cockroaches, each as big as Eloni if he were walking on his hands and knees. This hall was crowded with giant bugs.

"What's going on down here?" Syke asked.

"Dr. Frankenhammer has been testing out his sudithium antidote," I explained. "He makes insects big and then sees if he can shrink them."

"It's going well, I see," she said.

Ron laughed, and then stepped behind me for safety. I blasted the bugs with insect repellent, because they were standing right in front of the lab's door. The mantis lifted a spiked foreleg to take a swipe at us, but then backed off.

"Ron, take this," I said, giving him the canister. "I need to get

Dr. Frankenhammer to open the door. Keep spraying, I don't want to be eaten."

"I thought everybody left," he said.

"Dr. Frankenhammer never leaves his work. Once, the dungeon was filled with bombs and he had to be dragged out." I banged on the lab door. "Dr. Frankenhammer! It's Runt and Syke! Let us in!"

Ron blasted insect repellent at the bugs, and they didn't come closer, but the lab door stayed shut.

"He has another lab back there," I said, pointing to the way we'd come. "Dr. Frankenhammer!" I yelled, banging my fists on the rocky wall. There was a camouflaged keypad, but his secret code was ridiculously long and there was no way I'd remember it, so I kept banging

Syke tapped my arm. The corridor opposite the mantis and its friends was filling up with giant, black-shelled beetles, each as tall as my hip and just as wide. Their faces had pincer mandibles that looked like they could slice us in half. We all screamed, which only seemed to excite the insects into a hissing and clicking frenzy.

We had insects coming at us from both directions now. Ron swiveled to spray the beetles. A fog of bug repellent filled the confined space and made us cough. Syke and I kept screaming for Dr. Frankenhammer, but the door remained shut.

"Can's empty," Ron said through his pulled-up shirt. "What now?"

The bugs were inching closer as the spray dissipated. I threw a fish at them, but they seemed more interested in fresh meat.

"We have to run," Syke said. "Let's charge through the beetles."

"I agree," Ron said.

"Wait," I said, banging on the wall again. "He's got to be here."

The bugs inched closer.

"We need to run NOW," Ron said. Just as he was about to take off, a human figure pushed his way through the beetles. He was dressed head to toe in camouflage gear, a bandana covering his face. His gloved hands seemed to glow in the darkness.

He pointed a finger at the praying mantis. "BACK OFF!" he screamed, and all the bugs did.

I knew that voice, but my brain didn't believe me.

"Darthin?" I said, completely shocked.

"Runt!" he answered. "Syke! . . . Boris?"

"No, this is Ron," I said. "Can you get us inside?"

Darthin pulled down his bandana and began typing in the lengthy code. The praying mantis edged closer, but Darthin raised his hand. Without even looking at the terrifying bug, he said, "Back off," and it did.

"Darthin, that's amazing," I said.

"It's chemical," he said. He raised the glove, flexing his five fingers, each one a different color. "Insects send messages to each other using chemicals. Simple things like: back off, protect, flee, and follow me. I have a different message chemical in each finger."

"Genius," Ron said.

"Just don't ask me where the chemicals come from," he said as he opened the door. "Okay, I'll tell you. It's gut bacteria I collected from their feces."

Syke had been about to give him a hug of thanks, but she backed off. "You're wearing gloves loaded with bug poop?"

"Yes," he said, smiling wide. "And it works."

We raced into the lab and slammed the door shut on the insects. I nearly collapsed with relief.

Dr. Frankenhammer's lab was a mess. More unusually large insects filled the cages along one wall, and the stainless-steel counters and tables were covered with bubbling test tubes and papers scribbled with notes. A bunch of brightly colored steel drums were lined up at the end of the room, each one covered with warning labels.

Dr. Frankenhammer was huddled over a beaker at the far end of the room. Frankie was there, too, sitting at a lab table in the opposite corner, his arms a blur as he filled hundreds of test tubes with a thick, pale liquid. They were both so focused on their work that they didn't notice us come in.

"Frankie!" I said. "Dr. Frankenhammer, we need your help."

Frankie looked up and rushed over. "Runt, Syke, you're okay!" He lifted us both in his arms.

Dr. Frankenhammer looked from me to Ron and back again. "Clones! There'ssss two of you."

"No, Dr. Frankenhammer, this is Ron."

"Nice to meet you," Ron said. I don't know if he was still in shock from the bugs, but all his haughtiness was gone.

"Where is everyone?" I asked.

"They evacuated," Frankie said. "Darthin and I offered to stay behind and help Daddy finish his work."

"My work would be ruined if I left," Dr. Frankenhammer said, returning to his beakers. "We're sssafe here. We have everything we need." He pointed to three cots along the back wall, and a mini-fridge next to a door that I hoped was his bathroom, because I really needed to use it.

"Evacuated where?" I asked Darthin.

"The Kobold Academy. As you know," he said with a pointed look at me, "there's a vacant mountain fortress near there."

"Runt," Frankie said. "Where have you been? Everyone's been worried sick about you."

"Long story," I said. "But first, we need to get this cuff off Syke."

Dr. Frankenhammer stood up and grabbed her wrist, leading her over to one of his tables. Ron picked up a banana from its end.

"Don't eat that," Frankie said. "It's not safe for human consumption. If you're hungry . . ." He nodded to the corner. We both rushed over, because we were starving. We each grabbed an MRE (meals ready to eat) from a stack next to the fridge, and a can of soda. I ducked into the bathroom, and when I came out, Ron had eaten both MREs and Dr. Frankenhammer was still examining Syke's cuff.

"Can you remove it?" I asked him after grabbing another meal.

"That'sss a tricky little gizmo," he said. "It has a tracker, which I removed." He nodded to a small metallic circle on his table. "But I'm quite certain if I cut through the cuff, it would inject a poison into your wrist."

"That's exactly what it does." Syke looked at us. "Pravus is able to activate it remotely. He gives them to minions he feels have not shown true loyalty to him. He can't afford to have defectors from

163

that cult school of his. If someone tries to run away, he can stop them before they tell anyone what he's really up to."

"That's so evil," Ron said. "We must get it off you, immediately."

He looked very worried, which was nice, considering he'd just met her. I began to wonder how long it would be before he was telling me that Syke was his best friend.

Dr. Frankenhammer tried a few of his instruments, but nothing worked. Then he brought out a power saw that had a thick, serrated blade at the end of its gun-shaped handle.

"You can't cut off the cuff," Syke said.

"Er . . . I wasn't intending to cut the cuff," Dr. Frankenhammer said.

"What then?" I asked.

"I'm going to amputate her hand," he said. He gave the trigger a few pumps and the saw whizzed to life.

CHAPTER 24

My Life as the Bug Boss
—DARTHIN'S LIST OF POTENTIAL AUTOBIOGRAPHY TITLES

N O!" I screamed. Syke looked like she was going to faint. "There has to be another way."

"I was going to reattach it," he said, a little hurt. "There issss one other thing I could try. But you might not like it."

"Do it," Syke said. "I have to get this thing off."

"All right, if you insssist." He selected one syringe out of hundreds from his cabinet and jabbed her in the arm.

"What was that?" Syke asked, her eyes now wide with panic.

"My sssudithium antidote," he said. "It will shrink you and then the cuff will fall off."

"But, she hasn't ingested any sudithium," I said.

"Doesn't matter," Darthin said. "It shrinks everything. Look at this." He walked over to the cages lining the wall. They were filled with deformed animals that had been injected with the monsterizing virus. Darthin opened the cage.

"This is Dr. Frankenhammer's dragon," he said, holding the once-large beast in the palm of his hand. It was the size of a rat.

"You shrank your dragon?" I asked Dr. Frankenhammer.

"Many timesss now," he said. "The first sssserum, the one I just gave Syke, did not last very long. I adjusted the formula, sssso it would last longer."

"I'm going to be that small?" Syke said. I thought she was going to be angry, but she smiled. "That's so cool. How long does it take?"

"Sssince you are not a dragon, I'm not precisely sssure," he said. "But I believe you will begin reducing in twenty-four to forty-eight hoursss."

"The antidote works?" I said. "It really works? That's fantastic! We can stop Pravus's Undefeatable Minions by shrinking them."

"Actually, I've concocted an antidote for the virusss as well," Dr. Frankenhammer said. "Frankie and I are producing a combo sssserum that will return the UMssss to normal humansss."

"They're so huge, though," Darthin said. "We need a large supply."

"We're brewing as fast as we can," Frankie added. "But we need more time."

"You don't have it," Syke said. "Victus is going to find you. He's very suspicious of what could be hiding down here. They think the insects might be protecting something."

"I just ran off a team of werewolves," Darthin said. "But I have a feeling they'll be back."

"We've got to come up with a plan to distract Victus," I said. "And I've got to get Ron to Professor Zaida."

We were quiet for a moment, pondering our dilemmas.

"Pismo can take Ron up the river," Frankie said. "Like he did with us, remember?"

"Pismo's here?" I asked.

"He's in the lake," Darthin said. "He said he feels safe there, because it's so huge."

"He's a merperson," I explained to Ron. "Okay, Ron and I will find Pismo. Syke, you have to stay with Victus until your cuff falls off, so he doesn't suspect you're not loyal."

"Take this," Darthin said. "It's a DPS that I modified to give false information. We knew they'd be coming, so I've been trying to think up some protective measures."

"Great idea," Syke said, taking the gadget. She also stuffed the tracker in her pocket. "I'll take this with me. I can leave it in my room if I need to sneak out at night."

"Darthin, what about the rest of these DPSs?" I pointed to a pile of the pocket-sized gadgets.

"They work," Darthin said. "I collected them from the hub, so the Pravus team wouldn't find them."

"If your friend isss going to the Kobold Academy," Dr. Frankenhammer said, nodding at Ron, "perhapsss he could take the completed sssserumsss. It's not much, but at least the formula would be ssssafe there."

"Good idea," I said. "Do you have some ready to go?"

"Frankie will prepare a case," he said. "He will contact you when it'sss ready. Now, please, I must get back to work without distractionssss."

I grabbed two DPSs and left with Ron and Syke.

Syke led the way through the tunnels as we headed for the main office hub, where we could sneak out of the dungeon.

"What is this thing?" Ron asked, fiddling with his DPS.

"Dungeon Positioning System," I said. "It helps navigate the dungeon. It also has a flashlight, which comes in handy."

"Any weapons?"

"Everyone always asks that, but no," I said. "You can plug in your schedule and get homework reminders. Send messages. Take pictures."

He stuffed it in his pocket, uninterested.

We reached an intersection and Syke put a finger to her lips. She checked the tunnels, then motioned us forward.

"So, are we going to this mountain fortress then?" Ron whispered. "I'm ready to be away from this place."

"I can't go that far," I said. "My tether curse will activate. But Pismo will swim you upriver, and I'll tell you how to find Professor Zaida."

Another intersection. This time Syke motioned us to get flat against the wall.

"I heard something," she whispered. A second later a swarm of bats flitted by, and we exhaled in relief.

"It's so weird," Syke said, staring at us. "You guys really do look exactly alike."

I scowled at her. Ron did too. "I wouldn't say exactly," Ron said. "An expression of shocked bewilderment seems to have settled on his face, while mine tends to remain comfortably bemused."

Syke looked at me with an expression I knew meant, "Is this guy for real?"

"He's a work-in-progress," I explained.

"But you know what? He's kind of right," she said, smiling at Ron. He smiled back. It was the first time I'd seen him genuinely smile.

"And you do look nicer than in your family portrait," Syke said, motioning us forward.

"The portrait?" Ron said. "I've heard. That painter really hated me, just because I ate his piece of cake. He'd left it right next to his easel, and I was four years old."

We reached the entrance to the hub, but quickly backed away because it was full of Pravus minions.

"Ron and I will go another way," I said.

Syke nodded.

"We'll wait for the antidotes, and then I'll send Ron off with Pismo. After that I'll hide in Uncle Ludwig's secret library. You can join me when the cuff falls off."

"Why not hide in Frankenhammer's lab?" Syke asked.

Because I would have nightmares about cockroaches streaming through the vents, or giant muscle blobs suffocating me, or Dr. Frankenhammer using me as an experiment while I slept.

"Too crowded," I said.

She nodded. I took one last look at the hub. It had been completely wrecked: desks overturned, file cabinets emptied. Someone had stolen the painting from the conference room. I clenched my teeth and led Ron back the way we'd come, anger and fear fighting for my attention. I was angry that the Pravus kids thought they could get away with this, and I was scared that they might have done the same thing to Uncle Ludwig's beautiful library.

We were close to the kitchen, so Ron and I slipped upstairs through a dumbwaiter. I stole some cans of food and a few of the spare uniforms that Cook kept for me in the closet. I also snagged that Pravus uniform I'd stashed earlier and put it on.

"Got one for me?" Ron asked.

"Sorry, I just have the one. But you're getting out of here, so you won't need one."

We headed to the secret library to wait for the antidotes. If the library was still safely hidden, I could barricade the main entrance and hope that Clarence would keep the Pravus team away from the grotto entrance. With enough supplies, I could stay there until the Pravus minions left.

"Is this school always full of monsters?" he asked as we sprinted by the splashing tentacles in the grotto.

"Yes, isn't it great?"

Once inside the library, I found the light switch and held my breath . . . then exhaled in relief. Uncle Ludwig's beautiful library was untouched. Ron strode to the middle of the room and looked up at the fresco on the ceiling, spinning around to take it all in. His gaze traveled along the wooden balcony circling the space, then flitted around the gorgeous artwork and the books. So many beautiful books.

"Unbelievable," he whispered.

We dumped our supplies on a table, and then I turned on a computer. "Maybe we can get some news from outside," I said. "See what's happening in Stull City."

Stull had one EO-approved news site. It was broadcast from

Stull City and watched by nearly everyone in all the realms. I was surprised it was still running, after Dr. Pravus's attack. But based on the top news stories, it didn't take long to realize that Pravus had taken it over:

"Stull City falls easily to Dr. Pravus, Liberator of the Kingdoms"

"Show Your Support for Dr. Pravus and Be Rewarded!"

"Where to Turn In EO Sympathizers"

"Unbelievable Show of Force Leads to Quick Surrender"

"He's done it," I said. "I can't believe it. The most evil man in the world has taken over Stull City."

CHAPTER 25

My Life as a Science Experiment
—FRANKIE SAW DARTHIN'S AUTOBIOGRAPHY TITLE LIST,
AND STARTED ONE TOO

The last article was accompanied by a video, so I pressed play. It was hard to make out anything, because smoke filled the screen, but something huge, hairy, and extremely powerful was demolishing the stone mausoleum in the park. The video cut to more buildings being destroyed, mostly the homes of EOs in Castle Valley. We never got a full view of the attackers, only a limb or a claw, but it was enough to terrify us completely.

"I wonder if they've destroyed the embassy," I said.

"I'd destroy it myself if Janet and her father were inside," Ron said. "They locked me up for months, the evil little schemers."

"Seizemore was using me to get Cordholm's rebels to join him," I said. "I wonder what he would have done after we got to Andirat."

"He planned to establish a new government, with you as ruler once you came of age, and him as your top advisor. Then he would expose you as a fraud and take your place," Ron said. "It was what he was going to do with me too. Only with me, he planned to turn my people against me."

"With that video of you being awful?" I asked.

"That's right. At first I thought he just created it as a threat, but now I think it was his plan all along—to use me to regain power, and then discredit me and take my place."

"So you think he raised you to be . . . well . . . spoiled and arrogant, so he could record that behavior and use it against you?" I remembered what George had told me, that Seizemore had ruined the prince. Ron's stories about his birthdays seemed to confirm that.

I remembered how isolated Ron had been at the embassy, and wondered if that was also part of Seizemore's plan. Ron had grown up thinking he was better than everyone else, so he didn't know how to make friends, or allies.

Ron was silent, and I was worried that I'd gone too far by insulting his character.

"The video is a lie, you know," he said after thinking it over. "Seizemore told me that people believe what they see, and first impressions always stick."

I tried to think of a way to change the subject, but then the video feed showed a new announcement. Dr. Pravus was offering a reward for the capture and delivery of Dr. Derek Critchlore, and that reward was one EO gold bar.

"Seizemore gave Pravus's man a gold bar," I said. "What's one EO gold bar worth?"

"A gold bar weighs about thirty pounds," Ron said. "Gold is currently trading at a thousand Stulleons per ounce. Sixteen ounces in a pound. Sixteen times thirty is . . . four hundred and eighty. That's almost half a million Stulleons."

"Wow," I said. "Most minions don't make that much their whole lives."

"It's enough to throw an adequate party, I guess," he said. "You know, the kind with pop stars, gourmet food, lavish decorations, and expensive gift bags. And security, to keep out the . . . er . . ."

I stared at him open mouthed. "A party? Are you kidding? You could feed a village for a year on that." I shook my head. "Seizemore promised Pravus three more. Just how much money does he have?"

"That's a good question. Seizemore gets his money from the exiles, who are mostly rich people who got out of Andirat before the generals cut off escape routes. They converted their money into gold, for safety. Seizemore probably has access to many millions."

Darthin contacted me on the DPS to say he was on his way with the antidote case. While waiting, I told Ron about traveling by merperson, and how to find Professor Zaida once he made it to the Kobold Academy.

"There must be somewhere else you can go," he said. "Those monsters are going to destroy this school and kill everyone. And Seizemore might come looking for you here."

"He won't find me," I said, nodding at my secret hideout.

Darthin arrived with the waterproof backpack for the prince, and we headed out, sneaking back the way we'd come in.

As Darthin strolled through the giant bugs, touching them with his gloves and directing them where to go, Ron said, "That's got to be the bravest kid I've ever seen."

"He really is," I agreed.

Darthin left us at the bottom of the shaft, wishing Ron luck. Once Ron and I climbed back into the boathouse, I pointed to a row of wet suits hanging in the corner.

The ground shook, so I peeked outside to see what was happening. Bright lights were shining through the trees over by the dorms. Closer to us, I could see a troop of ogres charging in formation through the memorial garden. They knocked over statues and slammed their clubs through the Wall of Heroes. They were destroying the very heart and soul of my school.

I punched the wall of the boathouse.

"What's happening?" Ron asked, coming up behind me.

"Look what they did," I said, pointing.

He peeked out next to me. "Well, you knew they were going to destroy the school, right?"

He was right, I did. But seeing is different from knowing. That pile of rubble had been a statue of Grantor the Great. It was a statue I'd grown up admiring, hoping I could one day be even a tenth as great as him, and an ogre had just smashed it without a second glance.

I felt rage building up inside me with every ogre's stomp and swing. "I've got to stop them," I said.

Ron laughed, and I turned on him, overcome with anger. I don't know what I looked like, but he backed up a couple steps with his hands raised. "Sorry, but you saw them, right? You can't stop them."

"Wanna bet?" I said through clenched teeth.

"You're insane. Those are ogres."

"I know," I said. They were big ones too. I was only as tall as their knees.

"You're supposed to take me to your merperson friend. Remember?" Ron held up the antidote case.

"The lake is that way, you can't miss it," I said. "Stick your head in the water and yell for Pismo."

"Now, wait a second—" He grabbed my arm.

I yanked myself free. "This is *my* home, Ron." He looked me in the eye and then nodded, letting me go. "They're heading for the dorms. I have to do something."

I took off, sneaking through the cemetery. Ron followed, making way too much noise.

"How are you, a kid, going to fight a team of ogres?" he whispered when I stopped behind a tree.

"I have an idea," I said. I'd lived next door to the Dormitory for Minions of Impressive Size for three years. I'd learned some things about giants and trolls and ogres.

"You know, I've wanted to see you get a beating since I met you," he said. "But not anymore. This is suicide."

"I'm going to sneak through these trees to the dorm," I said. "Stay by the trees and they won't see you." I looked at him. "Where's the case?"

"I put it in the fish cooler," he said.

We made it to a clump of trees behind the D-MIS, where we had a good view of the clearing in the middle of the dorms. The ogres were warming up. The leader led them through some team stretching exercises and practice swings with their clubs. They were the giant, stupid kind of ogre, with huge bellies, underbites, and expressions of confused anger.

"Is that the building you wish to save?" Ron said, pointing to the D-Hum, the Dormitory for Humans. "It's a decrepit old pit."

I used to think so too. I'd always resented being placed there.

But now, the thought of my dusty little dorm being destroyed really bothered me.

"See that window on the second floor?" I asked. "That's my room." The building housed so many memories, it felt like they were going to smash a part of me. "I'm not going to let revolting Victus destroy it."

"Your funeral," Ron said, ducking behind a tree.

A flash of movement caught my eye—Syke flitting through the trees. She whistled at us before swinging down from branch to branch.

"Wow," Ron said, watching her.

"She's part tree-nymph," I said.

"She floats through the air like a feather. And her hair. It shimmers with so many colors. It's . . . mesmerizing."

Syke landed next to us. "Hey, guys."

"Hi, Syke," Ron said.

"Is everything okay with Victus?" I asked.

"Yeah, I told him it took me a while to come back because I was looking for a DPS to help his search crew. He was impressed with my efforts."

"Perfect," I said.

"He thinks I'm trying to recover some things from the tree house debris, since they burned it down before telling me, the jerks." She shook her head in disgust.

"You don't look smaller," I said.

"Not yet," she said, tugging at the cuff. It was still tight. "What are you doing here?"

Ron stepped forward. "We're going to try and stop these monsters."

I looked at him. We? Really?

"Remember when we were first-years?" I asked Syke. "And the Minion Games were postponed because of Hector?"

Syke knew exactly what I meant. "You're going to Hectorize them? That's nuts . . . but it just might work. Do you need help?"

"Yes," I said. "Do you know who's in charge here?"

"Victus is in Critchlore's office, conferencing with Pravus, but he'll be here later. In the meantime, his sasquatch lackey, Carl, is supposed to start things. He's over there, on the steps of the D-MIS. Oh, look, here come the ahools." She nodded at the sky. They swooped in and landed next to Carl, each one holding a camera to film the destruction.

"I need about thirty seconds," I said. "Think you can distract them?"

"No problem," she said. "I'm still mad about my tree house, and it was Carl's doing. I can start up our argument from earlier."

She climbed back up the tree, and we watched as the branches seemed to toss her in the direction she wanted to go. She landed gracefully, right next to the hairy monster.

"She's like a bird," Ron said.

"Okay, I'm going," I said. "Just stay here, out of sight."

"Hmm?" Ron reluctantly tore his gaze from Syke and nodded.

The ogres were about to get the go-ahead to start bashing. Arms were lifted, ready to swing those heavy clubs down on my dorm.

I took a deep breath, smoothed my Pravus uniform, and charged out of the clearing, acting like I wasn't at all terrified of the huge monsters standing in formation. I strode right through them like a general, noticing that no fewer than five of them wore giant orange cuffs. Pravus controlled his minions through fear. I could use that.

I saw Syke pulling Carl into the D-MIS to yell at him. Perfect. I reached the front of the ogre line and held up my hand for attention. "The cameras are here," I said. "But I've just received word from Pravus that we have a slight change in operations."

They looked confused, which was a change from their normal angry faces. This was good. All humans look alike to ogres, because they're farsighted. I was hoping they'd think I was Victus.

They were wearing the Pravus green uniform and, lucky for me, they had their names stitched in huge letters above their jacket pockets.

"Pulverizer," I said, addressing the one in front. "Step back. Rocktosser gets first bash."

For the ogres at Critchlore's, "first bash" is a highly prized privilege. They routinely fought over the honor. Rocktosser smiled and pushed his way to the front.

Pulverizer, who had led the stretching, was the clear leader of this group, and he did not care for the demotion. Nor did the ogres next to him, who probably thought that if Pulverizer was going to be demoted, then one of them deserved his slot. Angry protests erupted from the front.

"DO YOU DARE QUESTION DR. PRAVUS?" I screamed. "This sort of disobedience is why Pulverizer has lost his privilege!" I looked directly at Pulverizer, whose rage was only contained by his confusion. "A spy from Critchlore's got into our school last week," I said to him, quieter now. "Both Shattercrunch and Grindface told us it was your fault."

Pulverizer's face looked like it was about to explode with anger. I may have overplayed things, I realized, as his balled-up fist looked ready to smash me. But then a rock hit him on the back of the head. I saw Ron smiling before ducking behind a tree.

That rock detonated the ticking time bomb that was Pulverizer's anger, and I sprinted away as fast as I could. The ground shook as he charged, swinging his club wildly, just wanting to hurt someone, anyone.

He knocked down three innocent ogre bystanders, who rose up swinging their own clubs. Pretty soon the clearing was a scrum of wrestling, punching, fighting ogres.

The ahools took to the air, unsure of what was happening. One started screaming, "The building! You're supposed to demolish the building, not each other!" But once an ogre gets going, he's not going to stop until his opponent is down, or he is.

Victus arrived and tried to get their attention by yelling and throwing things, but he was too late. Soon, everything was quiet. The ogres were all knocked out.

"That was hilarious," Ron said, laughing.

"I'm just glad it worked," I said. "Nice throw, by the way." I held up my hand for a high five, but he left me hanging.

"Ok, let's go find Pismo," I said, "and get you out of here."

CHAPTER 26

*A remote valley in Carkley was home to the cruelest,
most vicious people around, until a strange virus started
killing them off a few weeks ago.*

—*PORVIAN NEWS TODAY*

Pismo was easier to find than I expected. He popped out of the woods as we neared the lake.

"Runt! You're back," he said. "Did you see that? Those ogres, they completely wrecked each other." He noticed Ron and said, "Who's your friend?"

"Prince Pismo, meet Prince Auberon," I said. "He's escaped from some people who'd been holding him prisoner. I was hoping you could take him to the Kobold Academy, upriver?"

"Now? Sorry, dude, I'm spent. Been fighting the kids from the School for Aquatic Minions all day. They've thrown in with Pravus, the little traitors. Can you wait 'til tomorrow?"

I looked at Ron, who shrugged. Then I looked at Pismo. "You up for a little sabotage?"

"I'm hurt you think you need to ask," he said.

"C'mon," I said, "let's go to the secret library."

We snuck into an abandoned dorm to grab some pillows and blankets, then picked up the antidote case in the boathouse on our way back to the library. Pismo jumped into the grotto lake to have a quick visit with Clarence while Ron and I made our beds for the night. I propped my pillow next to the end of a bookshelf and sat down to eat. Ron did the same.

"Hey, Ron?" I said, tossing him an apple. "Thanks for throwing that rock. You really saved my skin back there."

He smiled. "You walked through them like they were toddlers, not ferocious ogres," he said. "I couldn't believe it. I thought if you could do that, then at least I could help from the trees."

"Your aim was perfect," I said, laughing.

"I've had a lot of practice throwing rocks. I used to try to hit the flying monkeys at the embassy." He tossed a scrunched-up piece of paper straight into the wastebasket across the room. "Seizemore filmed me once, then edited it so that it looked like I was throwing rocks at people enjoying a picnic by the lake. The video shows me hitting a child on the head and then laughing hysterically about it."

I cringed. "You didn't really—"

"Of course not! But think about it. Seizemore set up that picnic scene and made someone else throw a rock at a little girl so hard that her head was bleeding."

"That's sickening."

"There's more," he said, and he told me all the ways Seizemore made him look bad in that video. It was awful. If that video got out before people knew Ron, it would destroy him.

"You have to stop him," I said.

"Are you really going to stay here?" he asked.

"I can't leave," I said. "I have to help Dr. Frankenhammer. He's our only hope of defeating Pravus's UMs. Plus, I want to be here for Syke, if she needs me."

"That Syke," he said. "Can we trust her?"

"We grew up together. She's like a sister to me. There's nobody I trust more."

Pismo joined us and Ron and I got up to sit with him at the table so we could watch the newsfeed, which was mostly shots of people and monsters running in terror from Pravus's Undefeatable Minions. We never caught a complete look at the beasts, but what we saw was horrifying. They attacked with a rumbling screech that was both piercing and low at the same time. Buildings were reduced to rubble effortlessly, and we saw giant, clawed hands swoop up fleeing people and monsters. Scene after scene of destruction and terror.

"Dr. Pravus is trying to scare the other EOs into surrendering," I said.

"Effective strategy," Pismo agreed. "No army would want to go up against that."

Dr. Pravus made a brief statement to the reporter, ordering the EOs to surrender or be destroyed. He stood on the steps of the EO Council Building with some of his troops.

"Look!" Ron said. "It's Seizemore and Janet. And Mr. Fox." They were just visible behind the row of Pravus's bodyguards, large men and monsters dressed not in his minion-green uniform, but in all black.

"What are they doing with him?" I asked. "I thought they were heading to Andirat?"

"Seizemore can't show up there without a prince. I bet he's hoping Pravus will help find us," Ron said.

Syke joined us then and sat down next to Pismo. "I've only got a few minutes," she said. "I left my tracker in bed, but I should get back in case anyone checks on me. I just wanted to tell you that the ogres are concussed, so they're out of commission until their symptoms pass. Victus was so mad, it was awesome." She looked at Ron. "Nicely done, Your Majesty. I saw you throw that rock."

Ron beamed at the praise. "Happy to help."

"Also, Pravus's UMs have taken over Stull," Syke said.

"We saw." I pointed to the computer.

Pismo turned the screen to face him and Syke, and showed her the shots of destruction.

"Did you ever see them?" I asked her. "Pravus's Undefeatable Minions?"

"No, but I heard them," she said. "It was awful. They were in so much pain. They'd gotten infected by something. Everyone in the remote region where they lived was dying, but then Pravus went there with medicine. He brought the survivors to his school and put them in quarantine. He saved their lives, and now they're fighting for him."

"He didn't save them," I said. "*He's* the one who made them sick. That's the first step in creating an Undefeatable Minion. Critchlore wouldn't do it because hardly anyone can survive the virus. Where did they come from?"

"Carkley. They were forced out of their homeland when Lord Vengecrypt took over, but they've never stopped fighting. Apparently, these guys were known as the worst of the worst. Extremely violent and hot-tempered. Vengecrypt's troops had kept them penned in some valley somewhere, but the illness killed most of them off. Pravus was able to sneak the survivors out after Vengecrypt pulled back most of his troops to keep them from being infected."

"And now they're working for Pravus," I said. "He doesn't need the spell if they think he saved their lives."

"He'd still want it, though," Ron said. "In case they ever found out the truth."

I nodded. We had to find some way to stop them. "Why did Pravus send minions here? He must know that Critchlore evacuated."

"Victus told me that Pravus gave him two tasks," Syke said. "One, videotape the destruction of the school bit by bit, ending with the castle. He thinks the footage will lure Critchlore out of hiding. And two, find Dr. Critchlore's Top Student trophy."

"He wants a trophy?" Ron asked. "Why?"

"It's a symbol, I think," I said. "Pravus has always thought he should have won Top Student of their Doctorate of Minion Studies program. Critchlore brags about it all the time."

"He puts it in his advertising, just to rub it in," Syke said. "Even so, it's weird how much Pravus wants that trophy. He's ordered Victus not to harm the castle until we find it. He said that the trophy belongs to him and he needs it. Not 'wants.' 'Needs.'"

"Do you know where it is?" Ron asked.

"In the attic," Syke and I said at the same time. We'd lived at this school nearly our whole lives, so of course we'd explored every nook at least once. We'd found an attic room that was stuffed full of Critchlore's memorabilia. The trophy had to be there. I don't know why he didn't put his awards on display, because they looked so impressive.

"If Pravus wants the trophy so badly, it could be a bargaining tool," Ron said. "Let's go get it, before his people find it."

"Um . . . I think it's safe where it is," I said, looking at Syke. There was a reason we'd only gone in that room once.

"Yeah," Syke agreed. "It's totally safe."

Ron looked confused. "Why? Because Dr. Pravus hasn't sent his best minions here?"

"Obviously, if Victus is in charge," I said.

"That's right," Syke said. "Pravus knew that Critchlore had bailed, leaving nobody to fight."

"Victus doesn't suspect that Dr. Frankenhammer is still here?" I asked Syke.

"He has no idea. If he did, capturing Dr. Frankenhammer would be his number one priority. Pravus has tried to steal him away before."

"That's true," I said. "We have to keep Dr. Frankenhammer hidden and give him time to make more antidotes. Pismo's going to take Ron to the Kobold Academy with the finished supply."

Pismo nodded. "And then I'll come back here to help you mess with those Pravus punks, Runt. I have some ideas. Like, what if we changed the signs around the grotto to say things like, 'Critchlore's Private Spa—Headmasters Only!' Those Pravus kids won't be able to resist taking a dip, and then Clarence can grab them and take them to the dungeon cells. There's an underground river that connects them."

"They'll drown!" I said.

"Only if they can't hold their breath for twenty seconds," he said.

"Okay. I'll make the signs while you're gone."

"I just hope they haven't destroyed the castle by then," Syke said, and we all nodded.

"Listen," Ron said after a few seconds of silence. "I can't have you sacrifice this much for me."

My mouth dropped open, because yesterday he'd been fine with us sacrificing everything for his cause. Syke smiled at him.

"I want to help," he said to her. "Then we'll all escape together. Well, except Runt, who can't go. But if we can make it safer for him to stay . . ."

Who was this guy? And what had he done with the obnoxious prince?

"That's so sweet," Syke said, and Ron's blush made me think that she had more to do with his change of heart than any concern for my safety.

"We need to get you to Professor Zaida," I said. "Like you said, Seizemore might suspect we came here. Pravus could send more minions here to look for us."

"Listen," Ron said, standing up, "as a minion, you are not trained to analyze situations from a position of leadership. That's one thing I learned from Seizemore, though it might not have been his intention. He was always strategizing, always looking at the big picture. He often said that one overlooked threat, no matter how small, can ruin everything you've planned.

"The way I see it," Ron went on, "Dr. Frankenhammer's antidotes are the only way to stop those monsters. They are so powerful, so terrifying, and it looks like they are going to help Pravus take over this continent, and who knows? Perhaps in the future, conquer

Andirat too. We have to keep Dr. Frankenhammer safe. Once we've done that, then Pismo and I can leave. Right?" he asked, looking at Pismo. Pismo gave him a thumbs-up.

"That's very noble of you, Ron," I said.

"It is," Syke agreed. "Thank you." She stood up. "I've got to go. I need to stay near Victus until my cuff falls off."

"Okay," I said. "Be careful."

I called Darthin and Frankie on the DPS so we could make our sabotage plans. Dr. Frankenhammer gave them permission to help us strike back at the Pravus minions while he continued his work.

Ron, Pismo, and I sat around the table, with the DPS in the middle. I was leading my first teleconference. I felt like such a henchman-in-charge.

"We need to lure Victus's minions into traps," I said. "If they're trapped, they can't find Dr. Frankenhammer, and they can't destroy the school. He's got ahools patrolling the skies, werewolves and lizard-men rooting out the dungeon, and a bunch of human kids guarding the grounds. The ogres are resting in the D-MIS, but two giants are standing guard at the gate. Victus also has a few minions with him. So . . . I think we should start with the ahools."

"The spies in the skies," Pismo said. "I agree."

"As for the ogres, I'll tell Kumi to stand guard outside the D-MIS and keep them from getting out. Darthin, you and your beetles can herd the dungeon patrols over to the grotto, where Pismo and Clarence will grab them and take them to the cells. But make sure the cell door is locked first."

"Okay," he said.

"Frankie, I think you can handle the giants."

Ron grabbed my arm, his face making an "Are you joking?" expression. He'd only seen my friend's skinny frame. He had no idea what Frankie could do.

"Don't worry, Frankie can handle two giants," I whispered. Louder, so Frankie could hear me through the DPS, I said, "Drag them over to Kumi and shove them into the D-MIS with the ogres. But wait until Ron and I take out the ahools. I don't want them to know you're here."

"Gotcha," Frankie answered.

We strategized for another hour, and then Pismo left. The prince and I got in our sleeping spots, but I couldn't sleep. I was nervous about our plan. Nervous about Dr. Critchlore. Nervous about everything.

CHAPTER 27

All good escapades need a catchphrase.
—INTRODUCTION TO ESCAPADES CLASS

The next day Ron and I dressed in our matching Critchlore uniforms, with beanies to hide our different hair lengths. We went over our plan during a quick breakfast of canned food.

"Can you whistle with your fingers?" I asked. He couldn't. "Have some rocks ready, then. Remember the places I told you. The key to this plan is to disappear; that's very important."

"I'm ready," he said, standing up.

I stood and faced him. "Prepare for trouble . . ." I said, raising my hand for a high five. Then I waited for him to say his part of the catchphrase I'd made up.

"I'm not going to say it," he replied.

"Fine, let's go."

After some quick reconnaissance, we discovered that the ahools each patrolled a different section of the school. We started with the one near the castle. I sent Ron to his spot and positioned myself near the hedge maze. I took out my lucky rock, the one I always kept in my pocket. I couldn't bear to throw my lucky rock, though, so I picked up another rock from the ground.

As soon as I saw the ahool overhead, I let my rock fly.

I missed. By a lot. I grabbed another rock and threw again. Another miss. Dang, he wasn't even that high. Maybe I should've used my lucky rock. The ahool kept moving around unpredictably and I couldn't hit him.

Finally I nicked his wing and got his attention. He swooped low to get a better look, and I threw a rock right at him, hitting him in the chest. Then I ran into the hedge maze, sticking close to the sides so I'd be harder to see. I raced to the middle and hid beneath the bench in front of the statue.

Through the slats on the bench I could see him scanning the maze, looking for me. I watched as he was pelted on his shoulder by a rock.

Ron was much better at this than I was. I had a feeling I'd be hearing about it later.

The ahool's expression morphed from confusion to anger and he swooped after Ron. I burst out of my hiding spot, found the secret exit, and dashed after them. Ron was luring the ahool toward the stable, and I watched him duck inside. The ahool, thinking Ron was trapped, swooped lower to follow him. While he did that, I whistled at him. (I was out of rocks.)

He turned and did a double take, from the stable back to me. I ran for the trees, looking behind to see him zooming after me and closing in fast.

Ron exited the stable and headed for the aviary.

Just as the ahool was about to grab me, Googa stepped forward

and wrapped him up in his branch arms. The ahool squirmed and screamed. Googa took two giant steps to the aviary and threw him inside. Ron slammed the door shut. The aviary was huge, and covered with unbreakable netting, to keep the wyverns and other flying creatures inside.

Kwami, the gray parrot, swooped over to me from behind the netting. "You don't need two princes, squawk!"

"He always says that to me," I told Ron. "I think it's what my kidnapper said when he left me at the gate. I never knew what it meant."

The prince shrugged. "The kidnappers knew you were the double. Not needed."

"Gee, thanks," I said.

He shrugged. "Sorry. I didn't mean—"

"It's okay." I smiled. He was learning to be more considerate. Maybe there was hope for him.

We used the same "double take" confusion to lure the other two ahools away from their assignments and over to where my toddler trees could grab them. Ron almost got snatched twice, but Whoosh swooped in to save him.

"That was so much fun!" Ron said when we were done with the ahools.

"We have more work to do," I said. "But at least now we can do it without worrying that something in the sky is going to swoop down on us."

Next we made footprint trails leading into the swamp, so Pravus's minions would think we were hiding in there. Hopefully the swamp creatures and leechmen would give a nice welcome to anyone investigating.

We booby-trapped the hedge maze. We lured Pravus's human minions into the organic garden, where they got tangled in the strawberry snares. We turned off the water to the castle and stole as much food as we could from the cafeteria.

Then we led Kumi over to the D-MIS. One of the ogres heard us coming and tried to come outside, but Kumi ran at him and roared, baring his enormous teeth. The ogre turned and dove back inside the safety of the building. With Kumi guarding the entrance, they were trapped. They couldn't bash their way out. The building's walls were triply reinforced.

Ron seemed to change into a different kid before my eyes. Gone was the condescending bossypants; now he was just a kid having fun. He actually giggled once, and then clamped his hand over his mouth. He got dirty and didn't fuss about it like he had in the barn.

"Prepare for trouble!" he said, after we were done for the day.

"Make it double!" I replied. Then I laughed, because he was right—it was a stupid catchphrase. And then he laughed, because he could tell I knew it was stupid. Soon we were both doubled over laughing at our stupid motto.

At nightfall we returned, exhausted, to our base in the secret library. Syke snuck down to join us.

"You still don't seem smaller," I said.

"There's a little wiggle room on the cuff now," she said, twisting it. "But not enough." She looked very nervous.

"What's happening with Victus?" I asked.

"He's livid," she said. "Kumi won't budge and the ogres and giants can't get out. The ahools have disappeared. He knows Critchlore has someone protecting the school, and he's focusing on the dungeon, but his minions keep disappearing down here."

Pismo joined us around the table. "Clarence and I caught four werewolves, six lizard-men, a shapeshifter, and three humans today," he said. "They're in the cells. And don't worry, Runt, I left them boxes of MREs I stole from the supply depot."

"That's awesome, Pismo."

"Victus is waiting for reinforcements from the School for Aquatic Minions," Syke said.

"Pismo, can you take them out?"

"Of course," he said. "They won't know what hit them. Strong, swift, stealthy. That's me."

Dang, that was a good catchphrase.

We watched the newsfeed out of Stull City, which had just begun its nightly broadcast. Dr. Pravus stood in front of the capitol building. All the EO flags had been removed from their flagpoles. He dropped a match onto the pile of flags and it burst into flames.

"Good evening, my friends," he said, smiling his winning smile as he walked toward the camera. "I know that some of you may be nervous about recent events. I want to assure you that my intentions are good. I only wish to rid the world of the Evil Overlords who rule everything with little regard for anyone but themselves. I will right the wrongs of these tyrants and free the people from their oppression."

He passed a group of children sitting on the capitol steps and patted them on the head. "I think that if you knew me, you would join my righteous cause. I only wish to serve the oppressed."

Wow, he was convincing.

"Since my takeover of Stull City," he said, "I know some of you are missing your regular entertainment programming. Soap operas like *All My Overlords*. Reality shows like *EO Dinner Theater*, *The EO Punishment Games*, and *Monster Obstacle Course*. I know this is inconvenient, and as an example of my consideration, I have created new entertainment programming for you. It will let you get to know me better, so we can continue this journey together.

"We call it *The Pravus Projects*. Every night I ask you to join me, your new ruler, as I deal with the many challenges of taking over a continent. Here's a preview of tonight's episode: 'A Time to Be Bold.' Enjoy!"

The screen turned black and then lit up with a shot of Dr. Pravus's back as he looked out of his Eye of Pravus building. You could see the whole world stretched out in front of him.

"He was just a man," the voiceover said. "A man with a bold plan to free the world from the oppression of the evil overlords."

"Oh, puke," I said.

"You know, I almost fell for that," Syke said. "He's so convincing. There's something about him . . . you just want his approval, you know?"

I didn't. He'd tried to kill me. Twice.

A series of shots showed Dr. Pravus at his school, training minions with a smile on his face as they performed well, or a sympathetic pat on the shoulder when they failed. It was all very corny, with a soundtrack to match.

The narrator continued: "How could one man take on a whole continent of Evil Overlords? It would take a special man. A very special man."

"Oh, double puke," I said.

A series of scenes showed Pravus bravely arguing with prominent EOs, scowling at Fraze Coldheart in the EO council chamber (so bold!), and working late at night in his office.

"His plan took years to develop," the narrator said. "But no sacrifice was too great for this man of vision."

The video cut to Dr. Pravus, looking dashing as he commanded his army into Stull City.

"Stay tuned to find out what happens next!" the narrator said. The show cut to a commercial for WartGrow, so I turned it off.

"They forgot the bit where he cuffs people and threatens them with death if they don't obey," I said.

"I've gotta go," Syke said. "Hopefully, my cuff will fall off by morning and I can join you guys. If not, I've got to keep pretending to help Victus."

I was really worried about Syke, so I suggested doing the one thing that scared me more than all of Victus's minions put together.

"We could get that trophy," I said.

Syke gasped. "No."

"If Victus suspects you, he'll activate that cuff. We need something to bargain with."

"I know. And Pravus really wants that trophy." She sighed. "Okay, if he threatens me again, I'll tell him that I know where it is, but I'll only hand it over to Pravus himself. That should buy me some time, at least."

"Good idea."

CHAPTER 28

Tree nymphs have a slower drug metabolism
than humans.
—SOMETHING DR. FRANKENHAMMER FORGOT
(EVERYONE MAKES MISTAKES)

The next morning, I woke to Syke shoving my shoulder. "I've been called into Critchlore's office," she said. "You have to come, in case I need help. I'm not smaller! The cuff won't come off!"

"We'll be behind the bookshelves," I said, getting up and waking Ron. We grabbed some food and raced out of there.

Ron and I reached our spying spot before Syke showed up in the office. We peeked through the bookshelves and saw Victus looking out the wide windows at Mount Curiosity. Two minions, a human girl and sasquatch Carl, stood nervously next to the desk, looking down at something.

Victus started pacing. He was clearly agitated. "He'll be here tomorrow," he said. "I'm so dead. I didn't capture Critchlore. I haven't destroyed a single building except that stupid tree house. My minions have disappeared, and I don't have that trophy. I'm so dead."

Dr. Pravus was coming here tomorrow? Oh, no.

"WHERE IS SHE?" he screamed. "She knows something, I know she does."

"The tracker said she was in her quarters," the human girl said. "But Carl saw her coming out from the lower levels."

"She's behind everything here," Victus said. He lifted a piece of paper. "This proves it."

I grabbed Ron's wrist, my eyes wide.

"What's on that paper?" he whispered.

"I don't know."

My heart sank even further when I saw three trophies arranged on Dr. Critchlore's desk. Two were generic gold trophies, but the third I remembered from years ago, because I'd helped Syke make it. It was a Best Dad trophy she'd given to Dr. Critchlore on Father's Day.

"Ron, you think you could hit that button on Critchlore's chair from here?"

"With what?"

I searched my pockets. The only throwable thing I could find was my lucky rock. I held it out to Ron, but then changed my mind and stuffed it back in my pocket. Then I changed my mind again and handed it to him. If there was ever a time to use it, it was now.

"This opening is small," he said. "And I don't have room to line up my shot, but I'll try."

Syke entered the office, looking flustered as everyone in the room stared at her angrily.

"What's up?" she asked.

Victus read from the paper in his hand. " 'A dad is someone who carries you on his shoulders, who reads you bedtime stories, who shows you how to tame a wild swamp monster. I know you're not really my dad, but you *are* really my dad. Love, Syke.'"

Syke laughed. "Is that why you called me? Please, I was a baby. I wanted a father. I didn't know that he'd killed my mom."

"Claudia here tells me you were seen in the dungeon. You told me you never go down there. Why are you lying?"

"I didn't lie. I never said I didn't go down there, I just said I didn't *like* to. All students have to go to the dungeon depot to collect supplies. Anyway, there's a cabinet in a meeting room down there. I wanted to check it out, but it was empty. Really, is this why you called me here?"

"Show her the picture," Victus said.

Claudia handed Syke a handheld device. I couldn't see what was on it, but Syke frowned, pursing her lips.

"You've been sneaking around the dungeon with a blond-haired Critchlore merperson. You, Syke, are a spy," Victus said. "You're sabotaging our efforts here. My minions are missing because of you. I am going to contact Dr. Pravus and tell him to activate your cuff." He pulled something out of his pocket.

"No, wait! It's not true—"

"Now," I whispered to Ron. "Throw it now—she's on the trap-door."

I stepped out of the way as he lined up his shot in the tight space. Syke was still pleading her case when Ron let the rock fly. It zipped out from our hiding place and hit Victus in the eye.

"*Ahh!*" Victus yelled.

Ron winced. "That one got away from me."

Victus's hands went to his face and he stumbled backward, right onto the arm of the desk chair. The chair had wheels and flew out from under him, right into Claudia. Victus fell to the ground, and Carl ran over to help him up.

I didn't waste any time. I opened the secret door.

"Syke, here!" I yelled. Syke just managed to escape Claudia's lunge as she ran for the secret passageway.

Victus looked at me with his good eye and screamed, "YOU!"

I shut the door and we bolted down the steps.

"FOLLOW THEM!" Victus screamed.

As we escaped, Syke kept repeating, "I'm dead. I'm dead. I'm dead."

At the bottom, she tugged on the cuff as hard as she could. "He's going to poison me, as soon as he can contact Dr. Pravus, who has the trigger. He'll type my number into his master control, and snap! I'm dead."

"Don't worry," I said. "We'll get you to Dr. Frankenhammer."

We sprinted down the dungeon halls. Syke kept frantically pulling at the cuff as we went. It was so close to coming off.

"Darthin!" I yelled into my DPS. "Open the lab. We're coming with Syke. The cuff has to come off NOW!

"I'm so sorry, Syke," I said. I knew that she was terrified about what Dr. Frankenhammer was about to do. "He'll give you something. I'm sure it won't hurt."

"Hurry!" she screamed, pushing us to run faster.

We reached the lab door, where Darthin stood holding the insects back. We rushed inside and saw Dr. Frankenhammer waiting by his stainless-steel table, power saw in hand.

"Get it off!" I screamed. "Now!"

"Put her arm down," Dr. Frankenhammer said. "Frankie! Bring me that bottle on the counter."

"There's no time!" I said. "Just take it off!"

Syke was so pale, so terrified. Ron, his eyes just as fearful, held her good hand and was whispering in her ear, trying to distract her. He put an arm around her waist as she held her hand out, tears streaming down her face. I'd never seen her so scared.

Frankie handed a bottle to Dr. Frankenhammer, who'd ditched the power saw for a cleaver. "The saw might take too long to cut through the bone," he said. Syke collapsed into Ron's arms at the sight of it. Dr. Frankenhammer sprayed the disinfectant all over Syke's hand, then he raised the cleaver. The blade hung there in the air and we all held our breath as we waited for it to fall. Syke closed her eyes, trembling.

Dr. Frankenhammer dropped the cleaver and grabbed Syke's arm with one hand. With the other he pulled the cuff off with one quick yank.

"Glob, gurgle, blug," Syke mumbled, collapsing to the floor.

"What did you spray on her wrist?" I asked.

"Sssalad dressing," Dr. Frankenhammer said, dropping the cuff on the table. "Her wrist just needed a little lubrication."

The cuff popped into the air as a ring of needles snapped out of the inside edge, each one dripping with a poison that burned holes in Dr. Frankenhammer's stainless-steel table upon contact. Syke stood up and hugged Dr. Frankenhammer.

"Flurg ur," she said, still in shock.

"You're welcome," he said.

‡‡‡

We all collapsed after that. It had been too close. Dr. Franken-hammer gave Syke something to drink, and we sat around his table, trying not to imagine what had almost happened.

"You sprinted here, yesss?" Dr. Frankenhammer asked, writing in a notebook.

Syke nodded as she drank.

"Fascinating," he said. "I believe the increased heart rate, caused by the physical exertion, may have sssped up the sssserum just now. That, or the adrenaline. You were experiencing extreme fear as well?"

"Oh, yeah," Syke said. She looked at her empty cup. "What *was* that?"

"Sssssudithium mixed with Critchlorade," Dr. Frankenhammer said. "The effect isss not immediate. You will continue to shrink, but now you will return to normal sssize faster than if we had waited for the sssserum to wear off, which could take weeksss."

"All of you have to get out of here," I said. "Dr. Pravus is coming tomorrow, probably with some of his Undefeatable Minions."

"Agreed," Dr. Frankenhammer said. "Frankie, you and Darthin will take the chariot." He walked over to Frankie and put his hands on his son's shoulders. "It's going to be quite a load for you to pull, but you can do it. Take my work to Dr. Critchlore."

Frankie nodded. "You have to come with us."

"I cannot leave my other specimenssss," he said.

"Then we'll stay too."

"No, you must take the antidotesss to sssafety. I need you to do this."

"What about Syke?" Frankie asked.

"Look!" Syke said, kicking off her tied boots like they were three sizes too big. "I'm shrinking."

"She's going to need some new clothes," I said.

Dr. Frankenhammer nodded. "I'm prepared for that." He turned to his cabinets and pulled out a little outfit on a tiny hanger.

"Victus saw you," Syke said to me, clutching the top of her pants to keep them from falling off. It was like she was shrinking before our eyes. "He remembers you from Polar Bay. He's going to tell Dr. Pravus that you're here. You have to leave too."

"And go where?" I said. "I can't go to the Great Library, my tether will activate."

"Just go for a few days, until Pravus is gone," Syke said. "When you came back before, the tether went away."

"No, I'm going to stay," I said. "I can hide from Dr. Pravus. And if he does come here with his UMs, maybe I can find a way to inject them with the serum. We have to destroy his army before he takes over the world."

"Then I'm going to stay too," Syke said.

"Okay, but stay with Dr. Frankenhammer for now," I said. "You guys get that chariot out of here before Pravus arrives."

CHAPTER 29

Rulers who demand loyalty don't understand how it works.
—DR. CRITCHLORE, ON LEADERSHIP

Ron and I ducked into the dungeon depot so I could load up on supplies before Pravus arrived. I combed the shelves, grabbing anything I thought might help and stuffing it all in a duffel bag while Ron kept asking me about stuff.

"'Tornado in a Can'? That's not real, is it?"

"Sure it is," I said, putting it into my backpack along with a pack of exploding gum. I raced to another section of shelves and came out with an armload of clothes.

"Are those dresses?" Ron asked. I didn't have time to explain, so I just nodded. A few of them went into my backpack, the rest into the duffel bag.

"Where are you going to hide?" he asked.

"I'll start in Mistress Moira's room, up in the tower," I said. "I can see everything from there."

Ron helped me drag the duffel up to the tower while we avoided the few Pravus minions we hadn't managed to trap. Then we went to the stables to help Frankie and Darthin load one of the chariots.

The chariot relay race had been a big hit in last year's Minion Games. They were big enough to hold an ogre, and now one was full of Dr. Frankenhammer's cases.

"You should see Syke," Frankie said. "She only comes up to my hip now."

Pismo had spent the day launching his battle catapult at anyone trying to come near the school by boat. He was exhausted again, and said he'd take Ron the next morning, before Pravus showed up.

Ron looked relieved. We were exhausted too. We headed back up to Mistress Moira's tower to settle in for the night.

"This room is amazing," Ron said, and he was right. Mistress Moira's tower was like a meadow floating in the sky, complete with a tree in the corner and frogs and birds and crickets chirping near the small pond beneath it.

We were eating dinner when Victus's voice echoed throughout the room. I ducked behind the couch in panic, but he wasn't actually in the room. He'd discovered the school-wide public announcement system.

"This is Victus Tarb speaking, henchman special class," he said. "Hello, Runt Higgins. Yes, I know who you are, Runt. I know you're the one who has been capturing my minions. Who put cayenne pepper on all the food in the cafeteria, and who left those rude messages on the walls."

"Pismo," I said, shaking my head.

"I am offering you a deal," Victus said. "Surrender now, release my minions, and I'll let you escape before Dr. Pravus arrives. I'll be honest, this situation doesn't make me look good, but it's much worse for you. Dr. Pravus is bringing enough monster power to find you, and then . . . well, I'll let you imagine what he wants to do to you. Oh, and I have Syke and your good doctor now."

I looked at Ron. "Oh, no. They got into the lab."

"There are two things Dr. Pravus wants me to deliver to him when he arrives," Victus went on. "You, and a certain Top Student trophy. He has a friend who is very anxious to see you again."

"Seizemore," Ron said, and I nodded.

"Bring the trophy to Critchlore's office," Victus said, "and I'll let you and your friends go. It's a win-win. You'll live, and I won't get cuffed for failure.

"You have until tomorrow morning. Eight a.m. There's really no other choice for you. Pravus'll be here by the afternoon."

I looked at Ron. "You have to get out of here first thing tomorrow morning," I said. "Before Pravus gets here."

Ron was quiet for a minute. "I think I'll stay," he said. "Listen, Runt. I know I've only known you a few days, but they've been the best days of my life. You're right, I've never had a friend before. I've never been allowed to misbehave or be immature. *I* put the cayenne pepper on the food. I wrote those things on the wall."

"You did?" I laughed. "But seriously, Ron, you'll be safer at the Great Library, with Dr. Critchlore and everyone else."

He sighed. "You're right, and Pismo can take me at the first sign of danger."

"All right," I reluctantly agreed.

"Tell me, what's in that attic room, really?"

"A lot of memorabilia from Dr. Critchlore's childhood," I said. "Artwork, trophies, and . . . his old toys."

"What are you afraid of? Ghosts?"

"No."

"Spiders?"

"No . . . well, yes, but that's not it."

"What then? What's up there?"

I took a deep breath before answering. Just thinking about them gave me the shivers. "Dr. Critchlore's doll collection," I said.

"His . . . what?"

"Dr. Critchlore has always been interested in training monsters. As a kid he collected dolls that had been possessed by evil spirits, and then he tried to train them." I paused for a second. "He wasn't successful."

"Possessed dolls?"

"Yes," I said. "The attic is full of them."

"That's creepy," he said.

I nodded. "I'm going to tell Victus that I can't get the trophy without Syke. And we need a backup plan in case Victus tries to double-cross us."

"In case?"

"You're right, of course he's going to double-cross us."

The next morning I went to Critchlore's office alone, leaving Ron and my "duffel bag of safety" in Mistress Moira's tower.

Victus had Carl and Claudia posted in the secretary's room outside Critchlore's office. I walked in and announced that I was surrendering. They took my backpack and led me inside.

Victus sat in Dr. Critchlore's wingback chair near the fireplace. His legs were crossed, and he wore a smug look on his face, like he'd just tricked a first-year into giving him his lunch.

"Well, well, well," he said. "You've seen the logic of my proposal. I wasn't sure you were that intelligent. Did you bring the trophy?"

"No," I said. "Give me Syke and Dr. Frankenhammer and I'll tell you where it is."

"I don't trust you," Victus said. "Get me the trophy. I'll keep my word and release Syke and the doctor."

"I don't trust *you*," I said. "I'll tell you where the trophy is hidden once I see that they are safe."

He nodded to Carl, who grabbed my arms, holding me tightly. "I'm guessing that if the trophy were easy to get, you'd have it now," Victus said. "So I'm going to insist that you get it for me."

Rats.

"Then I need Syke," I said. "I can't get it without her. And I need the supplies in my backpack."

"Fine," he said. "Carl, go get our prisoners and meet us . . ." He looked at me. "Where?"

"The fourth-floor landing," I said.

Victus enlisted another bodyguard to escort us on the trek upstairs, a kid so huge he looked like he could lift both of us and toss us out the window. Claudia came as well. We arrived at the landing before Carl, and while we waited for Syke, I opened my backpack and put on an extra piece of clothing.

"Is that a dress?" Victus said to me with a smirk.

It was, in fact, Verduccia's dress from the fashion show. The hem hit just above my knees, and I wore pants underneath. I thought it would pass for a tunic, but apparently not.

"Do you know how ridiculous you look?" Victus said, laughing.

"Really? I think it drapes nicely," I said, running a hand down

210

the silky fabric. The dress fit me perfectly, and the green color high-lighted my eyes. I watched Victus's face as I balled my fists and knives popped out of the sleeves. His expression was so worth it.

"What's taking them so long?" I asked, but Victus just sneered at me. Eventually Carl showed up, pulling Dr. Frankenhammer down the hallway toward us.

"Where's Syke?" I asked.

Dr. Frankenhammer pulled his lab coat pocket forward and Syke peeked out.

"Syke!" I said. "You're tiny! I thought—" I was going to say that I thought she'd been given an antidote to the sudithium antidote, but I didn't want to say anything in front of Victus.

"Hasn't kicked in yet." Dr. Frankenhammer shrugged. "Tree nymphs, who knew?"

Syke eyed me up and down. "I would have gone with the shield-dress," she said.

I opened my backpack and pulled it out. It came with a protective cape that could deflect arrows. I quickly switched out, draping the cape over my pack of supplies. "You ready?" I asked.

She nodded, but she looked as nervous as I felt.

"Get me the trophy," Victus said. "And we'll all leave happy."

I held my hand out to take her from Dr. Frankenhammer, but Dr. Frankenhammer was holding something else in his other hand—his miniature dragon. Syke hopped onto him and was soon hovering next to my head.

"Let's go," she said.

CHAPTER 30

"The castle dungeon may be creepy, but the attic is so much worse, so much worse, so much worse . . ."
—NINE-YEAR-OLD RUNT, WHISPERING INTO HIS PILLOW,
BECAUSE HE HAD TO TELL SOMEONE

At the end of the hallway we faced a brick wall. I stood next to a wall sconce and pulled down one of its candle holders, which sprung the mechanism that opened a hidden door. Behind the door a spiral staircase led to the attic.

Victus hit Carl on the shoulder. "You should have found that."

"Got anything else in that pack?" Syke asked, hovering near me.

I opened my stuffed backpack and showed her. "Exploding gum, Tornado in a Can, more dresses, a miniature tea set."

"A miniature tea set? Really?"

"Dolls like tea parties, right?" I said with a shrug. "I thought—"

"Take it out," she said, shaking her head. "And let's go."

"The trophy box is in the corner, remember?" I said, removing the tea set and putting on my backpack again.

Syke nodded. "We'll go in quiet. Maybe they won't notice. But if they do wake up, I'll distract them, you find that trophy."

"Sounds good. Let's go." I held the door open so Syke and the dragon could fly upstairs.

"I'm going too," Victus said. "I'm not leaving you two alone to escape."

"Fine," I said. "Just be very, very quiet. We don't want to wake them. Here." I reluctantly handed him a couple of Frieda's exploding rings. I hated to admit it, but we might need his help. "Bite off the gem and toss it. But only in an emergency."

At the top of the stairs I paused, facing the attic door. When we were all ready, I took a deep breath and opened the door very, very slowly.

Stale air rushed out at us, sounding like someone whispering "nooooooo" as it escaped the confines of that evil room. At my first step inside, the floorboards creaked, because of course they would.

The room stretched out in front of me. Dormer windows lined the wall to my left, each one draped with spiderwebs. Enough light snuck in, allowing us to see that the space was filled with sheet-covered furniture, old paintings, dusty candlesticks, and tons of boxes. I noticed a wooden armoire chained closed with a sign that read, "Shadows. Do not open."

And there, over by the window, four pleasant-faced dolls posed at a tiny table set for tea. I pointed at them as I looked at Syke. "See?" I mouthed.

She pointed to the wall on the right where boxes were piled up. I took another creaky step in that direction. I could hear my breathing, the room was so still. I kept watching those dolls as I crept past.

The last time we'd entered, we hadn't even tried to be quiet. We'd rummaged through lots of stuff before Syke squeaked with glee upon finding an old Walking Wendy doll. She'd grabbed it and lifted it to her face with a happy smile. But then the doll had grabbed her face, squeezing her cheeks as its happy doll face transformed into an evil scowl. Syke had screamed and thrown the doll across the room.

That had woken the others, and very quickly we were surrounded by possessed dolls, all with frightening faces and many armed with weapons—slingshots, small bows with arrows, tiny knives. One had a toy gun that normally shot soft, foamy darts, but she'd glued sharp tacks to the ends.

Fortunately, we hadn't come completely unarmed ourselves. We'd been nine years old, but we weren't idiots. I used the mini-flamethrower on my Critchlore pocket tool, which made them back off so we could get out of there, quick.

We never told anyone about the attic, because we weren't supposed to go up there. Even when I woke up screaming from nightmares, I didn't tell anyone. Not even Pierre, and he would have been so impressed.

I tiptoed over to the boxes, not wanting to disturb anything. Syke flew near my head, pointing out the ones she thought looked likely. I nodded. None of them were labeled. The first was full of holiday decorations. I moved to the next.

Something was waking up in the room. I could feel it.

I spun around, but didn't notice anything. Syke hovered near me. I could tell by her expression that she felt it too. Victus had stuck close to the door, twisting one of the rings on his hand.

I could feel *something*—an awareness zipping up and down my spine. A flash of cold swept through the still air, and my heartbeat quickened. I felt like I was being watched by something that wanted to hurt me.

I looked at the table set for tea. One of the doll's heads slowly turned around to look at me, a pleasant expression on her face. And then in a flash her expression twisted into an evil smile with narrowed eyes. I jumped back.

Just find it and get out of here! I told myself.

The next box contained a bunch of sweaters. I turned to shake my head at Syke, and that's when I noticed the Walking Wendy doll leaning against the wall near a window. I didn't think she'd been there before.

The next box was full of Dr. Critchlore's art projects from his school days. I pulled out a macaroni necklace, a few crayon drawings, and a shoebox diorama of monsters attacking a mountain fortress.

I turned to Syke, shaking my head. Walking Wendy had moved a bit closer, and the tea party dolls were now lined up, watching me. I nodded at the dolls. Syke gave me a thumbs-up. She turned the dragon around so she could keep an eye on them. Possessed dolls love to move when you aren't looking at them. They think it freaks people out.

They're right, it does.

The next box was full of financial papers. Then more schoolwork. Then old textbooks.

WHERE WAS IT?

Syke screamed. Walking Wendy now held a miniature bow and arrow and was firing at Syke, barely missing her head. The dragon blew fire at the doll, and Walking Wendy dove for cover behind a box. She moved like an acrobat. Two other doll heads popped up next to her, a clown and a ventriloquist's dummy. Smiling wicked smiles, they raised their weapons. One held a slingshot, the other a bouncy ball rimmed with tacks.

"Runt!" Syke yelled, her voice full of high-pitched panic. "Find that trophy!"

"Victus! A little help?"

But Victus was frozen; a trio of porcelain-faced dolls holding knives stood in front of him. His terrified gaze was locked on the dolls, and he reached behind him for the door handle. He was going to bolt, I was sure of it.

I began ripping open boxes, one after another. Three were full of trophies, but none was the right one. I was hit by a marble, and it really stung. I activated my shield cape and kept looking. I turned and saw Syke swooping around the dolls, trying to throw off their aim while the dragon blew fire at them. Victus threw one of the rings, and the explosion rocked the room, knocking me off my feet.

It also woke up the others.

Frantic now, I pulled open the next box and there it was: the tree-like trophy with pale blue-and-white branches. It stood out against the gold of the other trophies.

"FOUND IT!" I screamed. Two more explosions. Victus was out of rings, and the dolls were still coming for him, some of them missing limbs now, but still moving on him. "Let's get out of here."

My cape was yanked off from behind, making me fall backward. An army of skinny, plastic, blond-haired dolls raced my way, armed with pick-up sticks held high like javelins, ready to impale me. I spun away and rose to my feet, kicking out at the nearest ones, but there were so many.

What had Dr. Critchlore been thinking?

Wait, never mind. These dolls were terrifying. Why wouldn't he collect them?

I felt a warm trickle of blood drip down my arm and realized I'd been skewered. I pulled out the sharp stick just as I was hit by three more. These didn't penetrate farther than my clothes, but a metal dart grazed my cheek. Two rag dolls with red-yarn hair were firing the darts out of a propped-up crossbow.

I stuffed the trophy in my pack and jumped up, covering my head with my arms, able to peek through the small gap between them. The doorway was blocked by dolls. Victus was now hiding behind a couch, yelling at me to give him the trophy. Syke's dragon had run out of fire and was looking for a place to hide.

Some dolls were searching for more dangerous weapons, while others continued to pelt me with increasingly sharper objects. Another tack-ball glanced off my shoulder, ripping my dress.

I heard banging on the door as Victus's minions wondered what was going on inside.

"RUNT! TORNADO IN A CAN!" Syke screamed. "Blow them away from the door!"

"Okay! Keep back!" I pulled out the Tornado in a Can, twisted the cap, pushed the activation button on top, and tossed it at the door. I had three seconds before it exploded, so I ducked behind a barrier of boxes and waited for the boom and rush of air, but what happened was a boom and rush of water.

Oops. Wrong can.

"RUNT!" Syke yelled. "I said 'tornado'!"

The room rapidly filled with water from the Flood in a Can.

"The window!" Syke screamed. "Open one before the water gets too high!"

I trudged through the water as it rose from my knees to my waist in a flash. I fought through a floating sea of dolls that were swimming for me while still holding weapons. I had to get to that window. I reached for a roof beam and managed to grab it with both hands and lift my legs out of the water. Snarling plastic dolls wielding tiny knives in their hands covered one leg. I shook them off with frantic kicks as they started stabbing, but they were floating back toward me on water that was rising by the second. I aimed my last kick at the window and it flung open. I watched the demon dolls float outside on a waterfall filled with attic debris.

As the water subsided, I lowered myself back to the floor, standing in water that was as high as the windowsill. My arms ached and I was out of breath. I looked out the window to see where the dolls had landed. It was a long drop, and they'd shattered into pieces. And then I saw Dr. Frankenhammer being led toward the stables by two of Victus's minion guards.

That backstabbing, double-dealing liar! He'd had no intention of keeping his side of the deal.

"Give me the trophy," Victus said, standing by the door. I looked around for Syke. I saw Dr. Frankenhammer's dragon perched on a windowsill, but Syke was nowhere to be seen.

I looked out the window again, in complete panic at the thought that I'd just flushed my best friend out the window.

CHAPTER 31

The Catastrophe-in-a-Can novelty items include
Flood, Earthquake, Thunder, Tornado, and the just
released Sinkhole in a Can.
—DR. CRITCHLORE'S *MINION ACCESSORY PRODUCTS* CATALOG

Looking for her?" Victus said, holding up Syke with one hand. "Give me the trophy, and I'll guarantee your safety." He opened the attic door and let the rest of the water drain out.

All I could think was that Dr. Critchlore was going to kill me, so Victus's guarantee of safety wasn't making me feel any better.

"No, Runt, he's lying!" Syke's tiny voice screamed.

I knew he wasn't going to free her, and he'd probably planned all along to hand me over to Pravus. When Carl stepped into the room, followed by Claudia, I whistled for Dr. Frankenhammer's dragon, and climbed out the window.

Victus charged, but I made it outside before he could catch me. The dragon blew out a weak blast of fire in his face before joining me on the flat ledge in front of the window. I grabbed him and stuffed him into my pocket, then climbed onto the dormer's little slanted roof. From there I could climb up the pitched siding until I reached the flat top of the castle's roof. I pulled myself up and ran until I reached the wall of Mistress Moira's tall tower, a dead end.

"You're stuck!" Victus yelled. "Come back and give me the trophy. I'll go easy on you. If you try to escape, you'll regret it!"

"Ron!" I yelled up at one of Mistress Moira's windows. His head peeked out. "Throw me down the jet-pack dress! The orange one with the attached backpack. It's in the duffel!"

"I'm losing patience!" Victus yelled. He sent Carl out to climb up to the roof.

"Ron! Hurry!" I yelled.

Carl was on top of the window now, reaching with a hairy arm for the roof. The orange dress dropped down from the tower. I caught it and pulled it over my head, adjusting the jet pack. My panicky fingers struggled with the sleeves, which held the steering mechanism. Carl was running for me, getting closer by the second.

I blasted off just as Carl's fingertips brushed my legs.

I wished I could have seen Victus's expression, but hearing him scream was reward enough.

It was a short trip up to the window, and I quickly climbed into Mistress Moira's room.

"You're still trapped in that tower!" Victus yelled. "We're coming for you!"

"What happened?" Ron asked.

"I got the trophy," I said, putting my backpack on the table so I could remove the dress and put on a dry uniform. "Victus was never going to keep his word. Surprise, surprise. He took Dr. Frankenhammer away as soon as we went into the attic. He's got Syke too. We need to rescue them."

"It may be too late," Ron said. "Look out there." He led me to the windows facing the front of the school. "Something's coming. Something huge."

The UMs. Even though I was terrified of them, I couldn't help wanting to see what they looked like. What sort of monster could do all the damage that we'd seen on the nightly news?

They were miles away, and we could only see their shoulders poking out above the trees. They were hunched over, as if walking on all fours. Unlike the orderly marching of Pravus's ogres, these monsters were scattered and disorganized. Two humps veered off to the right, tearing through a field to smash the buildings there. Another group turned around, going back the way they'd come.

One of them stood to roar at the world, and when it did, I gasped. "Did you see that?" I asked. The monster's mouth was filled with rows of sharp teeth. Horns circled down around the ears, like a ram.

"They're horrific," Ron said. "I've never seen anything so terrifying."

"No—did you see its face?"

"Yes, it looked like it could eat a village."

"It looked exactly like Sara, like the vaskor," I said. "Only huge."

"Who are the vaskor?"

"They were your family's bodyguards. How do you not know that? Before the coup they lived with you. They looked like giant wolves."

"The wolves, yes. I remember them," Ron said. "But how do they relate to those." He pointed outside. "I'm not following."

"The vaskor take on a glamour that hides what they look like, but they look like those monsters, only smaller."

"But you told me Dr. Pravus made those monsters," Ron said, pointing outside. "That they were once human."

"Yes. The virus mutated them. Wait . . . That means the vaskor were once human too. Of course! Sara told me she was Oti, a human tribe that was wiped out centuries ago. I thought she'd just meant that her kind came from the same place."

"If the vaskor are like Pravus's beasts, only smaller, can't your Dr. Frankenhammer make them huge?" Ron asked.

"Yes. That's the easy part. Dr. Critchlore didn't want to make UMs, because you have to give the virus to humans, and it kills most of them. But now he doesn't have to. We already have the mutated humans—the vaskor."

I started pacing, because this changed everything. "The vaskor are under a spell of obedience to the royal family—you! And me, as your double. Do you know what this means? *We have them!* The vaskor are the original Undefeatable Minions. We've got the mutated humans, and the spell of obedience . . . We just need to give them sudithium, and then . . . oh, no."

"What?"

"The vaskor hate fighting," I said. "They're pacifists. We can't make them go into battle against monsters that are just as strong as they are, but a million times more vicious."

"What choice do we have?" Ron asked. "The safety of this continent rests on stopping those things."

"We have to get to the Great Library. I need to talk to Dr. Critchlore."

"How?" Ron asked. "Your friends left with the serums. And I thought you couldn't leave."

"If I go and come right back, I'll be fine. Probably. Come on." I led him over to the window facing the lake. "We need to get this dragon over to the pond at the FRP. There's sudithium in the water. He'll grow bigger and we can escape on him."

"That will take too long," Ron said. "And how are we going to get past Victus? He's coming up to get us."

"We'll jump out the window," I said. I pointed outside. There, standing in a nice little clump, was my emergency escape route.

"Googa! Catch me!" I said as I jumped. Ron followed, and we were caught in some very prickly arms.

"Take us to the FRP," I said. "We're playing hide-and-go-seek. Hurry!"

Googa giggled and ran while Ron and I held tightly to the swinging branches. I thought I was going to throw up from all the tossing about, but at last we arrived at the FRP, and Ron and I were lowered to the ground. We both stumbled for a few steps, dizzy, but I managed to place the dragon next to the pond. Tired and thirsty after the battle in the attic, he took a long drink of the water.

The ground shook. Pravus's enormous UMs were coming closer.

"You're right," I said to Ron. "This is going to take too long."

"What's going to take too long?" a raspy voice asked. Coming out from between my toddler trees was Sara, our girl explorer savior.

"I've been looking for Syke," she said. "She's not at the Pravus Academy, she's not in Stull City. I thought she might be here."

"She is," I said. "They know she's a spy. We got the cuff off, but

Victus captured her. Sara, we need to get out of here. We have to tell Dr. Critchlore what's happening. Can you take us to the Great Library?"

"And leave Syke here?"

"We have something Pravus desperately wants." I showed her the trophy. "Syke is his only bargaining chip to get it, so I don't think he'll harm her. We have to get it to safety. Once he has this, we're all dead."

She nodded. "I'll take you."

CHAPTER 32

If you want a job done right, don't hire Critchlore minions.

—AN ADVERTISEMENT FOR THE PRAVUS ACADEMY

S he doesn't look anything like those monsters," Ron said after I introduced him to Sara.

"Hold on to your medallion and look again," I said. "She has a glamour."

He pulled out his necklace and gasped. "Whoa."

We rushed to the stables to grab the second chariot. After attaching Sara to the harness, Ron and I jumped into the two-wheeled carriage. Then we raced out the unguarded front entrance. (Kumi still wasn't letting the ogres and giants out of the D-MIS.)

The journey was exhausting. And painful. Ron and I stood the entire trip, gripping the edge of our unstable transport as Sara bolted down deserted roads, across open fields, and through the Hills of Distraction. I had to keep yelling at her to slow down, and twice we were thrown out when she took a turn too fast. Sara grew frustrated by how often we asked her to stop so we could rest. She never tired.

It was late afternoon by the time Sara left us near the secret

entrance to the Great Library and went to join the rest of the vaskor in the forest. Ron and I sprinted through the mountain tunnels until we reached the door to the library, which stood open.

"This was the site of the Great Library," I told Ron. "The secret repository of all the world's knowledge. It was built to hold all the books that were smuggled out of Erudyten two hundred years ago, when the country was overthrown."

Inside, the seven stories of bookshelves were bare, and the place seemed so big and empty without the books.

"My ancestors built this?" Ron asked, his head tilting back to take it all in. "They built this, and filled it with books? Incredible."

"It shouldn't be hidden away," I said. "The librarians are waiting to return the books to libraries that everyone can use. They just need a realm with the right ruler." I looked him in the eye and said, "You."

On the first floor, the empty bookshelves had been pushed aside to make room for the Critchlore minions. Sleeping bags were arranged on the floor, and everyone was spread out, grouped by year, with the first-years by the door.

I found my friends a bit farther on. Frankie and Darthin had joined Boris and Eloni. Meztli and Jud sat between my friends and the werewolves. They all stood up as I approached.

"Eloni, Boris, this is Ron," I said. "Ron, these are my friends."

Ron took one look at Boris and said, "There are three of us? Egad, what a common face I was cursed with."

"Where's Critchlore?" I asked.

"He's in a conference room at the end of the library," Eloni said.

"Come on, Ron," I said, taking off. We jogged down the long

hallway until we reached the conference room. Inside, there were grown-ups sitting and standing around a table, looking at papers. A small group of teachers huddled by a side table that was covered with food. Dr. Critchlore sat at the head of the table. Near him were Coach Foley and Professors Murphy, Zaida, Dunkirk, and Twilk.

Dr. Critchlore stood up when he saw me.

"Runt, what are you doing here?" he asked.

Every head turned my way, all looking equally shocked.

"I was kidnapped by Janet," I said. "Her father was trying to get me to pose as the prince so he could take control of Andirat. This is the real Prince Auberon."

"Hi," Ron said with a shy wave.

"What?" Professor Zaida stood up. "You're not Prince Auberon?"

"I was his doppelganger. They used me in parades and stuff, which is why I showed up at Dr. Critchlore's dressed in prince clothes. But listen, we figured out—"

"Runt, you shouldn't have come here," Dr. Critchlore said, shaking his head.

"I know, but this is really important," I said. "I know how we can stop Dr. Pravus."

"We can't stop him now," Professor Murphy said. "He has the Undefeatable Minions."

"Yes," I said. "And so do we."

They looked at me with expressions that ranged from pity to sadness, which, I'll admit, wasn't the reaction I'd been hoping for.

"Dr. Critchlore will not give the virus to anybody," Professor Murphy said. "We can't make the Undefeatable Minions."

"He doesn't need to," I went on. "Have you seen them? The UMs? Have you seen what they look like?"

Everyone shook their heads.

"The reason Pravus doesn't show them in his propaganda videos is because he doesn't want Dr. Critchlore to see them. If you do," I said, looking at him, "you'll know. The Undefeatable Minions look just like the vaskor, only huge."

Professor Murphy gasped.

I took out my DPS and showed them the picture I'd taken. They passed it around.

"Son of a dragon, he's right," Professor Zaida said. "That looks just like a vaskor."

"You mean we can turn the vaskor into UMs?" Professor Murphy asked. "With just a dose of sudithium?"

I nodded.

"We'll have an equal force," Coach Foley said, pounding the table with his fist. "We can take on Pravus!"

"The vaskor are pacifists," I explained. "They don't want to fight."

"Doesn't matter," Coach Foley said, standing up. "They have to obey you, right? You can order them to fight."

I looked to Dr. Critchlore. He was watching me, and looked sympathetic. "They have to fight for us, Runt. I'm sorry, but we can't defeat Pravus without their help."

"What about the antidotes?" I asked.

"We'll try, of course," he said. "Dr. Pravus doesn't have the spell of obedience. Maybe his UMs will surrender without fighting. What are they fighting for, really?"

"They think Dr. Pravus saved their lives," I said. "Syke told us. He infected their village, and then took the survivors away, pretending to have cured them."

The room filled with a flurry of talking and excitement. Everyone was smiling now. I looked at Ron, who nodded at me, like he was saying, "good job." But inside, I felt terrible. I knew that they were probably our only chance to stop Pravus. I'd hoped that Dr. Critchlore would understand how I felt about forcing them to fight.

"You did the right thing," Ron said, as if he was reading my thoughts.

Dr. Critchlore ordered Professor Murphy to round up the vaskor so we could give them the sudithium as soon as possible. Then he asked Coach Foley and Professors Dunkirk and Twilk to continue to work on a way to get the antidote into Pravus's monsters. Most of the adults scattered with their new assignments, but Dr. Critchlore and Professor Zaida stayed behind.

The excitement of the last few minutes faded quickly as Dr. Critchlore came around the table to talk to me.

"Runt, you shouldn't have come here," he said again.

"I had to," I said. "I had to show you that we can stop him."

"No, you don't understand," Professor Zaida said. "Your tether, it's come back, on your neck."

My hand reached for my neck, which was silly because I wouldn't be able to feel it. "That's okay," I said. "I'll go back to school and it will disappear, like the others."

"Runt . . . I'm so sorry," Dr. Critchlore said. "Mistress Moira sent an urgent message after you disappeared. She told me not to let you

231

leave the school because . . ." He paused, not knowing how to finish that sentence.

"Because what?"

"Because if you activate your tether a third time, it won't go away," he said. "The third tether will kill you."

CHAPTER 33

Curses!

—THEY'RE THE WORST

WHAT?" I dropped into a chair. Was the room spinning? I felt like I'd been sucked into a whirlpool that was dragging me down into a dark abyss. "No. No. No," I said through hyperventilating breaths of panic.

Dr. Critchlore sat down next to me, draping an arm around my shoulder. "Runt, there's hope," he said. "Mistress Moira found the witch. We have a chance."

"She found my witch?" I asked. "In Skelterdam?"

"Yes. She'd sent a crow telling me that she was bringing the witch here, but then they were both captured by Pravus's troops a few days ago. Dr. Pravus needs the witch to cast his spell of obedience."

"The same witch?" I asked. "The same witch who cursed me can do the obedience spell?"

"Yes," he said. "She's done it before."

I gasped. "The vaskor? The same witch who cursed me also cursed the vaskor?"

"We believe so, yes," he said. "Her name is Dismorda. She goes by the title Enchantress, and she's over three hundred years old. The spell that cursed the vaskor has gone down in Grand Coven lore as the most powerful spell ever cast. It's been outlawed as RCE—Ridiculously Cruel and Evil. It's a spell of transgenerational obedience, which means that not only did the original vaskor have to obey the royal family, but their offspring and their offspring, and so on forever . . ."

"Until the witch dies," Ron said.

"Or the vaskor are freed by their master," Dr. Critchlore added.

"But she hasn't performed the spell for Pravus," I said. The UMs I'd seen were completely out of control.

"No. The last crow from Moira said that Dismorda will not perform the spell until Pravus can guarantee her safety and pay her extremely exorbitant fee. Once she performs the spell, the Grand Coven will know, and they'll come after her. She wants gold, lots of it, plus a castle and an army to protect her."

"Seizemore promised Pravus four gold bars," Ron said. "Would that be enough?"

"Four?" Dr. Critchlore said. "No. He'd need much more."

"Does Mistress Moira know why I was cursed?" I asked. Maybe she could convince Dismorda that it had been a mistake. It had to have been a mistake. I touched my neck. The last time I'd activated the tether curse, it had almost killed me in seven days. Seven days. Oh no.

"I don't know," Dr. Critchlore said.

"Is there any way we can get to her?" I felt dizzy, and nauseous.

"Pravus has her now," he said. "He sent me a video yesterday." He shook his head and looked away.

"Can I see it?"

"I'd rather not show it."

"Please, I have to see the witch who cursed me."

"Fine," he said, handing me his laptop. "But I must warn you, it's disturbing."

"You mean, he's torturing Mistress Moira?" I asked, closing the laptop because that was something I couldn't watch.

"Torturing her? No. He's torturing *me*. He's wooing her, and she seems to be falling for him. I can't watch it."

I opened the laptop. The latest episode of *The Pravus Projects* was queued up and ready to go. Dr. Critchlore turned away as Dr. Pravus, impeccably dressed in his dark suit, entered his interrogation room and saw Mistress Moira for the first time, bound in a chair. He looked smitten by her beauty, and when his henchman raised a hand to strike her, Pravus grabbed his arm to stop him.

As Pravus and Mistress Moira gazed into each other's eyes, the narrator's voice said: "All those years of hard work and planning had left little time for . . . love."

The show cut to Pravus and Mistress Moira strolling around his grounds together. She was no longer a prisoner. They ate meals together, laughing and toasting each other. He taught her how to use a crossbow. They danced beneath the moonlight. I snuck a few glances at Dr. Critchlore, who was pacing at the end of the room.

He caught me looking at him. "I'd written a letter to Mistress Moira. I was going to give it to her before she left for Skelterdam, but I . . ."

"Chickened out?" I offered.

He frowned. "Instead of giving it to her, I left it in my office. Pravus's minions must have found it, so now he knows how I feel about her. He's using that to lure me out of hiding."

"At least now we know why he's been so desperate to capture you," I said. "He knows that as soon as you see the UMs, you'll know that they're vaskor."

The episode ended on the steps of the EO Council Building, with Pravus and Mistress Moira standing in front of a cheering crowd. His usual contingent of black-clad bodyguards stood behind him. As the camera panned across the crowd, Ron reached over me and froze the video. He zoomed in on a tiny woman standing near Pravus. She was incredibly old and disfigured with scars.

"That old lady could be your witch," Ron said. "She's got sores all over her face, just like the ones I've seen on people who've been to Skelterdam. The air is poisonous there."

Dr. Critchlore was behind us in a flash, looking at the screen. The small woman was nestled among a band of monster body-guards. "She does look very witch-like."

"It's got to be Dismorda," I said.

"Let's go after her," Ron said. "Kill her and your curse is lifted."

Dr. Critchlore and I looked at each other, neither of us saying anything. I knew. And he knew I knew.

"What?" Ron asked. "What am I missing?"

"We can't kill her," I said. Dr. Critchlore nodded sadly. "If she dies, the curse of obedience dies with her. Without that curse, our vaskor won't fight."

"If they don't fight," Dr. Critchlore said, "Pravus will win."

"And we'll all live in a concrete-and-barbed-wire world wearing loyalty cuffs," I added.

The only way to stop Dr. Pravus was to keep the witch alive. The only way I could live was if the witch died.

CHAPTER 34

The Grand Coven governs witches. While supremely
powerful, even they cannot undo a curse.
—*HISTORY OF WITCHES* BY DR. VENKO COVERLY

I remembered the trophy and pulled it out of my backpack. "I think Dr. Pravus wants this," I said. "Maybe we could trade it for Syke and Dr. Frankenhammer."

"How did you find it?" he asked. "The hidden room . . . my dolls . . ."

I shrugged and he laughed.

"Why does he want the trophy so badly?" I asked. "Is he that petty?"

"He is. He hates that I have it and he doesn't. But that's not why he wants it."

Dr. Critchlore picked up the trophy and pulled off two branches. He switched their positions and then pushed the branches down until we heard a faint click. He twisted the base a few turns until the front of the base popped open, revealing a hidden compartment.

Dr. Critchlore pulled out a map and a key. "This is what he's really after," he said. "Directions to an extremely large treasure. All the money his father stole when he fled Riggen. The entire nation's treasury, in gold."

"Whoa. So, like, hundreds of gold bars?"

"Over twenty thousand," Dr. Critchlore said, and I nearly fell over in shock. "Pravus needs that gold now, desperately."

"To pay for the spell?"

"That, and it's very expensive keeping an army." Dr. Critchlore replaced the map and key. "Especially an army of huge, hungry monsters."

"Did you find it? The treasure?"

"Twenty-five years ago," he said, nodding. "I knew there was something odd about how obsessed he was with this trophy. I caught no fewer than seven spies trying to steal it. At school, Pravus had been watched closely by Fraze Coldheart's men. They knew who he was, and they wanted to find his father and the gold his father had stolen from their nation before he was overthrown. Coldheart's men wouldn't let anyone near Pravus without searching them thoroughly.

"The trophy was actually a clever way for his father to pass Pravus a message. Everyone thought he'd win it. Pravus's father's men made a copy of the real trophy, stuffed the map inside, and substituted in the new trophy before graduation."

"But then you won it, instead of him," I said. "What did you do with the treasure?"

"That gold belongs to the people of Riggen. Not to Pravus, and not to Fraze Coldheart. I am holding it until the right leader comes along."

"Holding it . . . where?"

"Now, Runt, you don't think I'm actually going to tell you where thousands of gold bars are hidden, do you? That would be breaking the fifth rule of hiding treasure."

I shrugged. "I'm going to die in a few days. Why not?"

"You will not die from that curse," Dr. Critchlore said, standing up. "I will see to that. Now, why don't you go see Cook? She's been very worried about you."

I left Ron with Professor Zaida and headed for the kitchen. I didn't want to think about my curse, but it was hard not to. I'd nearly died after a week in Polar Bay. That meant I only had seven days to find the witch and get her to remove it. Seven days.

Before I entered the kitchen I zipped up my jacket so the collar would cover my neck. When Cook saw me she nearly spilled a huge pot of chili as she raced over to give me a hug.

"Thank the skies and all the stars you're okay," she said. "I've been so worried."

Pierre sat down and slugged me on the shoulder. "Missed you, kiddo."

I didn't have the heart to tell them about my curse. Instead, I asked for a bag of doughnuts, because Sara was going to be mad at me. While Cook made them, I told them about my adventures at the Andiratian embassy. Then they told me about the evacuation, and everything that had happened since I left. I barely listened.

"Most of the kids went home to their families," Cook said. "The sirens, the giants . . ."

One week. That's all I have.

"Except the ones from Riggen and Lower Worb," Pierre added.

"Rumor has it that Pravus will attack those realms first, and the kids would be safer here."

I won't live to see what happens.

"Dr. Critchlore will find a way to stop him," Cook said. "Then we can all go home again."

I don't want to leave you guys.

I was about to burst out crying, so I grabbed the doughnuts and made an excuse to get out of there. I managed to hold back the tears until I got outside, but as soon as the door shut behind me, I looked up at the sky through the tall redwood trees and let out a primal scream. I picked up rocks and threw them as far as I could, yelling, "Why?" with each throw. "Why am I cursed?"

Eventually, I collapsed into a little ball, sobbing while I yanked up clumps of grass.

Dr. Critchlore sat down next to me.

"It's not fair, I know," he said, rubbing my back. "You don't deserve this."

I sat up and wiped my eyes. I could see dark shapes darting through the forest. "The vaskor don't deserve what's going to happen to them, either," I said. "They shouldn't be forced to fight."

"They might not have to," he said. "If we can figure out a way to inject the antidotes into the UMs. But their skin is like iron beneath that fur. Nothing penetrates it."

"There's got to be a weakness, a soft spot of some kind."

"If there is, the vaskor are our only hope of finding it," he said. "Professor Murphy is examining one now. But I feel that only our vaskor are strong enough to subdue Pravus's UMs and inject that antidote, and to do that, they will have to fight them."

"I know," I said.

"What's in that bag," he asked. "It smells delicious."

"Doughnuts," I said, handing him one. "I asked Cook to make some for Sara. I know it's a lame peace offering. 'Hey, Sara. We're asking your people to go against everything they believe in, but here, I brought you a doughnut.'"

He took a bite and stood up. "Tell Sara I'm sorry."

After Dr. Critchlore went back inside, I climbed up the mountain to a rocky ledge that offered a nice view of the forest. The sun was slipping away, like it didn't want to watch me break Sara's heart.

I knew Sara wanted me to free all the vaskor so that they wouldn't be bound to do things they didn't want to do. But there was too much at stake.

She jumped up onto the ledge when she saw me.

"I'm sorry, Sara," I said as I handed her the bag. She didn't reach for it, so I placed it next to her. I could smell the sugary goodness fill the air between us.

"What's happening in there?" she asked.

I didn't say anything. How do you tell someone that her people are going to be given sudithium and ordered to fight an army just as strong as they are?

"They're going to make us fight, aren't they?" she guessed.

I nodded. "It's the only way to stop Dr. Pravus."

"You are so selfish, Runt," she said. "Using us to get what you want."

"What I want is to stop Dr. Pravus. You know he's evil, Sara. Millions will suffer if he takes over."

241

She shook her head in disgust. "What's wrong with your neck?"

"I've been cursed," I said. "The same witch who cast the spell on you vaskor also cursed me. I've got about a week until this tightens and chokes me."

Her mouth dropped open and she stared at me for a long time.

"I'm surprised Critchlore hasn't suggested finding her, and—" She made a throat-slashing gesture.

"We can't," I said. "If she dies . . ."

Sara squinted as she realized my predicament. "If she dies, then we'll be free. We won't fight."

I nodded.

"You're going to die, just to make sure that we fight," she said. "That's so stupid, Runt."

"I'm just one person. So many other people will die if you don't fight. And Dr. Critchlore thinks they may surrender, because they don't have a spell. And we're not going to ask you to kill them. You just need to get close enough to inject them with the antidote."

"They will fight us," she said. "There will be deaths."

She picked out a doughnut and stuffed it into her mouth. A second one soon followed.

"Do you all like doughnuts?" I asked.

"Who doesn't like doughnuts?" she mumbled, her mouth full.

I shrugged. "Cook says doughnuts were invented as an excuse to have cake for breakfast."

"That's what makes them so awesome," she said. "It's something you're not supposed to have, but you can, because you've named it something different."

I laughed. Names are important. Funny, I still didn't know mine.

Everyone has called me Runt for as long as I can remember. And Higgins is Cook's last name. I wasn't a Natherly. Who was I?

"I'd like to know my real name before I die," I said.

"You deserve that," she said over another mouthful of old-fashioned deliciousness.

The next morning, Ron and I went to the conference room after breakfast. On the way there, I asked him about his meeting with Professor Zaida.

"She showed me the shrine and told me about her role in preserving the knowledge of my ancestors, who were forced to leave Erudyten. It's really incredible what they've done."

"It is," I agreed. The order of secret librarians had saved so many books that would have been destroyed by the invading evil overlords.

"Seizemore never told me about the librarians, or about Erudyten, and how it was a center for learning. It's . . ."

"Humbling?" I suggested. He nodded. "I think there are lots of things he didn't teach you," I said, remembering all the leadership lessons I'd gotten over the last year. "But don't worry, Professor Zaida will fill in the gaps. She taught me that leadership isn't about being in charge, it's about serving those who are willing to follow you."

"Zaida worked with my father and grandfather before the coup," Ron said. "They wanted to find a way to return Erudyten to its original glory by working with the EOs who had taken it over and split it up."

"Seizemore thinks Pravus will give him the realms that made up

Erudyten if he helps him defeat the EOs," I said. "But he's wrong. No way will Pravus give up his father's realm, Riggen."

"So more Andiratians will die for nothing," Ron said, shaking his head. "And the people here will suffer worse than before."

"We have to stop Pravus, but you need to stop Seizemore," I said. "If the generals do surrender to Cordholm, then Seizemore may take over Andirat's armies, with or without you."

"That's true. Zaida's been in contact with Cordholm's people," Ron said. "Cordholm has told them to support Seizemore, and Seizemore is already positioning himself as the leader of Andirat's reunited army. It hasn't even been reunited yet, but he's received pleas from the Evil Overlords to help them fight Pravus."

"Both Pravus and the EOs want Andirat's help," I said. "But they're both evil. Why can't they both lose?"

We reached the conference room, where everyone was watching another episode of *The Pravus Projects*. Another hour of him being a compassionate, charismatic leader by day, wooing Mistress Moira by night.

A breaking news story cut off a scene where Pravus was about to kiss Mistress Moira, which was good because I didn't think Dr. Critchlore could take any more. Fraze Coldheart had tried to single-handedly retake Stull City with his army of the dead. They were terrifying, and their huge numbers made them difficult to stop, but a shaky-camera view showed something bigger, more powerful, and more terrifying wipe them out completely.

The battle was a scene of complete panic for everyone who wasn't a UM. Pravus's other minions looked just as terrified as Fraze Coldheart's troops. In the background, we saw Pravus's minions flying through the air, having been swept aside with a mighty paw, just as the zombies had been. The UMs were fighting because that's what they liked to do. Pravus didn't really have control of them, and the rest of his army was suffering because of it.

The room was still. I don't think that anyone had ever seen a monster so powerful or devastating. The UMs had just taken out an army that was feared throughout the continent in minutes.

If Dr. Pravus's Undefeatable Minions could do that, only the vaskor could stop them.

CHAPTER 35

If you remember the first rule of Hiding Treasure,
you might guess where Critchlore hid the gold.
—HINT: *POLAR DISTRESS*, CHAPTER THIRTY-ONE

D r. Critchlore broke the silence. "Can't say I'm sad to see that," he said. "Fraze Coldheart is a brutal, vicious ruler."

"Was," Coach Foley said. "He's done now."

Professor Zaida came over and pulled Ron and me aside. "I've just talked with Seizemore," she said. "Did you know he's asking to be called 'The Commandant'?" We nodded. "He doesn't know I have you both here. He does know I'm a Covert Librarian, and that I'm in contact with other rebel groups."

"What did he say?" Ron asked.

"He said that he's now leading the united rebel group himself, and he expects my support. He told me the prince ran away from him, and he's desperate to find him. He presented himself as the long-suffering caretaker of a really difficult and delusional prince who is a danger to others."

Ron shook his head.

"Seizemore admitted that he took Runt away because he wanted to use him in his old role as doppelganger. The safety of his beloved, if troubled, prince is so important to him. He's worried you boys may have misinterpreted his actions. Everything he's done has been for the safety of the prince."

"Ha!" we both said.

"To prove his point, he sent me a video of the prince behaving in a way that would have anyone believe he was completely evil."

"It's all lies," Ron said. "You know that, right?"

"I believe that, yes," she said. "But it was a very well-made video. He's positioning himself as the best option to lead the rebels, and to lead a reunited Andirat, while the prince gets the help he so desperately needs. Seizemore was a close advisor to the royal family, with privileged knowledge of how they ruled so successfully for so long."

"My father was going to fire him before the coup," Ron said.

"Unfortunately, nobody knows that," Zaida went on. "Seizemore wants to join with Dr. Pravus, because Pravus is going to defeat the EOs, and he must be on the winning side. He thinks Pravus will be so grateful for our support that he'll respect our wishes to reclaim Erudyten, which is absurd. He never will."

"Did you tell him that?" I asked.

"No. I told him it was a great plan," she said. "Egomaniacs love praise."

That was true. It's one of the first things you learn as a minion.

"Plus, I don't want him to know I can see through his lies." She turned to Ron. "He finished the call by telling me that he hoped I wasn't helping you, Your Highness. He said that if he found out I was in contact with either of you, and didn't tell him, then he would make sure that the Covert Librarian Order was squashed out of existence."

"He threatened you?" Ron asked.

Professor Zaida nodded. "He must be stopped. I've heard from the EO Council that they are offering to surrender control of Riggen, Fraze Coldheart's realm, in return for help from Andirat. The United Armies of Andirat, should they actually unite, could regain part of Erudyten by coming here and helping defeat Pravus. It's a fantastic opportunity for our people.

"But we have to stop Seizemore from taking over and ordering his army to help Pravus," she said.

"How?" Ron asked.

"I need to contact Cordholm," she said. "But it's been impossible, since he's traveling. I have to get the word out that Seizemore can't be trusted. But everything is mayhem right now, thanks to Pravus."

Over the next two days we waited for the vaskor to grow, and I watched the ring around my neck get darker and darker. Swallowing became difficult. My friends tried to keep me distracted, but it was hard not to feel overwhelmed with doom.

Meanwhile, after seeing Fraze Coldheart's army so easily defeated, two EO armies quickly surrendered to Pravus: Delpha and Euripidam, countries that bordered Stull. Despite those victories, Dr. Pravus was growing crueler, maybe because his control of the news outlets was slipping. Fugitive websites showed footage of dead Pravus defectors wearing orange cuffs.

Or maybe he was panicking. Another site posted a video of three UMs destroying the Eye of Pravus, his award-winning building, which was further proof that he didn't have complete control of the UMs, because he loved that building. There was a rumor that a few UMs had returned to Carkley to destroy Lord Vengecrypt's castle. Pravus claimed he had sent them there, but we doubted that was true.

Even *The Pravus Projects* had taken a dark turn. Pravus's tone had gone from "You have nothing to fear" to "Anyone who stands against me will suffer greatly." And the reward for the capture of Dr. Critchlore had gone up to two gold bars.

"He's desperate to capture you," Professor Murphy said. "Why?"

"The longer I'm free, the better my chance of figuring out that we have an army that could defeat his. He can't control his UMs, as we've seen."

"I don't get it," Murphy went on. "He has the witch. Why won't she perform the spell for him?"

"He must not be able to meet her demands," Professor Zaida said.

I caught Dr. Critchlore's eyes, and he made the money sign by rubbing his thumb and fingers together.

"Are the vaskor large enough to attack yet?" Murphy asked.

"Almost," Coach Foley answered. "And we've found a soft spot in the UMs' hides, right between the shoulder blades. That's where the vaskor have to inject the antidotes."

"There's just one problem," Dr. Critchlore said. "As soon as Pravus sees the vaskor coming for his UMs, he might do something desperate."

"Like what?" Professor Zaida asked.

"He might kill the witch himself," he said. "He knows the vaskor are under a spell of obedience. Pravus controlled them for years before Runt lured them away from him. He probably knows that they're pacifists, that they won't fight if the spell is broken. If we are to defeat his army, we need the element of surprise. A misdirection of some kind. So that he doesn't notice until it's too late."

As my time grew shorter, I realized I wanted Pravus to kill the witch. I wanted to live.

But I knew I had no choice. I couldn't let him take over the continent, killing masses of people and monsters along the way. I would be dooming everyone to life ruled by a monster and his loyalty cuffs.

At last the vaskor were ready, and Dr. Critchlore said it was time to contact Pravus. We were called back to the conference room as he prepared to make the call.

"The plan is to lure Dr. Pravus away from Stull City," Dr. Critchlore told us, "so our vaskor can inject his UMs with the antidote." He stood up and started pacing. "I will offer to meet him at my school to give him the trophy in exchange for my people, my school, and the witch."

"He'll never relinquish them," Professor Murphy said. "You'll be walking into a trap."

"I know. But I *will* be a distraction," Dr. Critchlore said. "We just need to distract him long enough to defeat his army in Stull City."

Dr. Critchlore was going to sacrifice himself. He was going to walk right into the trap of his worst enemy just so the vaskor would have a small chance to defeat Pravus's UMs. He opened his computer to call Dr. Pravus. It didn't take long, and soon that evil man's smiling face appeared on the screen.

"All right, Thiago," Dr. Critchlore said. "I hear you've put a price on my head. I'm willing to turn myself over to you in exchange for the release of my people."

Dr. Pravus chuckled. "Say it, Derek."

"Say what?"

"Tell me that I've won," he said, leaning forward. "I have everything that was yours. Your school, your top scientist, the woman you love, and your beloved ward. I beat you."

"Fine," Critchlore said. "You won. Now can I have my people back?"

"I suppose I could be the bigger man and release them, but I'd need something in return. Hmm, what would be a good token of your defeat?" He pretended to think about this for a few seconds. "I know, give me the Top Student trophy and I'll let them go. It's rightfully mine. You know it and I know it. Give it to me, and I'll let you live. I'll let Syke live."

"Counteroffer," Dr. Critchlore said. "I want the witch you lured out of Skelterdam to remove the curses on Runt Higgins."

"Denied," Dr. Pravus said. "Dismorda was actually quite pleased when she sensed that third tether activate. If he dies by her hand, then the vaskor will belong to her. That's how the spell works. If the vaskor's master is defeated, then they must obey the person who defeated him. Your young prince is the last ruler of those beasts."

I wasn't, actually, and I found it interesting that his good friend Seizemore hadn't told him about the real prince. Maybe Seizemore didn't trust Pravus after all.

"I want to see them," Dr. Critchlore said. "Dr. Frankenhammer and Syke."

"Also denied." Dr. Pravus sighed. "You're in no position to make demands. I'll give you twenty-four hours to come to Stull City. If you don't, I'll kill them and destroy your school."

"Do that, and I'll keep this," Dr. Critchlore said, holding up the trophy. Dr. Pravus leaned forward, his expression showing just how desperately he wanted it. He recovered quickly, but we'd all seen it.

"We'll make the exchange at my school," Critchlore said. "The trophy for my people."

"No," Dr. Pravus said. "Somewhere neutral."

I whispered in Dr. Critchlore's ear.

"The Andiratian embassy, then," Dr. Critchlore said. "In Castle Valley."

Dr. Pravus's smile grew wider. "Deal. Tomorrow. Noon." He disconnected, and the screen went black.

Professor Murphy stood up. "Dismorda wants to control the vaskor, and she thinks she'll have them when Runt dies."

"But she's wrong," I said. "Why can't we tell her about Ron?"

"I don't want Pravus to know that just yet," Dr. Critchlore said. "He thinks he's close to getting the witch to perform that spell—a spell that will give him complete control of an undefeatable army. The only obstacle in his way is our vaskor. But he's greedy. He thinks he can have them all."

I felt sick. I didn't want to force the vaskor to fight, and I didn't want to die, but my time was running out.

Dr. Critchlore stood up. "We have four goals: Get the witch to remove Runt's curses, keep her from performing the curse of obedience for Dr. Pravus, rescue Syke and Dr. Frankenhammer, and defeat Pravus's UMs.

"Dr. Pravus keeps Dismorda close, so they will both be at the embassy in twenty-four hours. He'll bring Syke and Dr. Frankenhammer as well, knowing I'll need to see them before I make the trade. My spies say that most of Pravus's UMs are in Stull City. His other minions bring in trucks of food for them daily.

"I'll take the trophy and bargain for the hostages. While I'm distracting Pravus, a team led by Professors Twilk and Dunkirk will try to locate Dr. Frankenhammer and Syke at the embassy. Runt, you and Prince Auberon will provide them with the castle's layout. Meanwhile, Coach Foley will lead the vaskor into Stull City and surprise the UMs. Once we defeat Pravus, we'll convince the witch to come here. We have everything that Pravus could have promised her."

"I want to go," I said. "I want to talk to the witch."

"You must stay here, Runt," he said, "with Professor Zaida and the prince. Do not leave this mountain."

CHAPTER 36

Creative Complimenting, Fawning Flattery, and Groveling
—MUST-HAVE SKILLS FOR MINIONS

Dr. Critchlore and his team left that evening, taking two of the school's vans that had been hidden at the Kobold Academy.

I sat in the old Natherly shrine, which was now empty. The statues of famous Natherlys that used to sit in the alcoves along the hallway were gone. So was the life-sized family portrait at the end. Everything had been moved to the new location of the Great Library.

Ron joined me.

"Hey," he said, sitting beside me.

"Hey."

"I don't want you to die, friend," he said.

I nodded. I didn't want me to die, either. "When I first came here and Professor Zaida told me I was the missing prince of Andirat, I wasn't super happy about that," I said. "I finally knew who I was, but my family was gone. All of them. Gone. I felt as empty as this hallway is now, and so alone. Now I know that I'm not the prince. And that the life I'd imagined for myself over these last few months is gone. I don't know who I am, and I feel like I'm nobody."

"Listen," Ron said. "I thought that too, when I met you. That you were a nobody. But since I've been with you, I know I was wrong. You are a leader, Runt. At the embassy, you gathered allies around you—the manticores, the ghosts, George. George could have helped me escape months ago, but I'd treated her so badly. You shared your cookies and told her stories. And as a result, she was willing to risk the wrath of the Commandant to help you."

I shrugged.

"And then at your school, creature after creature came to your aid—those trees, that giant gorilla, the mer-fellow, the guy with the bugs, Syke."

"They're not creatures," I said. "They're my friends."

"I know," he said.

"And you are too."

"I know. And here I am, realizing that *I'd* do anything to save you from this curse. Why should I care? You're the son of a lowly castle worker. Why do I care?"

"Because it's the prince's duty to care about his people," I said.

"That's right. It is. And you taught me that. So, thank you." He handed me my medallion, now on a new chain.

"Thanks," I said, putting it on. The medallion had always been my only tie to my past, and it felt good to have it back.

Thumping footsteps echoed down the corridor. We looked up to see Darthin, Frankie, Boris, and Eloni sprinting around the corner to find us. Darthin squeezed between me and Ron and opened his laptop. "I think I saw something," he said. "Pravus is already at the Andiratian embassy. Look at this."

He showed us a video taken by one of Pravus's ahools. The aerial view started near the front gate, then swept over the field in front, over the giant *E* and *A* made of flowers in the grass, and the topiary animals. The camera flew over the massive castle, and we saw the backyard, the gardens, and the lake. The ahool turned around and approached the back of the castle.

The terrace was filled with Pravus minions. Dr. Pravus himself stood with a group of officers, looking like he was giving commands. A huge, black-hooded man stood behind Pravus, holding a scythe.

"There'll be a special episode for tomorrow evening," Dr. Pravus's voiceover said. "I'm going to show everyone what happens to those who stand against me. Stay tuned."

"He's going to broadcast Dr. Critchlore's execution," I said.

"Yes, but keep watching," Darthin said as the camera swept closer to the castle. I could see the third-floor balconies. "There!" He froze the image and we all saw her. The small, stooped figure standing on my old balcony, her face a map of sores.

"She's in my room!" I said. "Er . . . Ron's room."

"I have an idea," Ron said. "You, Sara, and I go back to the embassy. We'll get George to sneak us into my room. We can tell Dismorda that her plan won't work. We'll explain that she won't have the vaskor, because you freed them all already. You can order Sara to do something and she'll refuse."

Darthin nodded. "She needs to know that as soon as Dr. Pravus finds out that we have the UMs, he'll probably kill her."

"And that Critchlore will keep her safe, if she removes your curses," Frankie said.

And we could also tell her that Critchlore had the gold that Pravus was planning to pay her with. It was all so logical. I stood up as I thought it through. I could sneak back into the embassy, of course I could. I could get into that room, easy. This could work. We just had to get back to Castle Valley.

We heard footsteps running our way, the click of boots on the floor echoing in the cavernous space. We all stood up, ready to face what was coming.

It was Syke, back to normal size. She raced right past us, heading for the conference room, but I shouted at her and she skidded to a stop.

"Runt, thank the Goddess." She put her hands on her knees as she caught her breath.

"You escaped," I said. "How?"

"Victus is an idiot," she said. "Where's Critchlore?"

"He went to bargain for you and Dr. Frankenhammer," I said. "With the trophy."

"We have to stop him," she said. "Pravus is going to kill him. And Dr. Frankenhammer went back to Critchlore's. I freed him."

"How'd you get here?" I asked.

"Kumi," she said, still panting. "He's resting near the river." She collapsed onto the bench seat next to mine. "I'm so tired. And hungry. Tell me what's been happening."

Frankie dashed to the kitchen while we recapped Critchlore's plan. He was back with a huge plate of food before I finished my second sentence.

"Before I left," Syke said, grabbing a bagel, "I managed to spy on Pravus and Victus and that angry, sour-faced weasel-man who's following Pravus around."

"Seizemore," Ron and I said at the same time.

"He and Pravus, they're panicking. Big time." She took a bite and we waited while she chewed. "Those UMs think they've done enough to repay Pravus for saving them. They want to go back to Carkley and retake their home. Pravus has agreed, but wants them to come for one last 'Thank you' banquet in Stull City. He says he'll give them enough sudithium so they can stay huge and defeat Vengecrypt. Do you have some water?"

Frankie dashed around the corner and was back in a flash holding a water bottle.

"Thanks." She took a long drink and continued eating.

"Pravus plans to spell them before they leave," Ron said. "At the banquet."

"And then he'll control them forever," Syke said. "We have to stop him."

I watched Syke take another bite, and an idea popped into my head. "A banquet for the UMs. Guys, it's perfect! What if we put the antidotes in a food they all love? We could sneak it into the banquet."

"Ingesting the antidote would work," Darthin said. "But their food supply is guarded by Pravus minions."

"But this banquet will be the perfect cover. We could get Sara and a few other vaskor to carry the tainted food right into Stull City, and say it was a special surprise for the banquet. She looks just like a UM, and she'll be coming with food, so they won't raise an alarm."

"What food?" Syke asked.

I knew what food. After being fed a diet of meat from Dr. Pravus for all those years, Sara craved doughnuts. *Who doesn't love doughnuts?* she'd asked me. Pravus's UMs might feel the same craving.

"Burkeve is right on the other side of this mountain," I said. "The land of giants. We find a bakery and get as many huge doughnuts as we can."

We continued to plan, and I felt my whole body fill up with excitement. It was so much better to be working on something rather than just sitting around waiting for my throat to feel tight. I had to keep moving, keep fighting. Dr. Critchlore had to understand that.

Frankie and Eloni volunteered to get the giant doughnuts from Burkeve and take them to where Coach Foley was hiding with both the vaskor and the antidotes, near Ogre Rock. They planned to recruit Frieda and the other ogre-men to help carry all that food. Everyone was sick of being stuck inside and eager to do something, anything.

"Find Penelope," I told Eloni. "She's a second-year girl from Burkeve. Ask her where the nearest giant bakery is and get as many huge doughnuts as you and the others can carry. Syke, while they're getting the doughnuts, you run ahead and tell Coach Foley about this new plan."

Syke smiled. "Got it."

"The prince and I will sneak into the embassy and try to convince the witch to switch sides," I said, standing up. "Everybody ready?"

Ron came out of a closet wearing the ceremonial Andiratian royal attire—a long, pale-blue jacket trimmed with dark-green piping over black slacks. The jacket had gold cuffs and epaulets, a dark-green sash, and quite a few medals hanging from his chest. A ceremonial sword hung at his hip.

"Are we playing dress-up now?" I asked him.

He stood a little prouder, side-glancing at Syke. "Professor Zaida hasn't shipped everything from this mountain," he said. "This was my brother's. I thought I'd like to feel like a prince before we begin our attack. It might be the only chance I ever get."

"You look very nice," Syke said, and Ron beamed. "Very commanding."

He *did* look commanding. I smiled, because our plan just might work. But then Ron tripped over his sword.

CHAPTER 37

A minion's work is never done.

—ANCIENT MINION PROVERB

We knew Critchlore wasn't planning to meet with Dr. Pravus until the full twenty-four hours was up, to delay as long as possible and give his team a chance to find out where Dr. Pravus was keeping his hostages.

I wanted to arrive at the embassy before dawn, and before Dr. Critchlore. Hopefully we'd be able to find him and tell him about Syke and Dr. Frankenhammer. Hector, a seventh-year hobgoblin I'd met in detention, was going to drive us back to Castle Valley in one of the vans so we could sneak into the embassy and find Dismorda.

Syke came up from the forest to wish us luck.

"You know what to do?" I asked her.

"Don't worry about me."

"I'm not," I said. "And I think our prince has a bit of a crush on you."

"I know," she said, looking over at him. "If only he weren't so goofy-looking."

"Hey," I said, because he looked just like me. She laughed.

"Syke?" I wasn't sure how I was going to say what I wanted to say, but I knew I had to say it.

"Yeah?"

"I just want you to know, in case anything happens . . . You're my best friend."

"And you're mine," she said. "Bestie." Then she punched me on the shoulder. "Go on, you can do this."

I smiled and got in the van.

We drove through the night. As we neared the embassy, we saw a long line of trucks carrying Pravus minions heading slowly through the embassy's arched entryway. Pravus was readying the place for a full-scale assault, it seemed.

"Are you sure you want to do this?" I asked the kid who was my perfect reflection. We were dressed in black, with matching beanies. He nodded.

It was still dark when we jumped out of the van, well before the gate. I found the brick with the scratch mark, the one that hid the button to open the entrance in the wall, and we snuck through. I didn't see any patrols this far from the gate, but we moved slowly and carefully through the woods, just in case.

As we neared the front of the castle, I saw that it was crowded with Pravus's minions: ogres and werewolves and humans, with more coming up the road. Pravus's ogres were pushing Seizemore's own ogres away from the entrance so they could take their places. The Seizemore troops were fighting back. Some humans were trying to settle them down, while the smart ones just stayed clear of the shoving match.

It was a good distraction, and we were able to race undetected through the forest by the edge of the field. We reached the stables, and I saw that the door had been barred from the outside, but nobody was guarding it.

I unbarred the door and we slipped inside. The manticores weren't the only ones locked up in here. Mrs. Ambrose, George, and some other loyal embassy staff were huddled near the door. Professors Dunkirk and Twilk were there too. I guess their hostage rescue operation had failed.

Everyone was asleep. I shook George awake, and then nodded for her to join us outside.

"George," I whispered. "We need to sneak into my room. Can you help?"

"I knew you'd come back to save us," she said. She called down one of the gargoyles with a whistle. "Rothor can take you up, one at a time. You want me to come with yourselfs?"

"No, stay here," I said. "Leave the door unbarred, but wait a few hours before letting anyone out, okay?"

She nodded, gave my leg a hug, bowed to my partner, and slipped back inside.

"I'll go first, okay?" I said, stepping into the gargoyle's arms. Once we were both on the terrace, I said, "Let me do the talking. You stay safely outside this window. She only needs to see you. If I give a signal, yell for Rothor and escape."

"Got it." He nodded. He'd been very quiet this whole trip. I began to feel a little antsy. This was too dangerous. Maybe I should have left him safely back at the library.

Rothor opened the door with a claw, and I quietly edged inside.

Dismorda was sitting up in bed, looking so tiny and frail amid the giant pillows that I didn't notice her at first.

"Enchantress," I said as I entered the room. My heart raced. This was it. This was my one chance to live.

She turned to look at me, this incredibly old woman with a wrinkled face covered in sores from living in the poisonous air of Skelterdam. She reached for something on the nightstand next to her.

I raised my arms in the air. "Is that a wand?" I asked as she pointed it at me.

"This? No," she said. "But don't come any closer."

I lowered my arms. "I'm Runt Higgins, the kid you cursed. I don't want to hurt you."

"As if you could," she rasped. She squinted as she looked at me. "Not too bright . . . are you? Letting the tether . . . activate three times." She talked very slowly, as if each word took enormous effort to utter.

"My friends needed me," I said. "I don't regret it."

She harrumphed at that.

"I don't want to die," I said, pleading now.

"You don't have . . . much time, Runt . . . Is your throat . . . feeling tight?"

"Yes. Please lift the curse."

"No. I am waiting . . . for you to die," she said. "Then I'll have my vaskor . . . and my safety."

"The vaskor won't be yours," I said. "The real prince Auberon lives." I nodded to the balcony, where my friend stood safely just outside.

She squinted her eyes at me, looking from one of us to the other. She seemed to deflate. "Moira told me," she said. "I didn't believe her . . . but she was right . . . I'll never be safe."

"Yes, you will," I said. "Remove all your curses. Can't you see? Your desire for revenge has hurt you more than the people you've cursed." I pointed to the mirror above the fireplace. "Look at what's become of you. Cursing has rotted you out from the inside."

She looked in the mirror, sadness plain on her face.

"Lift the curses," I said.

"I cannot," she said. "I've made promises. My safety—"

"I'll make sure of your safety."

"So promises the little boy," she said with a scoff.

"I have the vaskor. I can order them to protect you."

"I'd sooner believe . . . the promise of a toad," she said. "Everyone lies to me."

"Let me prove it to you," I said. "Anything. I'll do it."

"I need the gold . . . that Dr. Pravus promised me," she said.

"He doesn't have the gold," I said. "Critchlore does."

"And Dr. Pravus . . . will soon have Critchlore . . . won't he? Pravus is the most powerful person . . . in this game. I always choose to side . . . with the most powerful."

"What if we defeat him?"

"Defeat Pravus?" She cackled at that, then reached for her wand. "Sure . . . do that . . . and I'll remove the curses."

"Please," I said, stepping closer. "Lift my curse. You cursed me by mistake, I know you did. You meant to curse him." I nodded outside. Ever since I'd met Ron, and saw what a brat he was, I knew that the curse I bore was meant for him.

"No, child . . ." she said. "The curse was meant for you. I don't make mistakes."

Before I could ask her why, the door to the room slammed shut. I turned and saw Seizemore standing next to it. He'd heard our conversation.

CHAPTER 38

Don't bite the hand that feeds you. Please.

—SIGN INSIDE THE MANTICORE STABLE

Dismorda laughed again. "It's not a wand," she said, waving her device. "It's my emergency call button . . . in case I fall . . . and cannot get up."

I ran for the balcony door, but Seizemore's voice stopped me cold.

"Leave now and you'll die without ever knowing why you were cursed," he said.

I kept my hand on the door, but turned to him. "Tell me then," I said. "What did I ever do to her?"

"Is that the prince out there?" he asked. "What were you planning?" He stepped forward, so I opened the door. He held up his hands and backed up. "Ah, you wanted to show Dismorda that the vaskor would not be hers." He called out, "Come inside, Your Majesty."

"He's fine where he is," I said. "Just tell me why I was cursed."

"You were cursed," he said, turning back to me, his face ablaze with hatred. "Because *you* are the boy who ruined *everything*."

"What are you talking about? I was four when I showed up at Critchlore's with the curse."

Seizemore walked over to the fireplace, turning a knob that lit the fire. He sat in one of the wingback chairs, never taking his gaze off me. I stayed near the balcony door, ready to bolt if he made any sudden move.

"I was a chess master," he said. In the firelight his narrow face was filled with shadows, and he looked more sinister than the ghost who haunted this room. "I had all my pieces perfectly positioned. The king and his family had been taken out by my pawns."

"The generals," I said.

"Yes. I suspected they might turn on me, but I was prepared. I'm always prepared. The generals wanted to cut me out and rule Andirat themselves. But I had a plan to ensure their loyalty.

"Days earlier I had contacted an old classmate for help. He's a brilliant minion trainer, and a trusted friend."

"Pravus."

"Correct. He came to Andirat just before the coup, and together we concocted a brilliant plan. He'd been researching the Unde-featable Minions, and he'd heard rumors that the beasts could be controlled by a spell of obedience. That spell had been outlawed for centuries, but he knew of a witch who would perform it on the generals, for a price. Once spelled, they would obey me, and I would control the mighty armies of Andirat. I would then use my power to help Pravus defeat the EOs. We would split the realms on the Porvian Continent. I would get the four realms that made up Erudyten, he would get the rest."

"That sounds like a good plan," I said, remembering Professor

Zaida's approach to dealing with egomaniacs. I wasn't going to tell him what I really thought: that only a fool would trust Pravus. "What happened?"

"The royal family was killed, except for the young prince," he said. "I assured the generals that I would take care of him myself and bring his lifeless body to the clearing. Of course, I was lying. I had planned to keep the prince, for insurance. I was going to bring *your* lifeless body instead, but your father had hidden you away."

With the dogs. I gasped as the memory came back to me.

"Still, I had everything in place. The generals insisted on watching the burial of the royal family, which was perfect, because I'd have them all together. We'd chosen a clearing just outside the castle wall. The king and his family would be buried in a hidden grave. No shrine, no place to worship them. Dismorda was waiting in the shadows to perform the spell. She just needed a flicker of moonlight.

"We'd brought some castle workers with us, to dig the graves. But we hadn't told them what they'd been brought there to do."

The witch cackled.

"One of the workers pulled back the sheet covering the largest body. This worker was a big, strong man, but when he saw the king's corpse, he fell to his knees like a child, crying. Pathetic.

"He threw down his shovel and refused to dig. The generals beat him, but still he refused."

"He was loyal," Dismorda said. "Like the dogs he trained."

"Oh, no," I whispered. I saw it too. I had been there, hidden in the trees. I had watched them beat my father. I must have blocked the memory.

"They beat him with their fists, with the shovels, with their boots," Seizemore said, watching me wince with every word. "It was perfect. The generals were distracted just as the clouds, were parting. The clearing was bathed in moonlight."

I felt my whole body fill with rage. While my father was suffering, all Seizemore could think about was how the beating was helping his plan.

"I saw Dismorda raise her arms and begin her chant," he went on. "I was about to have everything!"

"*We* were going to have . . . everything," Dismorda said.

"But then a high-pitched wail echoed through the woods and a small boy raced into the clearing, heading for the unconscious, bloody man. The boy was followed by a pack of dogs, who trampled over Dismorda, dragging her into view."

"They were mountain dogs," the witch said. "Huge, disgusting beasts."

"You threw yourself over your bloody, unconscious father," Seizemore went on. "The generals' men came forward to intercept the dogs, and they saw Dismorda. Of course they recognized her. Everyone in Andirat knew her. She tried to finish her spell, but the generals' men grabbed her arms. She looked to me and then they knew. The generals knew what I'd been planning.

"They forgot about the disobedient houndsman and his pathetic, crying brat of a son. Now they were focused on me. Just like that"—he snapped his fingers—"I'd gone from having everything, to being a dead man. Because of *you*."

"What happened?" I asked, but I knew. Someone had lifted me

from my father's unconscious body. I'd kicked and screamed, but strong hands had covered my mouth and pulled me away.

"Pravus saved us," Seizemore said. "He created a distraction and we escaped. He grabbed you, thinking you were the prince. I hadn't told him that I'd already shipped the real prince overseas, to safety. You were still wearing his parade clothes. Pravus then helped us leave Andirat.

"I wanted to kill you," he went on. "But that wouldn't be punishment enough. You had to suffer. Better to have you die once you'd learned to appreciate life. I paid Dismorda to curse you. And then I had my henchman take you to a family in Stull who'd agreed to keep you for a fee. Later I found out my man had kept the fee himself and left you at a minion school instead. I just didn't know which one."

I looked at Dismorda. "You cursed me to die because I protected my father?"

"I was happy to do it," she said. "Plus . . . he gave me quite a bit . . . of gold."

"What happened to my father?"

"The generals should have given him a medal," Seizemore said with a laugh. "It was thanks to you that they were saved from the spell. But they aren't smart enough to see beyond their own egos. They probably threw him into jail. Or killed him.

"After that, Dismorda had an even higher price on her head, so she fled to Skelterdam, where no bounty hunter could reach her. I took the real prince to the Forgotten Realm." He paused and we stared at each other in silence. "How foolish you were to come back here. Dismorda, I think we have stalled him long enough."

She nodded.

"Stalled me?" I asked. They were both smiling in a way that filled me with panic. The room door burst open and Mr. Fox stepped inside. I rushed out to the balcony, and right into the arms of a flying monkey. Four more hid in the shadows, surrounding my friend.

"Kill the prince," Dismorda said. "If he's alive when Runt dies . . . the vaskor will go to him . . . instead of me. I only have enough strength . . . for the spell. Or I'd kill him . . . myself."

"We'll go to the capital," Seizemore said. "I will bravely fight off Pravus's guards, risking my life to save the prince. Sadly, I will be unsuccessful. The prince will die, but my heroics will be broadcast live, and the people of Andirat will see me as a hero."

To me, he said, "You will get to watch your friend die before you." He laughed. "This has worked out better than I could have imagined!

"Take them to the vans," Seizemore yelled.

CHAPTER 39

We're doomed.

—SOMEONE WAS THINKING THIS

Dawn had broken, and the monkeys flew us down to the front of the castle. We were thrown into a van that already held two prisoners: Dr. Critchlore and Mistress Moira.

"Mistress Moira," I said. "You're not . . . you weren't . . ."

"She was pretending to fall in love with Pravus in order to gain information," Dr. Critchlore said. "I knew it all along."

"I needed to stay close to Dismorda," she said. "To try to convince her to remove your spells."

"I guess your plans didn't go well, either," I said to both of them.

"I wasn't expecting to see you two here," Dr. Critchlore said. "I thought I told you to remain where you were."

"I wanted to know why I was cursed. And I thought we could convince Dismorda that my death wouldn't give her the vaskor," I said. "I brought the prince to prove it."

"Ah," he said, nodding. "But didn't you realize that if they caught you, they could just kill you both? Come to think of it, why haven't they?"

"They're going to kill him at the capital, where Pravus's cameras can record Seizemore trying to save his life," I said. "When the curse kills me, the vaskor will have to obey Dismorda, because I'll have been their last ruler."

"And once that happens," he said, "she'll cast the spell for Pravus, and the Undefeatable Minions will be completely in his control."

Two large guards jumped into the van, then the van door slammed shut and we were off.

"Syke and Dr. Frankenhammer are safe," I said.

"Good. Did you at least get your answer?" he asked. "About why you were cursed?"

"Yes," I said. "Apparently I ruined everything for Seizemore, Pravus, and the witch eight years ago."

He smiled. "I would have expected nothing less from you. Well done."

We rode on in silence.

Getting to the EO Council Building was tricky, because the roads had been destroyed by the UMs, but we followed Dr. Pravus's truck as it zigzagged slowly around potholes and chunks of demolished buildings. It was torture, heading toward our doom at such a slow crawl. It gave me time to think about all the mistakes I'd made, starting with the kid sitting next to me. Why had I brought him? He could die because of my stupidity.

Pravus stood on the flatbed, using a megaphone and every ounce of charisma he had to get the UMs to follow him.

"Well done, my loyal friends!" he shouted. "I saved your lives and you've repaid me by destroying everything in your path! Just like I asked you to! Let me show you how grateful I am! I will give you enough sudithium to help you conquer any land you want! Come to the park in front of the EO Council Building and we'll feast!"

He repeated this message as we drove through Castle Valley and into Stull City. A few enormous monsters followed us, and my pulse quickened at the sight of them.

We reached the city square, and the devastation there was unbelievable. The EO Council Building was the only structure still standing. The library, the government office buildings, the museum, and the performing arts center were all reduced to rubble. Smoke rose from multiple fires, filling the air.

My throat, my chest, everything felt tight as we slowly moved through the wreckage. I couldn't understand why anyone would unleash so much destruction on the world.

As we neared the EO Council Building, we could see that the park was filled with UMs. Every instinct in my body was screaming "RUN!" But the guard sitting next to me was not going to let that happen.

The monsters were restless, shoving each other for room on the field. A few were still smashing defenseless buildings with huge chunks of concrete. The bangs echoed through the smoky air.

Rubble covered everything, and soon our road became impassable, so we climbed out, surrounded by guards. We prisoners were forced to follow Dr. Pravus and his guards as he walked down a cleared pathway to the EO Council Building. The huge, angry UMs were on our left. I could feel their breath on us. On our right, row after row of troops were lined up where buildings had once stood. There had to be thousands of soldiers, all saluting Dr. Pravus as he walked by.

These were the massive armies of the two realms who'd surrendered: Delpha and Euripidam. I noticed most of the soldiers wore the orange loyalty cuffs. His own minions, dressed in their green uniforms, stood closer to the EO Council Building.

Pravus strutted at the head of our procession, keeping his focus on the stage that had been set up facing the park. There was a microphone stand in the center, and giant speakers and cameras flanking the sides. His elite, black-clad guards and the EO Council Building served as a backdrop.

I turned to look at Dr. Critchlore, but his face was unreadable. I knew he was feeling what I was feeling—despair, anger, fear, and helplessness, but he wasn't going to let Pravus see him defeated.

As we climbed the steps, I looked for any sign of my friends. While planning, I hadn't factored in the size of Pravus's army, and it was huge. *One mistake is all it takes*, kept repeating through my thoughts. My throat tightened so much I couldn't breathe, and it already felt like I was breathing through a straw.

A rumbling hum approached the city center, and we saw a line of flatbed trucks approach the blocked area. They were piled high with food, some of it falling off the sides.

The guard next to me grabbed my arm to keep me from moving. Pravus walked straight to Dismorda, who was standing at the top of the steps, waiting to cast her spell. The guards led Dr. Critchlore to the front of the stage, next to the microphone and the hooded executioner. The rest of us were pushed into a group of guards off to the side. We would have a front-row view of his execution.

The Pravus minion next to me nudged me on the shoulder. I looked up into Rufus's face, the big traitor. "I knew you weren't a prince," he said. "What a joke, the lamest kid in school, a prince?"

He was wearing an orange cuff, and I felt more pity than anger for him. But mostly I felt light-headed and weak, my throat tightening with every breath now. I looked up at Mistress Moira, standing next to me. A tear fell from her eye.

"It's okay," I whispered.

She grabbed my hand, squeezing it. "I'm sorry I failed, Runt. I'm so sorry."

"We haven't failed," I said. "Not yet." I wasn't going to give up until I took my last breath.

Dr. Pravus removed the trophy from a bag and approached the microphone. The minions on stage snapped to attention, and the monsters on the field quieted down. Before he reached the microphone, Seizemore grabbed him by the arms.

"Finally, Thiago," he said. "It's all going to be ours."

"Yes, my friend," Pravus said with a huge smile. "Are you ready? My man will kill the prince while you valiantly try to save him. The cameras will catch it all."

"Perfect. Andirat is filled with posters that say, 'We Want the Prince!' Soon they'll say, 'We Want Seizemore!' I'll show them what true leadership looks like. Let's do this."

He moved to the side of the stage, crossing right in front of me. I tried to trip him, but the guards pulled me back. Seizemore made it

to his spot and practiced an expression of anguish while mouthing "NO!" Then he shook his head, like he wasn't satisfied with his acting, and tried again. I felt sick and looked away.

Dismorda looked to the sky. The moon was a faint crescent in the early-morning light. She was ready to cast her spell.

Pravus strutted to the center of the stage. He was full of smirking self-confidence as he approached Critchlore, who stood tall and defiant in front of him.

"I'm so glad you'll be able to watch," Pravus said. "This is the moment I will get everything I've ever dreamed of, enough power to rule the world. And you . . . you will die."

"You're a sick man, Thiago," Critchlore said. "You destroyed a beautiful city so you could rule a pile of rubble. Congratulations."

"I'll rebuild it," Pravus said. "Pity you won't be around to see it."

"Well, it's been a good life," Dr. Critchlore said. "I only have one regret."

"Only one?"

"Yes," he said, nodding to the trophy. "I was hoping to live long enough to see your face when you travel to the Ventorgen Caves and discover your father's fortune . . . gone."

Dr. Pravus frowned. He fiddled with the trophy and pulled out the map. His face paled as he realized Critchlore had discovered the trophy's secret.

Dr. Critchlore smiled. "Look at that. I guess I have no regrets after all."

Dr. Pravus crumpled the map and threw it to the ground. "You think I won't get it out of you? Besides, soon I'll control them, and

I'll be able to take anything I want." He pointed to the UMs, who had finished off the food on the trucks and were looking around for more.

One of the monsters smashed an empty truck trying to leave. They were still hungry. Pravus's other minions surged closer to the stage, trying to put some distance between themselves and the UMs, in case the monsters mistook them for part of the food offering. I saw quite a few minions—the uncuffed ones—flee the area in panic.

Pravus noticed too. He raised his hand, which held a small, black device. "If any of you flee, you'll regret it!"

"Thiago, the spell," Seizemore said. "We need to do it now, before those UMs eat us all."

"Guard, bring the prince," Pravus said, then he beckoned his executioner closer.

A guard yanked me forward, but Seizemore shook his head. "Not him, the other one. Rufus, take him over to Pravus."

Rufus nudged me out of the way as he grabbed the boy next to me. I felt the blood rush out of my head. My heart raced as I reached out to grab my friend, but the guards pulled me away. He was going to die, because of me.

What had I done?

CHAPTER 40

A fool and his minions are soon parted.

—ANCIENT MINION PROVERB

"This isn't the prince either," Rufus said.

"Yes, it is," Seizemore answered impatiently.

"No, it's not," Rufus said. He ripped the beanie off, and the wig came off with it.

"What?" Pravus said.

"This is Boris Tumblewrecker," Rufus said. "He's a third-year ogre-man, and he's definitely not a prince."

Seizemore ran over to me. "Where is he?" He shook me, hard.

"The prince must die . . . before Runt," Dismorda said. "Or I won't get the vaskor . . . and I won't do the spell."

"WHERE IS HE?!?!" Seizemore screamed at me.

"I don't know," I said. "I thought he'd be here by now."

Pravus rushed over and grabbed my throat, squeezing hard. "What have you done?"

"The prince must die . . . before me, remember?" I said, and his grip eased a little.

"I will kill everyone you know," he said, throwing me to the ground. He turned to Dismorda. "Enchantress, everything will be as I promised—"

"The prince . . . is not here . . . your gold . . . is not here."

"I will get them both, I promise, but you must do the spell, I beg you."

The UMs were approaching the stage. One of them picked up five Pravus minions and looked like he was going to eat them. Most of Pravus's new army had scattered, apparently preferring a death by loyalty cuff to being eaten.

And then a trumpet sounded, and we all looked toward the end of the park.

"There he is!" I said, pointing up the road.

There, approaching through the ruins of Stull City, was a very dashing young prince in his full Andiratian military attire. He rode the largest, whitest horse I'd ever seen. His face was serious, and his hair flowed out behind him like some fairy-tale prince. He rode at full speed, charging into Stull City. Frankie ran behind him, blowing a trumpet.

The huge monsters turned to face him, but the prince was unafraid. Of course he was unafraid; all of the UMs on the field were under a spell of obedience to him. And to me.

They were all vaskor. I'd known it as soon as we entered Stull City. Sara had done it. She'd snuck in with the doughnuts and told the UMs to leave or they'd be cursed with a spell of obedience. She'd told them to return to Carkley, and then the vaskor had taken their place.

(Hopefully, they'd gone after eating the antidote-laced doughnuts, so they'd transform back into normal humans by the time they reached their homeland.)

Sara now ran alongside Ron, snarling and swiping her paws at him as he rode for the steps of the EO Council Building, pretending to be one of Pravus's UMs. But when Ron reached the steps, he swung his horse around to face the monsters. He was angry and raised his voice:

"I am Prince Auberon Gabriel Titus Natherly! Rightful ruler of Andirat and Erudyten, and I command you to surrender!" And then, to the shock of everyone, the horrifying beasts he faced all raised their arms in surrender.

It had worked. Our plan had worked!

"NO! Kill him!" Pravus screamed at the monsters.

"They won't," I said. "They can't. He controls them all."

"NO!" Pravus turned on Dr. Critchlore. "You figured it out, didn't you? That the vaskor were the original Undefeatable Minions. And now you have them too."

Dr. Critchlore shrugged. "Too?" he said. "Actually, *we* have them. Yours appear to be gone."

"First impressions are so important, don't you think?" I asked Seizemore. "We're going to make sure this scene is broadcast in Andirat, so everyone can see their brave prince in action."

Pravus spun around, looking for something to attack, for some way to wrestle success out of this crushing defeat. His gold was gone. His UMs were gone. A field of vaskor stood between him and his army. Just as he was about to grab Dr. Critchlore in a fit of rage, a giant, furry hand reached over his bodyguards and lifted him away. Kumi had snuck up behind the EO Council Building, with Syke perched on his shoulder. The giant gorilla roared louder than I'd ever heard him roar. Pravus's guards ran for their lives.

"Kumi, Syke!" I said. "Well done!"

I watched as Pravus's remote control dropped from his hand. Rufus saw it too. I was a half-step closer and a half-step quicker, so I beat him to it and snatched it up. He tackled me, but I held on to the device.

"Rufus, Pravus lost," I said. "Come back to us. Let me release the cuffs."

He snarled, but then let me up. "It's the blue button on the bottom," he said. "I saw him use it once, to remove someone's cuff. Press it twice to 'Select All,' then hit 'Release.'"

I handed him the remote. "You do it."

And he did. He stood in front of the army and pressed the buttons. "You're free!" he told them. "You don't have to do what he says!"

The armies threw off their cuffs and cheered.

Frankie blew his horn, and more Critchlore minions stormed into the square from where they'd been hiding in the rubble of demolished buildings. They quickly subdued the remaining loyal Pravus forces, which numbered maybe twenty out of the thousands that had once filled the square.

I noticed Seizemore, Janet, and Mr. Fox trying to slip away, and nodded to Sara. She bounded over to them in one leap, her mouth and arms wide open. She swooped them up with one hand and brought them back.

"Can I eat them?" she asked. The three traitors screamed, but I had no sympathy for them.

"Maybe later," I answered.

Dr. Critchlore looked up at Pravus, who was squirming in Kumi's grip. "Impressive, aren't they?" he said, indicating the whole, giant group of Critchlore minions, now surrounding Pravus's much smaller group. "And so loyal."

The witch shuffled over to where I stood with Mistress Moira and Dr. Critchlore. "I have . . . decided to agree to your proposal," she said. "I will . . . remove Runt's curses . . . in return for . . . what we agreed."

"Start with the tether," Mistress Moira said, nodding at me.

The witch cast a spell, touched my arms, my chest, my neck. She said a few more things, then reached into a bag attached to her belt and blew powder in my face.

My neck immediately felt looser.

"Now the death curse."

She spat at my feet and said, "Begone, curse."

"That's it?" I asked.

She nodded. "You are free to live your life and die at the appropriate time."

"Thank you," I said.

I took a deep breath and smiled. I was free. Then I laughed out loud. "I'M FREE!"

Syke rushed over to hug me. My friends cheered. The vaskor cheered. All the minions on the steps cheered. Kumi roared and pounded his chest, which couldn't have been fun for Dr. Pravus, who was still gripped in Kumi's fist.

We were too exhausted to go back to Critchlore's, so we spent the night at the Andiratian embassy, where Mrs. Ambrose welcomed us with a huge banquet.

The next morning, rested and refreshed, we ate another huge meal in the dining hall. As I looked at Ron sitting at the head of the table, I felt so relieved. Not only had the curses been lifted from me, but also the responsibility of being a prince. I won't lie, I was going to miss some of the perks. It had been thrilling to think that this enormous castle belonged to me, that I could have anything I wanted. But that wasn't me. All those perks came with responsibilities I wasn't ready for.

Mistress Moira entered the dining hall and called to me. "Runt, you need to come outside." She was smiling.

"Why?" I asked, but she'd already left.

When I caught up to her, she stood on the gravel driveway, nodding to the road, where a car approached the castle.

"Who's that?" I asked.

"It's Miss Merrybench," she said. "After I was captured in Skelterdam, she escaped to Andirat."

"Why?"

"Runt"—she was smiling so wide I couldn't help but smile back—"she went to find your parents."

The car stopped and a man and woman got out. The man wore jeans and a faded leather jacket with the sleeves pushed up. His arms were tan and he looked strong. He had short brown hair and dimples that showed because he was smiling. The woman was smiling and crying at the same time. Miss Merrybench got out from the back. She was looking right at me.

"Is that . . . Are those . . . ?"

"Runt . . . yes. Those are your parents."

I didn't wait to hear anything else. I ran over to them, stopping a few feet away to search their faces for something familiar. In a flash, images rushed at me:

My mom, singing me to sleep, rubbing my belly when I felt sick, smelling like freshly baked bread.

My dad, carrying me on his shoulders after I ran to greet him coming home from work, reading me stories in a bed that was too small for the both of us, playing hide-and-seek in the stables.

"Maverick!" they said. Tears were streaming down their faces, and mine too. We hugged each other, all of us sobbing.

And then I let them go. Miss Merrybench stood next to the car, wobbling as she watched us. I walked over to her, held my breath, and gave her a hug too.

A good, long hug.

EPILOGUE

Syke stood between me and Prince Auberon on the terrace over-looking the backyard of the Andiratian embassy. I was wearing my fancy-dress Critchlore uniform, and I don't know if it was my excitement or the warm day, but I could already feel sweat drip down my spine.

We were waiting for the ceremony to start. I don't think the embassy had ever hosted a crowd as huge as the one that was gathered on the lawn in front us. Rows of chairs covered the lawn, almost to the lake, and they were all filled.

The front rows had been reserved for important guests like Irma Trackno and other EOs, the siren syndicate mothers, and repre-sentatives from Andirat. Behind those dignitaries sat the many members of the Critchlore family. Then came the embassy staff and their families, followed by rows and rows of teachers and workers from Dr. Critchlore's school, and then the entire Critchlore student body. Imps and flying monkeys had climbed into the trees for a better view.

Giant monsters stood in the back. I saw Roger and the other manticores, now happily well-fed. Dr. Frankenhammer's dragon was there, as were Kumi and Amaruq, the Woolly Gigantoth from Polar Bay. Alasie was perched on his shoulder, waving at me. Or at Syke. Probably Syke. Even Clarence the fish monster had come. He was frolicking in the lake with the hydra.

"Are you still grounded?" I asked Syke. I hadn't seen her for a few days, so I wondered.

"Oh, yeah," she said. "Tootles and Riga gave me two months for running away from Critchlore's, my hamadryad relatives added another month because I ran away from the Great Library, and then Critchlore added a month because I put my life in danger by enrolling at the Pravus Academy."

"Ouch. So, we'll be able to hang out sometime in November?"

"Hopefully they'll all forget by the time school starts again," she said. "Did you hear about the size of the incoming class? Everyone wants to go to Critchlore's now. And the EOs all want Critchlore minions. They're raving about how loyal his minions are."

"You just have to make it through the summer then." I laughed.

"At least they're letting me attend special events when they come up," she said. "Like this one."

Ron, standing on the other side of Syke, leaned forward to address me. "And she's been granted permission to visit us here next weekend," he said. "For . . . what did we make up?"

"I'm going to help you plan your inauguration," Syke said.

"Really?" I asked her. "Critchlore bought that?"

"Critchlore wants to stay on the prince's good side," she said. "After all, Ron convinced the EOs to hire most of Critchlore's graduating class to help rebuild Stull City. So I'll get to come here for a few visits this summer. Thank the Goddess, too, because otherwise I'd be stuck at that empty school with only Darthin and his poop gloves for company. Everyone's abandoning me for summer break." She added that last part with a hard glare at me.

"You can't blame me for wanting to live with my family," I said, and I waved to them. My parents were sitting in the embassy worker section with my siblings—I have siblings! Two younger sisters and a baby brother. And they all lived at the embassy now. Ron had hired my father as the embassy's Royal Creature Keeper, and my mom worked part-time in the business office. I was going to live here for the summer, then head back to Critchlore's in the fall.

"What a year, huh?" I asked.

"It was crazy," she said.

"The world we grew up in—it's been destroyed," I said. "I used to dream of being a junior henchman, and then I thought I'd be a prince. Now, I don't know . . . I can't go back to being a minion."

"You were never going to be a minion," she said. "Everyone could see that but you."

"That's not what I meant," I said. "It's just . . . I've lost all my dreams."

"You're going to be fine, Runt."

"Maverick," I corrected her.

"Yeah, I'm not calling you that," she said. "Listen, everyone has dreams that don't come true. You just have to keep dreaming until one of them does. There are lots of dreams out there. Find a new one."

"Is that what you're going to do, now that you've seen that the life of a spy is ridiculously dangerous?" She didn't say anything, so I added, "Right? You know that now, right?"

"Sure," she said. "But look where it got us. We saved Critchlore's school, we stopped Dr. Pravus, and we saved Ron from being Seizemore's puppet. Worth it, I'd say."

I noticed Mr. Cordholm in the crowd, and a new dream popped into my head.

"We should become Covert Librarians. Like Professor Zaida. We can help spread knowledge throughout the realms. Repair the damage done by the Evil Overlords. Get books out into the world."

"That's . . . not a bad idea," she said. "It's got danger and stealth, plus we'd be helping people."

Music started playing, and a woman wearing a fancy robe stepped forward to begin the ceremony. We took our spot in a line next to Dr. Critchlore, who was wearing his most formal uniform. On the opposite side of Dr. Critchlore stood a line of what I assumed was Mistress Moira's sisters. They were dark-skinned like her, and wore robes with gold sashes that matched the gold bands in their hair.

Everyone stood and turned to watch Mistress Moira walk down the aisle, dressed in the fanciest white dress I've ever seen. The toddler trees, now small again, began the procession, dropping rose petals down the aisle. Dr. Critchlore couldn't stop smiling. Even his mother smiled briefly before covering it up.

I don't think I'd ever been happier. Now, instead of having no family, I had two. And I could see them all whenever I wanted.

I'd even convinced Ron to install that zipline. After the wedding, we were really going to have some fun.

ACKNOWLEDGMENTS

Well, we've reached the end, and if you've made it this far with me, I hope that you've enjoyed the journey as much as I have. Thank you for reading.

I would also like to thank everyone at Abrams for their hard work on the Dr. Critchlore series. My editor, Erica Finkel, was a delight to work with throughout, both for her brilliantly insightful notes and also her encouragement. Thanks to Chad Beckerman and his team for packaging my words into such a fun little bundle. Thanks to Nicole Schaefer and Patricia McNamara for their support and work with promoting the books.

I am eternally grateful to my agent, Molly Ker Hawn, whose enthusiasm for this story during our first phone call is something I will never forget. I'm also grateful to have worked on this series with Joe Sutphin, who is not only a gifted illustrator, but also an extremely generous person who goes above and beyond for every single book. I'm so glad that we met through this project.

Thanks to my kids, Rachel, Ricky, Alex and Daniel, for signing up to be in the Wizard of Oz all those years ago. It was while working backstage that I began to wonder where the Wicked Witch got her minions, and who might have trained them. Thanks to my husband Juan, who amazes me with his generosity every day and without whom I never would have become a writer. Thanks also to my parents, Joan and Bob Jack, and my siblings, Lisa and Gordy, who have been so supportive and wonderful.

And finally, thanks to all the independent bookstores and schools that invited me into their spaces and allowed me to talk to kids about writing and reading. Standing in front of smiling faces, seeing hands waving in the air with questions—those are the kind of things that make it all worthwhile.

ABOUT THE AUTHOR

Ever since she saw *The Wizard of Oz*, Sheila Grau has been curious about one of life's great mysteries: Where do evil overlords get their minions? Also: Who trains them? Unable to find the answers, she thought it would be fun to make them up.

Sheila currently lives in Northern California with her husband and four children and, sadly, still no minions.